WHEN

THEY

COME

TRUE

WHEN THEY COME TRUE

SARAH FLEMING MOUNTFORD

Atthis Arts, LLC

WHEN THEY COME TRUE

Cover design copyright ©2017 Jennifer Zemanek, Seedlings Design Studio
Editorial services by Abigail Hodges
Editorial services by Christabel Barry, Quill Pen Editorial

Published by Atthis Arts, LLC
Centerville, Ohio
www.atthisarts.com

ISBN (paperback) 978-1-945009-08-2

Library of Congress Control Number: 2017943964

For Greg, with my love.

CHAPTER ONE

SLAMMING THE CELLAR DOOR, I shoved my shoulder into the rough wood and braced my foot against the bottom to jam it closed, my fingers fumbling in the dark for the bolt. I found the solid metal rod and slid it home, while my breath caught, rasping in time to my racing heart. I relaxed my pressure on the door with caution. The bolt was solid and the door was old, hard wood. Both were stronger than I was and I hoped they were enough to keep the ghosts out.

I listened, shivering at the answering silence. Where were they? What were they planning? I ran my hand up the wood frame and found the string that led to the single overhead light bulb and pulled it, illuminating the small cellar with its feeble glow. Leaning against the door, I tried to slow my breathing so my chest wouldn't hurt so much. I considered my surroundings. The cellar was carved into the ground next to the house, a narrow room meant for keeping root vegetables through the winter, and sheltering us from summer tornados. It had one entrance, which was currently overrun with ghosts.

A couple of them had attacked me while I was on my way to the root cellar to get potatoes and I'd used my power against them. The fire in me had evaporated them, sending their souls to the next world. Unfortunately, it had also seared through my rib fractures which were still healing from my last encounter with ghosts. I'd collapsed into the snow from the pain as another pack of them materialized. Glancing around the tiny space I now occupied, I began to regret my decision to run instead of fight.

I jumped as a dreadful scratching resonated through the rough-hewn wood. Backing up until I felt the cold wall behind me, I watched the door. They were ghosts, and I'd seen more than one float through solid walls. Others could move solid objects. Not too long ago, one had tried to carve me up with my kitchen knife. I didn't think it was a common skill, but lately too many of the ghosts I'd run into had dangerous abilities, like picking up tractors and crashing helicopters.

Why didn't they just dematerialize and come through the door if they wanted me so much? I hoped that these spirits weren't smart enough to come up with the same idea. I could protect myself, but I wasn't eager to use my power again, not with my sternum fractures wired together, still healing. It hurt to use my power on a good day and with my body still recovering it was agonizing.

I'd released my first ghost when I was a child and thirty years later I still didn't know much about the power I had. There was a core inside me, like a miniature nuclear reactor. Wherever it came from, when I used it, it burned inside me like fire.

It sounded as if a pack of rats was gnawing on the wood of the door and I shuddered in revulsion. It was a solid door, so if they were chewing their way through, it would take them a few minutes. I had a little more time to recover. Daggers of pain still seared my chest as the healing bones objected to the remains of my power. I sank to the ground, clutching my knees to my chest to control the shivering.

Why didn't I see them coming? The thought flitted through my mind as I tried to gather myself. Either they'd come out of nowhere, or I'd been distracted. My second sight allowed me to sense the amorphous blobs of the ghosts on the other side of the door. There were too many of them packed into the small stairwell for me to count.

Is Adonijah with them? My stomach twisted at the thought of having to face Jed's brother again and I cursed myself for daydreaming earlier. Like a bad ex-boyfriend, Adonijah was lurking around somewhere, waiting for his opportunity to take me again. I felt stupid. If I didn't pay attention, I couldn't protect myself.

Having Jedediah here would help. I couldn't imagine we'd have been trapped down here if he'd been with me. It was too convenient that they showed up the one day he'd left to get groceries.

They've been watching us. They must have been to catch me at the one moment that he wasn't here. My mind raced through the worst possibilities. If they'd been spying on us, they could have attacked him when he left. Maybe they'd just been waiting to get us while we weren't together. Was he hurt? If Jedediah came back to me, would it be him or would he be possessed? I wasn't entirely sure it was even possible for another ghost to take control of Jed. Anxiety clenched deep in my belly at the thought. I forced myself to slow my breathing. Hyperventilating would not help me.

Ghosts could possess normal people but Jed was anything but normal. My fingers traced the path of the scar from the top of my collarbone halfway down my right breast. I flinched at the memory of Jed's ancient sword reflecting the moonlight before he embedded it in my collarbone when Adonijah had possessed me. The moment his sword entered my body its power had burned through me and forced Adonijah out. It had nearly killed me, but I didn't blame Jed for that. I'd thanked him for doing what had to be done, and was more than a little grateful that he'd gotten to me with his sword before Ned had with his gun. The magical sword somehow seemed like a better option than being shot.

Something crashed against the door and I braced my feet against it, my back still pressed against the far wall of the tiny cellar. I should be able to overpower them if they got through, but I wasn't eager to try in my current state. The single bulb flickered overhead, but there were plenty of flashlights down here. There were also home-canned vegetables and a few cases of bottled water on the shelves lining one of the walls. Crates filled with sand lined another wall with layers of potatoes, beets, and carrots nestled in the loose grains. I could survive down here for a few days if I needed to, but living on sandy carrots and canned beans in the cellar wouldn't be fun. I needed an exit strategy.

I shrieked as something grabbed my left ankle. A skeleton hand tightened around it, bony fingers pressing into my flesh, squeezing with inhuman force. I stomped on the arm with my right foot, a futile gesture as its grasp tightened to the point that tears wet my face. Anger surged through me at the thought of this ghost breaking my ankle.

Fury caused my power to boil in my chest, and energy seared out of me in a rush, running through every unhealed fracture like water through cracks in rock. I cried out as the hand on my ankle squeezed a final death grip and then evaporated as if it had never been there.

I scrambled away from the door as the ghost that had been partway under it dissipated until there was nothing left but the echo of its squeals, heralding its final death. I strained to hear anything else from the other side of the door. Nothing. Maybe the others hadn't realized what I was capable of. That thought brought me an ounce of hope.

I pulled off my house shoe and stripped my sock off. To my dismay, the space above my ankle showed the imprint of the skeletal hand. My ankle was already beginning to swell, and it felt hot now that the pressure had been released. I flexed my foot with a grimace, making certain I could still move it in all the right directions. It hurt, but I was pretty sure it wasn't broken.

The barrage against the door resumed with vigor, the wood rattling under the onslaught. I rubbed the tender scar on my chest, hoping it would ease the burning sensation that still clung to my healing tissue. In my panic to get rid of the thing around my ankle, I'd used more than I should have. My power regenerated itself, but that took time. It wouldn't have taken much to dispel one ghost, but I'd poured out a lot in that moment of anger. Most of the energy had been deflected by the door. Based on the noise outside, I hadn't even dented their numbers.

I was at a distinct disadvantage, trapped as I was in the cellar. I could sense the cluster that remained in the stairwell, but there could be more above ground. My normal range was around half a mile, but I couldn't sense that far from my spot underground. I patted my pockets looking for my cell phone, but I must have left it in the kitchen when I'd come out here for potatoes. Not that it would work underground, nor were there many people who would be able to help with this particular problem.

Except for Jedediah, who could return any minute. Or in a few hours. Or never, if they'd managed to harm him in some way. I pushed the thought aside, not allowing myself to dwell on that possibility. Jed had to be fine because he was the only other person I knew who could fight ghosts and I didn't want to have to manage without him.

You're on your own for right now, Anna. Figure it out. The good news was I could walk on a bruised ankle. The bad news was my power didn't conduct through wood. I couldn't guarantee I'd be able to evaporate all of them if I took the time to open the door, but as long as I was trapped underground my options for strategy were limited. I rubbed the indentations on my ankle in an attempt to slow the swelling while I tried to figure a way out of my predicament.

The pounding on the door increased in intensity as if the ghosts were being spurred on by something I couldn't see. I pounded both fists against the door back at them and there was a pause. If I wasn't currently trapped with no means of escape, it would have been comical. I had enough power for one more good blast, I just needed a clear shot at them all. I knew I could banish all the ones left in the stairwell at once, but then I wouldn't be able to use it again for a while. Not without weakening myself too much. I couldn't afford to be that vulnerable again. Last time I'd done it, it had killed me. I didn't have a defibrillator and a medical team standing by to save my life this time.

A high-pitched squeal emanated from the stairwell, followed by the sound of metal striking bone, and then another scream. Using my sixth sense, I saw another being enter the stairwell, its soul brighter than the rest. The ghosts stopped hitting the door and I heard grunting, and the shrieks of distressed spirits. Jed must be back. I settled myself back against the wall and relaxed a notch.

The stairwell fell silent. I held my breath until I heard the heavy footfalls of someone coming down the steps.

"Anna." Jed's deep voice was a dissonant echo after all the noise. "Are you all right?"

I nodded, which didn't help much given that he couldn't see me. A few tears of relief leaked onto my cheeks and I wiped them away on the sleeve of my sweatshirt. I didn't want Jed to see me cry. I hated appearing weak.

"Anna, are you in there?" He inquired as if he were a neighbor coming to visit, and wasn't in the midst of rescuing me. Again.

"I'm okay." I realized I was whispering and raised my voice. "I'm fine."

He pushed against the door with enough force that the slide bolt strained against its screws. "Can you open the door?" Exasperation tinged his tone. "It's safe now." I'd gathered that much given that he was talking to me from the other side of the door and not still fighting the spooks, but I hadn't been able to move from my safe spot against the wall yet. I pulled myself up on one foot and threw the bolt before he decided to break through it.

"You're injured," he observed, ducking through the doorway. Jed had the build of a professional football player and the tiny cellar felt claustrophobic with him in it. He took in the small space with a quick glance. Despite the battle, he looked relaxed. The only signs that he'd been in a fight were the curls of dark hair that had escaped from the short ponytail at the back of his neck. He sheathed his steel blade inside his trench coat as I shied away from it. It had power that I didn't want to encounter ever again.

My strange ability sent ghosts on to where they should have gone when they died the first time. Jed's sword was an ancient kilij from the era of his birth. It had the power to weaken spirits, neutralizing the immediate threat. My solution was more permanent, but Jed was the only other person I knew who had a way to fight the dead. I needed him.

My body bore the healing scars from his blade and what it had taken to bring me back to life, but what I truly feared was the peaceful stillness of death. My memory of it was of incomparable beauty, the brilliant sky filled with stars that called to me. Was it the stars that spoke to me, or something greater? The secret that I could not allow myself to admit was that a part of me yearned for that perfect calm, craved that sense of peace.

"I'll be fine." I forced myself to ignore the after effects of the fire that still seared through my veins. I'd hurt for a while from having used my power, but there wasn't anything I could do about it.

Jed regarded me with thoughtful brown eyes that made me wonder if he knew what I was thinking. I stared back. It occurred to me that if there was anyone I could tell my secret to, it would be this man. He was one of the few people in the world who had tasted the sweet call of death, but rejected it. I wondered if he desired that silence, the closeness with the stars the way that I did. I couldn't bring myself to discuss it with him because saying my thoughts out loud might make them more real. Jed blinked and stepped back, breaking the tension between us with such ease that I wondered if I'd been the only one to feel it.

"They're gone for now. It's over."

I cast my senses out and didn't feel anything nearby other than the beacon of Jed's soul. Since I'd met him, I'd been using my sixth sense more. It had strengthened to the point that I could see the souls of the living as well as the dead. The living looked brighter than the dead did. Jed was a ghost, but since he was possessing a real body his soul looked more like those of the living.

"Do you need me to carry you?"

"No, I can make it." There wasn't any way he could carry me that wouldn't make my ribs hurt, and I was too independent to let him when I could still walk. I pulled my sock back on and stuffed my sore foot back into my shoe.

"Do you think they'll be back?" I asked.

"I do."

Jed didn't often elaborate, so I wasn't surprised by his abrupt response. I didn't bother to ask him what we should do about it. He'd been clear about his opinion, but I wasn't ready. He worked for a council of ghosts, a group of old souls who were supposed to be keeping bad ghosts, like the ones who'd just attacked me, under control. Jed wanted me to go to Europe to meet the Council in person, and I'd agreed to after my near-death experience. We'd been ready to leave two weeks ago, but I'd refused at the last minute. I wasn't ready to trust Jed's council. They'd sent Jed to find me, which I was thankful for, but improving relations between the living and the dead was going to have to wait for a better ambassador than me.

I gathered a small sack of potatoes as if nothing had happened and made my way back up the stairwell, surprised to see that it was still light out. It felt like I'd been down there for a long time, but it must not have been more than half an hour. *Hard to keep track of the time when you're scared shitless.* I didn't feel like cooking dinner anymore but we were far enough from town that we couldn't order out for pizza.

"How about leftover lasagna for dinner?" I asked and Jed glanced at the bag of potatoes. I could see the question form and watched as he decided to discard it.

"That would be fine." He paused. "I could make supper tonight if you would prefer."

"I'd been thinking of steak, but I lost my appetite when that ghost grabbed my ankle with his nasty hand." *Stop being sexist. Not all the bad ghosts are male.* An image of a spirit with blond locks and a fondness for blue silk flashed through my mind. That ghost was not nice, and she was decidedly female.

"Perhaps by the time I prepare supper, your appetite will find you again." His speech was odd sometimes, the result of being an ancient spirit who had learned English over the centuries, and who at present was inhabiting a Swiss body. When I first met him, I thought it was strange, but I was getting used to the assortment of accents that cradled his words. "Do we have enough steak to share with Carrie and Ned?"

"I'm sure we do."

Jed did make a mean steak, and I had craved meat since my accident. I assumed it was an after effect of the electrolyte imbalance that ghosts caused when they possessed someone, because I hadn't lost enough blood to make me anemic. My friend Chaz had also confessed to craving red meat after being possessed by Adonijah, although that wasn't abnormal for him. The third person Adonijah had possessed was my ex-boyfriend, Eric. I hadn't contacted him after our ordeal, and he hadn't reached out to me. I regretted that he'd gotten involved, but it was hard to call someone and say, 'Hey, I'm sorry you were possessed by a homicidal ghost. That was my fault.'

Jed quirked an eyebrow at me, inviting a reply to his offer to cook and I realized I'd stopped walking halfway to the house and was getting cold.

"Sorry, I was lost in my thoughts." I cleared my head with a vigorous shake. "The steak would be great, if you don't mind."

"I don't mind."

"I could go feed the horses while you're cooking," I teased and he whirled on me in horror.

"You will not." His tone was adamant. "I will feed the horses, and then I will cook. You are still healing." He shook his head in disbelief. "They warned me, doctors truly are terrible patients."

I choked on my laughter. "You're right. You cook, you feed the horses." He decided too soon that I was serious and turned towards the barn with a satisfied grunt. I couldn't resist. "Then I'll have time to bring up the ladder and change those light bulbs that are out..."

"If you touch that ladder, I will not be responsible for my actions," Jed growled.

"I'm teasing you," I assured him. The sack of potatoes I was carrying was starting to feel heavy. I wasn't up to manhandling a ladder or a bale of hay.

He glanced down at my slipper-shod feet. "Go to the house and get warm."

I shrugged, not wanting to admit that I didn't want to be alone. My ankle had settled down to a mild throb and the burning sensation was dissipating into my bones. Jed didn't protest when I followed him down the path of hard-packed snow to the barn.

"Did you know the ghosts were here when you came back?" I asked. I was still getting used to violent ghosts. Jed, once known as King Solomon of Judah, had lived in a tougher time. I needed to learn to be more like him.

"I did. I felt them when I was driving in. In fact..." He paused and I heard the sound of a truck coming down the drive. "That'll be Ned now. I sped past his place. He'll be wondering if something's wrong."

"I hope he didn't leave Carrie home alone." My neighbors couldn't protect themselves against ghosts and they'd been attacked before, just for living next door to me.

Jed turned back to me. "Why did you ask if I could sense the ghosts when I got back?"

"I didn't know they were close." I shivered. "Not until I was almost to the cellar."

"I wondered why you were down there." His gentle tone took me by surprise. Tenderness seemed at odds with his size, his sword skills, and the era in which he'd been raised.

"I wasn't paying attention." We walked into the barn, and I relished the musty warmth that smelled of horses, dried hay, and dust. Like comfort and home. The mares nickered a gentle welcome, their bodies shifting towards the gate of their stall, hoping for attention. I buried my face in the gray mare's mane and breathed in her warmth while I rubbed her face with my fingertips.

"We must remain vigilant. I shouldn't have left you alone." The words he didn't say resonated inside me. *Adonijah is still out there.*

"You can't be with me all the time. Besides, I can take care of myself." I was saying it for my own benefit as well as his. "I just need to be aware of what's around." I stepped away from the mare as I saw the bright soul of a living person coming towards us. There was another flare of light in front of the house and I knew Ned hadn't left Carrie alone.

"You must be more careful," Jed agreed with a note of reprimand.

"So why do you think they were here?" I directed the conversation away from my lapse in vigilance.

"Who was here? The Feds?" Ned interrupted, stepping through the doorway with a burst of cold air. Ned felt as comfortable waltzing into my barn as he would his own. Our childhoods had been spent racing our horses up hillsides and getting in trouble for taking the cows on impromptu cattle drives. We'd shared our first uncertain kiss in my circle drive when we were thirteen and been inseparable until we went to college. I'd been certain growing up that I'd marry Ned, but he'd chosen Carrie. He was a remarkable man; an organic farmer who loved guns almost as much as he did his wife.

"I thought it was too cold for the Federal guys out here." Ned hadn't been very impressed with the lead investigator who followed up on the helicopter crash.

"I haven't heard from them in a week," I informed Ned. The weather wasn't as brutal now as it had been the week I met Jed, but it hadn't improved very much. The coldest winter we'd had in years lent itself to a variety of global warming jokes. Snow still clung to the ground and the wind had blown it into drifts that had all but covered the crashed helicopter in the front field. It still lay where it had fallen from the sky, brought down by Adonijah and his army of ghosts. "All I could get them to say was that they'd remove the helicopter when their investigation is complete. I don't see much point in calling them again." The National Transportation Safety Board would take whatever time they wanted, and there was nothing I could do to speed the process up, despite the fact that the helicopter was sitting on my land.

"My guess," Ned speculated, "is that their investigation will be finished sometime after the weather improves in the spring."

"You can't blame them for that," I argued. "I don't know how they could get the helicopter out right now, as buried as it is in snow."

"Wait until mud season," Ned suggested.

"They may have to wait until it dries out in May."

We hadn't seen the sun in so long, I wasn't sure that I remembered what it looked like. Some days it was hard to imagine that spring would ever come. Knowing Missouri winters, it might well be April before the sun resurfaced.

"You never said who you were talking about." Ned wasn't one to let something slide.

I hesitated, unwilling to confess to him that a bunch of spooks had taken me by surprise, but Jed had no such reservations.

"A dozen ghosts had Anna trapped in the cellar when I returned," Jed told Ned and then turned back to answer my original question. "I'm not sure why they were here. Perhaps they knew you were alone." He sounded cheerful. Getting to use his sword had put him in a good mood.

"Damn it." Ned turned around and stormed back out the barn door, shouting Carrie's name as he went. He had his shotgun slung over his shoulder, but he'd been wearing that since the big attack a few weeks ago.

"I shouldn't have let my guard down," I spoke into the silence Ned left behind. "You said they'd be back."

Jed tossed a few sheaves of hay over the railing to the mares, who'd been waiting for us to finish our conversation. Their satisfied munching filled the quiet of the barn and covered the fact that Jed hadn't responded. I appreciated him not rubbing my nose in my foolish mistake.

"Anna!" Carrie bounded into the barn, filling it with her energy and brightness. Some women were introspective when they were pregnant, but Carrie was invigorated. Her pale skin had a rosy glow and her brown hair seemed longer and shinier than it had a few weeks before. "Are you all right? Ned says you had some trouble today."

"I suppose that's one way to put it. Is everything okay at your place?"

She gave me a teasing grin. "We haven't had any problems since Ned put the sign up that says, 'No ghosts allowed.'"

"When they stop by, I just send them this way," Ned added with mock cheerfulness.

"Well, next time call and let me know they're on the way. I didn't even have time to get the coffee cake out for them."

"That would be a terrible waste of a perfectly delicious coffee cake." Carrie's voice was filled with horror.

"Indeed, it would. Don't worry, there's plenty left." Carrie took her cooking seriously, and it showed. She'd dropped the cake off yesterday and I'd enjoyed a slice of it for breakfast. Jed had tried to convince me that just because it was called coffee cake did not mean that I was supposed to have it with my morning coffee, but I'd ignored him. Anything with coffee as a part of the title was clearly meant to be consumed before noon.

"I hope you blasted them into the next world." Ned was rubbing the barrel of his shotgun with jealousy. Shotguns didn't have any effect on ghosts and he'd been itching to take a more active role in the defense of our mutual properties since the spirits of the dead invaded his home a few weeks prior.

"I only got two of them." I nodded towards Jed. "He got the rest."

"Your method is better than mine," Jed observed.

I thought about the way his sword had released my soul from my body, freeing me and the spirit possessing me into death. His curved blade had sliced into my chest so deep that my collarbone and ribs would forever carry the marks of his blade.

"I don't know, Jed." I turned away from him to go back to the house, attempting to keep my voice light. "Your sword works pretty well."

Jed stopped me with a hand on my upper arm. I could feel the heat of his skin through my sweater. "I am sorry, Anna."

"You don't have to apologize. You did what you had to do." I'd asked both he and Ned to kill me if it came to that, and it had. "If…" I tried and found I was unable to say Adonijah's name out loud. "If he had maintained control of me it would have been very bad for all of us."

"It's awfully cold out here," Carrie changed the subject. "How about we all go in?" She looped her arm through mine and led me back to the house.

CHAPTER TWO

"**WILL YOU STAY** for supper?" Jed offered as he pulled a large bundle wrapped in white parchment paper and twine out of the fridge. Ned recognized the signature look of his home packaged beef and brightened. I slid my aching body onto a chair that gave me a view of the kitchen.

"We don't want to inconvenience you two lovebirds," Ned drawled, helping himself to an IPA from the fridge and settling onto his usual chair next to me.

"Ned." Carrie silenced him with one sharp word and then smiled at Jed. "How can I help?"

Ned turned his attention to his beer, as if ashamed. I wasn't buying it. The fact that Jed and I hadn't declared the nature of our relationship bothered him. He was pretty sure we were a couple but wanted us to confirm it. He wasn't right, but I wasn't sure he was wrong, either. There was something undefined between us. We'd had one searing kiss, but since my injury, we'd shared my house and my bed in a platonic partnership that showed no signs of changing. Since neither Jed nor I had addressed our connection, Ned's comments put us both in an awkward situation. I avoided looking at either of them.

The fact was, I'd told Jed he'd kissed me without my permission, and not to touch me again, so I was going to have to tell him if I wanted that rule to change. Then I'd find out if he wanted more from our relationship or not. Recovering from dying and being resuscitated had taken a toll on my body and my mind. I hadn't been ready to contemplate a relationship. I rested my head in my hands, lightheaded from adrenaline. My body burned as the power leftover from releasing the ghosts sizzled through my system like electricity through water.

"Eat this." Carrie laid a plate with a generous pile of her pecan butter and a few apple slices in front of me. I tilted my head up to give her a grateful smile.

"You're an angel. Thank you." I dipped an apple slice in the creamy pecan spread and took a bite, humming with gratitude. Carrie's homemade version was so much better than store-bought peanut butter.

"Would you like to cook the steak or the potatoes?" Carrie asked Jed, inserting herself into the cook space and taking control of dinner preparation in one smooth move.

Jed stepped back, accepting Carrie's right to be the head chef with humility. She was a great cook, and keeping her out of the kitchen when food was being prepared was impossible.

"I've got a craving for a potato gratin. Does that sound good to you?" Carrie asked as she snagged the sack of potatoes without waiting for Jed to answer.

"Always," I answered for Jed and his lips curved up in amusement. "Carrie, there's some cheddar in the fridge—"

"And cream. I know." She was quick to interrupt me. "I checked your supplies when I was here yesterday," she confessed. "I figured if you needed anything else I could pick some stuff up while I was out."

"I'm not incompetent, you know." I wasn't used to people looking after me.

She raised an eyebrow at me. "Well, you look like you could use a bit of help these days." She shouldered Jed out of her way and dumped a bunch of potatoes into the sink to wash them.

"I'm sorry," I apologized, dropping my eyes to my hands. "I appreciate your help, Carrie. I'm just tired of being an invalid. Other people get sick, not me." *Christ, Anna. You sound like one of your patients. Stop whining.*

"You aren't sick, honey. Just healing." Carrie had more patience than I did. She scrubbed the brown potato skins, freeing them of grit, and transferred them to the counter, forcing Jed to back out of her way. "Sorry, Jed."

"No, please, stay there. I can work on this side. I'll just cook the steaks. Like you said." He sounded amused, but as large as he was, there wasn't much space that Carrie could claim without making him move.

"If you'll give me an onion or the garlic I can chop it up for you," I offered. My farmhouse kitchen wasn't spacious. The only work surface was a stretch of counter space on either side of the sink. Since there wasn't room to stand at the counter with the two of them there, I felt justified in sitting at the table. I'd feel better about it, though, if I was helping.

Jed handed me a cutting board, a couple onions, and my favorite knife. I had all of us crying onion tears in short order, which led to laughter and casual conversation while Carrie and Jed cooked.

"What exactly happened today?" Ned asked later, looking down at his plate of steak and potatoes as if my answer wasn't that important. I was impressed that he had been able to wait. It was a sign of how battle-weary we were. A few ghosts didn't seem like a big deal. He wasn't going to get too excited unless there were a thousand of them trying to kill us all at once.

"I don't know." My voice lilted up in exasperation. "I went out to the cellar to get some potatoes and got ambushed. I didn't see them coming until they were on me. I ran down the stairs and bolted myself in."

"Why didn't you blast them?" Ned asked. Ned had seen me release a spirit in the woods when we were little, but his cynical young mind hadn't allowed him to accept what he'd seen. He'd even laughed at me when I attempted to explain it to him. After that, I'd stayed quiet about my abilities until ghosts attacked them in their own home. He'd seen his tractor fly through the air and a helicopter crash in the south field. Ned believed in ghosts now.

"They came at me from all directions, it was so fast," I explained, hoping I didn't sound pathetic. "Then I couldn't, once I'd closed the door." I paused and then tried again. "I was a little bit afraid to use my power. Because of how much it hurts, and because of what happened last time."

"Ah. You did the right thing, you know. Sometimes when you're surrounded, the smartest thing you can do is hide." Ned met my eyes and nodded, so I knew he didn't think worse of me.

"So, Jed got them?" Carrie sounded as nonchalant as Ned did, but I wouldn't be surprised if they considered staying the night.

I decided to leave out the scary part where the ghost reached under the door and grabbed me with a skeleton hand. That was the stuff of nightmares and she didn't need more of them. "Yeah. He pulled his King Arthur routine and rescued me."

Jed looked confused. "King Arthur?"

I smiled. Jed was a few thousand years old, as near as I'd been able to figure based on my study of the Bible and a few furtive Internet searches. As a man, he'd been King Solomon, the one from the Bible, who apparently had not been a very nice guy in real life.

I had several unanswered questions about his life before, but he'd stayed silent on most of them. The legend of Arthur, though, was in between Jed's original and current life.

"Arthur was a mythological king in England, around 1,500 years ago. There are many stories about King Arthur, a magician, and a sword." It was the quickest explanation I could come up with. Jed's grasp of modern day cultural references was lacking. He'd told me once that he'd lived other lives, too, in different bodies whose souls had passed on, but he hadn't been forthcoming on those details either.

"Was *he* there?" A tone of worry crept into Carrie's voice.

"Adonijah?" I forced myself to hide the fear his name instilled in me, shying away from the memories of him cutting away metaphorical strips of flesh inside me. I'd died to get rid of him because I was too weak by then to do it any other way. I was still haunted by the violation of him forcing his way inside of me, being powerless to fight him. When I woke from the nightmares where I relived those moments, I cradled myself in the empty expanse of night. Waking brought no relief, I was living the nightmare. There was no doubt in my mind that Adonijah was still around. The only question was, would I be strong enough to fight him when he came back for me? "He wasn't there. Maybe they were friends of his. I didn't have time to ask."

"Adonijah should need more time to regain his strength. The power of the sword has weakened him," Jed interjected.

"You think he'll be back." Carrie's tone was flat, belying the fear that Adonijah's name instilled in us all.

"It is possible. His obsession for Anna is strong. He won't be able to tolerate the fact that a woman bested him."

"How long will it take for him to gain his strength back?" I asked.

"I don't know exactly, but it's only been a few weeks. That's not much time. The spirits of the dead can't recharge by plugging into the outlet like your phone," he explained. "The generation of energy comes from the soul itself, and builds up over time. The sword takes that energy and bleeds it out so that the soul has to start again, similar to when they first died."

"That makes a lot of sense." Carrie sounded as appreciative as I felt.

"Do some ghosts charge at different speeds?" I was worrying about how long it would take Adonijah to regain his strength and hunt me down. More or less time than it would take to heal my broken ribs?

"Of course. Some spirits are simply stronger than others."

"If Adonijah isn't calling the shots right now, who is?" Ned slid his empty plate a few inches away from him. I was amazed by how much he could eat. He still had the same lean body he'd had in college. Then again, the life of a farmer was more active than that of a physician. I backed away from my half-eaten steak. I wasn't getting any exercise and my jeans' waistband wasn't very forgiving.

"There was another force behind Adonijah," I reminded them.

"Who?" Carrie asked. "Or what?"

"We don't know." Jed and I had spent hours covering this ground without any answers.

"Are there more of them out there?" Ned stretched and stood up to get seconds.

"Right now?" I clarified. "No, not that I've sensed." I looked to Jed for confirmation in case my extra sense was on the fritz.

He nodded his agreement. "No, I have been watching for them as well. We are safe right now."

"Can you see as far as our house?" Carrie's voice caught. I let Jed answer because his ability to sense ghosts at a distance was better than mine. Maybe because he was one.

"I can. Everything is quiet." Jed assured her.

"Good. I'm exhausted. Let's go home, Ned."

Ned gestured with his empty plate. "I'm not done yet, babe." He stepped to the stove and spooned another heap of gratin onto it.

She shook her head in resigned amusement. "Anna, if he keeps eating like this he's going to need his stomach pumped."

"It's not a job I want," I admitted as Ned stabbed the leftover steak off my plate and added it to his. "I guess you could take him into town."

"I don't need a doctor. I'm just hungry!" Ned shoveled a defiant forkful of steak into his mouth and chewed with determination.

"You guys could stay here tonight," I offered.

Carrie shrugged. "I thought about that, but I'll be more comfortable at home."

"Maybe it's time for you to go visit your mom again," Ned suggested.

"Without you?"

"I have to protect the farm," he insisted.

Carrie refrained from mentioning the fact that Ned couldn't do much to defend their property against a ghost. "You can't get rid of me just because I'm pregnant," she informed him. "I'm not going to my mother's." She turned back to me. "If you sense anything coming, you'll call us?"

"We will," I assured her.

They stayed long enough to help Jed wash the dishes and put leftovers away while I sat at the table feeling useless.

"I'll check in with you tomorrow if I don't hear from you first," Carrie promised as she gave me a gentle hug goodnight.

Jed saw them out and then joined me at the table. The cat appeared and leaped onto his lap. Now that the scary people were gone, Luna was ready for some quality time with her favorite person. Until she met Jed, I'd been her favorite.

"It's after eight. Aren't you tired?" He directed his words to the cat, a habit I found endearing.

The reality was that I'd been tired since the night the ghosts attacked us and the helicopter crashed in my front yard. My friends and I had been possessed, someone had died, and I'd not been sleeping all that well since. Jed was right to ask, though. I needed more sleep while I was healing. Everything took more effort.

"I'm a little tired but I'm not ready to go to bed yet." Jed accepted my answer with silence as he concentrated on rubbing his fingertips across the top of Luna's head until she collapsed across his legs. "Why did they come today?"

He shrugged, his eyes still focused on the cat. "I told you they would come looking for you again." His tone held a note of censure because he *had* warned me, and he'd tried to get me to leave.

"If we'd gone to Switzerland, what would we have done there?"

"I would have let you heal. The air in the Alps is healthier. It would have been good for you." He looked up, but his dark eyes didn't tell me anything more than his words. "You would have been safer than you are here."

"And then what, after I'd healed?"

"We would have gone to Turkey."

"To facilitate a conversation with the Council?"

"That is correct."

"I don't trust them."

"You have made that clear." Jed's eyes were back on Luna, his posture stiff with anger. After I'd refused to leave two weeks ago we'd argued. Jed had unpacked the car, silent with frustration, and carried our bags back up to my room. Part of me had expected him to leave me because that's what I was used to men doing, but he stayed.

"I didn't want to." He softened suddenly, leaning across the table and brushing his fingers across my cheek. His touch sparked through my skin and for a moment I remembered what it felt like to be alive.

"Didn't want to what?" I asked to distract myself from his touch. He pulled his hand away and the place where he'd touched me tingled. I wanted to settle my face in the palm of his hand and ask him to hold me but I didn't know how to say the words.

"To hurt you. I didn't want to do it." My chest ached with the sudden reminder of what his blade had done to me.

"You had to, Jed. There was no choice."

"If I'd waited, your power would have rebuilt and you could have banished him yourself."

"He already controlled me. If you had waited even one more second he would have banished you instead." We'd had this conversation before.

"I would rather that I had been injured."

"I'm fine." That wasn't quite true so I added, "I'll be okay. You did what you had to do."

Jed watched me, his brown eyes shining through his mane of dark hair. I turned away from the truth in them. I wasn't ready for what I saw. If he looked disappointed, or sad, or angry, I didn't want to know. I was too damaged from dying and coming back to life. When I closed my eyes, it was Adonijah I felt inside me, the terrible violation of him controlling me.

I reached out and touched Jed's arm to distract myself from the bad memories that crowded my mind. "I think I'll go take a bath."

"Very well. I'll stay here until you're done." Luna kneaded nonexistent claws into his lap, humming with happiness and Jed arched one eyebrow in resignation. I couldn't help but chuckle at his predicament as I walked away.

I stood naked in front of the mirror while water poured into the tub and evaluated the changes the last month had wrought. Brown hair hung in limp waves over my shoulders and my skin was paler than normal, making my dark eyes look larger than they were. I looked overwhelmed, but the thick red scar down the right side of my chest was the most obvious change. I wouldn't feel comfortable wearing a bathing suit in public anytime soon.

Jed's sword had embedded in my clavicle, in between my shoulder and the slope of my neck while the thicker curve of his blade sliced through the top of my breast and lodged in my ribcage. I remembered the sickening sensation of blade separating from bone when Jed pulled it free. I hadn't been able to take my butcher knife to a chicken since.

It had been an even slice, well placed so as not to kill me from the blow alone. I was lucky that Jed was an adept swordsman. The chest wall has lots of major arteries and veins, but my collarbone and ribs protected them so I hadn't lost too much blood. My friend, Ty, wouldn't have been able to resuscitate me if I'd bled to death.

The sublime heat of the bath beckoned and I shuddered away from too many uncomfortable memories, shielding myself in the joy of hot water. I stayed there until my skin had aged twenty years and the chill of winter had been eradicated from each and every bone.

When I came out of the bathroom, I found Jed in our bedroom. *My bedroom,* I reminded myself. I had a king size bed, wedged in between the eaves so that there wasn't much room on either side of it. The bed itself had plenty of room to share platonically without getting awkward. Sleeping next to Jed might not keep my nightmares at bay but it helped to know he was there when I woke from them.

He perched on the very edge of the sleigh bed as if he didn't belong there. His large frame made every small room in my little farmhouse feel cramped. His mass of curly dark hair was pulled back with a hair tie so I could see the thick scar over his right eye that I'd stitched up the night we met. Now that it was healed, it was a rugged addition to his face. His wide cheek bones and large nose made him look somber, sometimes almost fierce. Luna, his constant companion, was curled up on my pillow and I scowled at her for the inevitable dusting of black fur she would leave behind.

"You've been sleeping well at night," Jed observed.

"Sometimes." I didn't sleep *well* unless I took a handful of carefully mixed prescriptions for night terrors. My night terrors, according to Jed, were the Council of ghosts that wanted to help me defeat Adonijah. They hadn't bothered me these last few weeks although I didn't know why. I didn't share with Jed the nightmares I had about Adonijah.

"It would be best if I move back to the guest room, then." He looked across the room to me, as though asking for permission.

"Of course," I answered too quickly. I'd asked him to stay when we'd gotten back from the hospital and he had agreed. I'd thought it was mutual, the desire to be together. Apparently, I was mistaken.

I flushed with embarrassment and hoped he couldn't tell that I was upset. His bag wasn't leaned against the wall anymore, so he'd already moved his things to the guest room. Talking to me about it was an after-the-fact formality.

"That's great." My voice sounded strained. "The bed's all made up. If you need anything else, just let me know."

"Are you all right?" His voice was full of concern. Was he playing with me? It had been too long since I'd had someone in my life, but I couldn't let my hormones make decisions for me. They were unreliable.

"I'm just tired. I'll see you in the morning." I walked back into the bathroom hoping he bought my calm routine.

Had I missed something? Imagined that he wanted to be with me? Why was it that every man I liked wound up rejecting me? I brushed my teeth with vigor while words Jed said to me the first week I'd met him flashed through my mind.

"I was once a warrior, and a king."

In his previous life, he'd loved one of the most famous women in the world, the Queen of Sheba. He didn't speak of her much, but his brother Adonijah had wanted her too. The rivalry over her and their throne was the cause of Adonijah's hatred of him.

Her real name was Makeda, and she must have liked Jed well enough, because she and Jed's descendants were the rulers of some African nations today. By some accounts, she'd ruled her kingdom for fifty years and captured the fascination of the world, along with two brothers whose spirits stayed on Earth thousands of years after they died. Adonijah had lost the girl, the throne, and his life to Jedediah and was looking for revenge. Thousands of years later, I was in the middle of their feud.

Maybe I'd deluded myself into thinking that Jed was interested in me. After flossing until my gums bled, I crawled into bed. The cat meowed accusations at me. She wanted Jed back. I did too.

Fighting back tears, I argued with myself about whether or not to go to him. *I'll tell him how I feel in the morning. If he decides to leave, at least I'll know.* The last thought I had as I drifted into sleep was, *He might stay.*

I woke in a panic. The room was about fifteen degrees too cold, as though the heat had gone out. I realized with a start that I wasn't alone. I tried to shout for help, but my lungs produced only a soft squeak. There were two ghosts, the dim light of their wispy forms settled on the end of my bed. I scooted away from them, my back braced against the headboard.

"You deny us." The thing that hovered where my feet had been lingered on the last consonant, and it became a reptilian hiss. The ghost reached out as if to touch me and when I swung an arm to block it, it laughed at me.

Release them, you idiot. I reached for the core of power that lay inside me.

"Do not be hasty," the spirit to my left ordered, and I hesitated. Two ghosts weren't a real threat. I could release them in an instant. If they wanted to hurt me, they should have done so while I was still sleeping. I could afford to hear them out. There was no reason to do it blind, though. I flicked on my bedside lamp.

The form on Jed's side of the bed flickered, materializing enough so that I could see its skeletal shape with my eyes, not just my special sight. I stared in horror and amazement as the bones appeared to solidify, changing from transparent to opaque. Layers of ropy pink-ish tissue adhered itself to the raw bones. Organs formed themselves into existence starting with kidneys on either side of the spine. The stomach, spleen, and loops of bowels shaped into position and a fine layer of tissue, the peritoneum, grew over them. Muscles came into form, molding themselves over bone and then expanding into gener-ous breasts on her chest wall, declaring her sex.

I'd dissected a body in medical school, but I'd never seen one regenerate in front of me. I was so fascinated I forgot to be afraid. Fat and skin grew over the muscle and filled in the gaps. The skin of her belly developed over a taught stomach. I guess if you are able to make your own body, you have the right to give yourself the proportions of a supermodel with double D implants. The missing teeth grew in, straightened themselves out, and the flesh of a tongue flexed in its mouth. It was gruesome, but possibly the most incredible thing I'd ever seen.

Fingernails filled out over the tender pink skin on her fingertips, long and shaped, and her hair flowed out like water in thick bronze and blonde colored locks that spilled down her back. She looked like she'd just stepped out of the hair salon after spending a considerable amount of time getting highlights. Hair didn't come in two shades like that naturally. Her hands tightened into fists and then opened again. She looked down at them, turning her palms down and examining her fingertips. For the first time, she blinked her new eyelids. She had eyelashes that were so long they looked fake. She looked different in real life, but I knew I'd seen her before.

My mind raced with the implication of what she had done. Did her heart beat? Had she regenerated organs that worked or was this some sort of metaphysical illusion? I had never encountered a ghost who could form their own lifelike body before.

"You cause us much trouble." Her honey tones rolled off her newly formed vocal chords with ease.

"I've seen you before, in my dreams." She was the mean one. The one that enjoyed scaring me. She tilted her chin as her lips twisted in a cruel imitation of a smile. "Who are you?"

"I am Christiana," she said, disappointment evident. Apparently, she considered her name worth remembering.

"How did you do that?" I asked, my voice full of begrudging wonder.

"I am more powerful than you imagine. You disrespect me by not coming when called."

"I'm not a dog," I replied automatically, but my mind was swirling with questions. If all ghosts could create their own bodies, Jed wouldn't have needed to possess his body. It must be a different sort of talent that not many ghosts have.

She blinked her eyelids over turquoise blue eyes. "Perhaps not, human, but I tire of being sent to fetch you. I don't think you will ever be useful. We would be better off without you alive." Her words lacked substance. She looked more like a pretty peacock showing off its feathers than a terrifying ghost. We were in the real world, and unlike in the dream world, my power worked here.

"Then we feel the same way about each other. I would love it if I never saw you again. Why do you keep bothering me?"

The other one answered in a raspy, whispering voice. "You have business with us. We are the Council." Since this one hadn't pulled off any miraculous growth of human tissue, it must not be as powerful as Christiana was.

"All two of you?" I snorted. "I think you need more than two ghosts to qualify as a council."

"You will deal with us," it replied. I decided to call it Snake since it didn't introduce itself and spoke with a lisp like a small child missing its front teeth.

"Who are you and what are you doing in my house?" Why couldn't ghosts be like vampires who had to be invited in? It was damned inconvenient. Though since ghosts were real and vampires weren't, ghosts got to make their own rules, I supposed.

"We go where we please." She was combing her fingers through her long hair while she took in my bedroom. When she turned away from me, I had to roll my eyes. It looked like she'd spent years perfecting squats.

"That wasn't an answer to either of my questions. If you want me to cooperate with you, you'll have to do better."

"You are too impertinent," Snake informed me.

"What level of impertinence do you feel is appropriate?" I didn't bother to keep the irritation I felt out of my voice. "You come into my house in the middle of the night, without an invitation, and you threaten me. You've given no explanation for why you're here or what you want. I don't like it when ghosts lie to me."

It made a hissing noise, like the warning end of an angry rattlesnake. Christiana raised a calming hand towards it. "Be at peace," she ordered. Snake quieted, though it maintained the impression of an irritated viper.

I focused my ire on Christiana. I suspected she must be incredibly powerful to create her own body, and didn't know what else she was capable of. Part of me itched to release them so I could go back to bed, but I needed to let them stay long enough to figure out why they were here and what they wanted from me. I might be able to get valuable information from them. Scientific curiosity prompted me to maintain control of my power. I was desperate to know how she had recreated what appeared to be an actual living body.

I shook myself out of my scientific fascination and tried to focus on the matter at hand. There were two ghosts in my bedroom that were behaving in an unusual manner. I wished Jed was with me. If they were from his ghost council, then he'd know them. Given my last interaction with him, however, I didn't want to ask him for help. He wouldn't always be around to come to my rescue, it was time for me to handle these things on my own.

Snake started arguing with Christiana. "When the Council calls, it is supposed to come," it whined. I wasn't sure if it wanted permission to harm me or just to argue with me some more. It was clear that Christiana was the leader of this particular duo. Good leaders inspired people to follow them, she was ruling based on fear and power alone. If she didn't watch it, her pet would turn on her.

"It doesn't respect you." Snake appealed to Christiana and I thought it was funny that we both thought of each other as *it*. Not human, not ghost, not deserving of the humanity associated with a politer pronoun. Less than all of those things: *it*.

Christiana seemed inclined to agree. "Perhaps it did not get our messages." She inclined her head to me with a coy smile and I shuddered. "Did you not get our messages, sweet Anna?"

I was tired of ghosts playing games, haunting my dreams, trying to kill me and possessing my friends.

"Do you want something to wear?" I changed the subject. She hadn't gone to the trouble of regenerating clothing along with her beyond-perfect body. The room was cold and her statue perfect form was real enough that I could tell she felt it.

"Am I not pleasing to you?" She gestured the length of her body.

I arched an eyebrow. Pleasing didn't begin to describe how I felt about her. Everything about her made the hair on the back of my neck stand up.

"Is this a game to you?" I countered. I was glad I'd worn sensible pajamas to bed: sweat pants and a faded t-shirt. I felt like I had an advantage over her, since I was dressed.

"No, Anna. I did not come all this way to play games with you."

"All evidence to the contrary," I informed her. "I'd like you to get out of my house." Snake laughed at me, but it let her talk.

"You will come to the Council, Anna. Jedediah will bring you to us. It is past time." Her voice was low and smooth.

"I'm not going anywhere." I managed to scoot past Snake and was out of the bed and across the room before either of them could touch me. I hadn't realized I could move that fast with all of the broken ribs, but I made it. I must be healing.

I grabbed my robe from its hook and pulled it on over my pajamas. Having more clothes on made me feel less vulnerable.

"If you want to talk to me, you can talk right now. What is it you want?"

"What I desire and what the Council wants may not always be the same, but I am here at their behest. You will go to them without further delay."

"I will not."

Christiana took a step closer to me, tilting her head sideways so her hair poured over one shoulder in waves. I had a feeling that every move she made was planned. She was used to using her body to get what she wanted. Unfortunately for her, I wasn't impressed. "I had hoped that yesterday's events were enough to get your attention. Perhaps stronger measures are called for."

"They were yours? The ghosts that attacked me?"

Her voice purred with satisfaction. "Did they frighten you, poor girl?"

They had, but I didn't want to admit it to her. "There are easier ways to get me to talk to you. You could try the phone, for example."

"I tire of these games. You waste my time. Go to the Council."

I pretended to contemplate her request for a moment, then looked her dead in the eyes. "No."

"Still you defy me!"

I heard footsteps coming down the hallway and managed to move out of the way before the door burst open. Jed was still dressed in a black t-shirt and jeans, as if he'd never gone to bed. His sword glinted in the lamplight.

"What is this?" He assumed a ready stance in between Christiana and me.

"Jedediah." She murmured his name with a level of familiarity that made me uncomfortable, and I wondered what she was to him.

Check your jealousy, I reminded myself. *You don't have any claim to him.* To his credit, Jed looked confused.

"These two claim to be friends of yours, Jed. From the Council," I supplied helpfully. His eyes narrowed.

Her laugh had a coquettish tinkle to it. "Jedediah. Don't you recognize me?"

He accorded her his half bow but didn't sheath his sword. "My apologies, Christiana. It has been a long time since I saw you in human form. Why have you come?" His speech sounded stilted as if he'd stepped back in time. The fact that he hadn't recognized her added to my confidence.

"She won't tell me her friend's name, but maybe you know it." I kept my tone flat, so she wouldn't think she scared me. Jed glanced at the Snake's wispy hues and shrugged, dismissing it.

"I have come to find out why you fail the Council, Jedediah. They want to see the girl." She stalked towards him and at the last moment, he dropped the tip of his sword so that she didn't spear herself in the abdomen. Pity. She had overstayed her welcome.

He ignored her jab. "This is not a convenient time for a visit. Anna is not yet well."

"She looks well enough," Snake hissed from its place on my bed.

"She is not yet well," Jed reiterated. Christiana stuck out a lower lip so plump it looked like it had been injected with Botox. She rubbed her hand up Jed's arm possessively. Anger bloomed in my chest but I stamped it down.

"You are becoming soft, Jedediah. Has she made you her pet?" Her voice was liquid silk, contrasting with her hateful words.

"I am not soft." He shook her hand off and stepped away from her, towards me, and my inner bitch cheered.

"You have failed the Council," she repeated. "You were supposed to bring the girl to them."

"She listens to her dreams now. The Council can again communicate with her that way."

"It's too late for that. We sent you to bring her to us, not to restore that archaic method of communication." She turned back to me with a speculative look. "Although I am interested, how did you block me from your dreams for so long? You are not that strong."

"Maybe I am," I told her, and she laughed.

"You cannot be, but your years of silence have not gone to waste."

"She is not a child, Christiana." The cordial tone had left Jed's voice. "You have been dead too long if you think to gain her cooperation this way."

"The Council sent me to find her, Jedediah, as they did you. I am here to do what you could not."

"I have protected her as charged, under constant attack. Is the Council so out of touch that you do not know what happened here?"

I didn't see much value in rehashing our battle against Adonijah's army. "Hey, ghosts!" I interjected and they all looked at me. "You both need to leave my house immediately. Stay out of my dreams and do not come back into my house without a formal, written invitation."

Christiana's chest jiggled with rage. "That's not—"

"I'm not done yet," I informed her. "The next time you show up uninvited, I will blast you into the next world." Snake's form diminished slightly under my threat, but Christiana wasn't frightened.

"You will not," she commanded, haughty as a queen.

I laughed. "I will do as I please."

"Anna!" Jed interjected with alarm. Jed's warning tone seemed to convince Christiana that I was a force to be reckoned with, and she backed down.

"Maybe you would, then. Although it would be foolish of you. An event you would come to regret."

"Having to speak with you for this long is cause for regret."

Christiana crossed her arms, causing her breasts to roll up over them. "I see that this one is not as malleable as her mother."

"My mother?" My voice went up an octave. "What could you possibly know about my mother?"

"We know many things," she informed me with a steely smile. "None of which we will share if you continue your current path."

I'd lost my edge in the conversation and reacted with anger. She'd thrown me by bringing up my mother. "Venus de Milo here and her reptilian friend need to either tell us something useful or get the hell out of my house."

"Why have you come, Christiana?" Jed intervened. "Anna is not your servant to be ordered about."

"Do you take your commands from mortal women now? Have you forgotten that you are a king?" Her voice seemed to caress him and I was struck again by the familiarity of her tone. Had she been alive when he was? I hated to think of him spending time with her.

"No one orders me." I'd never heard his tone so cold. "Those times, however, are irrelevant now. King, or whore, what we were when living has no bearing on our roles in death. Anna is a respected healer. She possesses power over the dead, as you well know. Were I you, I would not trifle with her."

"Am I to be trifled with, then, Jedediah?" Her voice had a dangerous purr to it, but he continued as if he hadn't heard her.

"As an advisor to the Council, I would be remiss if I failed to assist you in your attempts to communicate with Anna." Jed was beside me now.

"You *have* failed the Council," Snake spoke, although this time it didn't linger on the soft consonants. *It was just trying to scare me.*

"I do not answer to your pet," Jed informed Christiana, addressing his dialogue to her alone. "I have protected her. I have encouraged her to meet with the Council. That is all I will do for them."

I flinched. I was an assignment. A job. Nothing more than a favor he'd taken on for his precious Council. I'd do well to remember it.

"I now have other priorities," Jed stated in cold tones.

"We did not change them," Christiana inserted.

"Adonijah is here."

"So, this has become personal?" Her voice went up a full octave. "You will use the resources of the Council to pursue this ancient vendetta?"

"You knew he was back, and you did not tell me." His voice was a dangerous whisper and I stepped away from him, and his sword.

"I feared that knowledge would distract you from your task. It appears I was correct."

"He has already attempted to possess Anna. She could have died. He will try harder to hurt her now that he knows she is with me."

"If she were with us, she would be safe."

"Would she?" Jed gave voice to his doubt and I wondered how long he'd had it. Had he intended to take me to them, knowing that they might try to hurt me? If the rest of the Council behaved like Christiana, I was glad I hadn't agreed to meet them. She hadn't tried to physically harm me, but she didn't act like someone who had my best intentions at heart.

"Do you doubt us, servant?"

"I find that I no longer trust you."

"It is not your place to choose!" Snake's transparent form shook with edges of blue. A cold wind rustled the curtains and I wrapped my robe tighter around me.

Jed stepped in front of me, sword held at his side in a relaxed display of the power that he held. "I do not serve the Council now." He sounded resigned as if he'd known it but hadn't been willing to say it out loud. "I stand with Anna Roberts. To the extent that the Council's noble goals are aligned with ours, we will be allies. Try to harm her, and you will have both of us to deal with."

Christiana's pretty face turned red with anger. "Now you defy us along with her. You will both regret it."

Jed's only answer was to shrug.

"Give the sword to me. It is not yours." Snake swirled towards him and I stepped forward and stretched out my hand.

"Are you ready for the next world, Snake?"

It hissed at me and the wind in my room increased to a roar, rattling the windowpanes and knocking over the framed photos on my desk. I heard glass shatter and released my power on the ghost as my anger surged at its lack of respect for me and my things. It screamed as my energy coated it in a fine net, and it exploded into a thousand drops of light. Tendrils of heat seared through me.

I turned to Christiana, my power still ready. Rage filled her eyes, but she acted wary as if she'd just realized that the creature in front of her was rabid.

"Anna." Jed's tone cautioned me, and though I wanted to see her dissolve into a million molecules of nothingness, I held back.

"They came into my house, threatened us, and damaged my property." My voice shook with anger. The photos that had fallen were of my own dead: my mother, my aunt, and my uncle. "You'll take a message to your Council for me," I informed her, "or you'll join your friend in the next world."

She thought this over for a long moment and then nodded, a

graceful acknowledgement of defeat. Whatever it was that held her to this world, she wasn't ready to give it up. "What would you have me say?"

"Tell them that I don't belong to them. I won't be summoned, and I won't do what you tell me to. Unless it fits in with my plans. I don't know who they are, and I don't know what they want to accomplish. If they want to have a meaningful discussion over these matters, I am willing to do that, but it must be on my terms. You will not ambush me like this again. You will stay out of my head, and you will stay out of my dreams."

"That is our easiest method of communication," she protested.

"You can email me. Or call me on the phone. It's not negotiable."

"Most of the dead cannot use a telephone, Anna."

"You seem like you could manage it."

She nodded. "And if you find our goals are aligned?"

"Then I may help you. It depends on what you want me to do, and whether you are willing to help us."

"I see." Her voice sent a shiver down my spine.

"Show up in my bedroom in the middle of the night again and I won't wait to hear you out," I warned her.

"I understand." She coated her words in ice.

"Good."

"Jedediah—" she began.

"You will release me from the Council's service," he told her.

"Is that what you want?" I asked before she could. Two days ago, I thought I'd known that he wanted to be with me but the last few hours had me filled with doubt.

"I would stay with you, if you will have me. Our fight is the same."

Maybe it still was. "No more secrets. You'll tell me everything. If we aren't equal, we can't do this." There were times when I wasn't sure that I could be on the same level as a man who'd been around for three thousand years, but I was going to have to get past my insecurities.

"I will tell you all that I can." His eyes assured me of his sincerity but I noticed he hadn't agreed to tell me everything—just what he could.

"This is very sweet." Christiana's words dripped with ridicule. "I do hope you'll invite me to the wedding."

"It's time for you to go," I reminded her.

"There is much at play that we should discuss."

"Then set up a time to discuss it, but don't pretend you came here today to do anything other than antagonize me." Her lips twitched in a smirk and I resisted the urge to kick her in the shins.

"Your ignorance makes you weak, human. You have delayed for too long." Her shoulders lifted in a shrug and she smiled. "Nevertheless, I will return within the week so that we can discuss these matters."

"Stay out of my head or I'll destroy you the next time I see you."

"So you've said." Her affect was bored. She'd be careful with me now that I'd shown her that I wasn't afraid to release a member of her Council, but she wouldn't show fear.

"If you come in person, you'll come to the front door, like any normal visitor." I looked her over. "With clothes on."

She lowered her chin in a brief moment of agreement and then, with no more difficulty than it took to blink, she was gone. The room sizzled with energy and warmed again.

I drew a deep breath to calm myself. My hands were shaking but I didn't want Jed to know. "How much trouble are you in?" I asked.

"I'm not sure," he admitted. "She did not release me from the Council but I don't believe that she has the power to." He heaved a sigh and sat on the edge of my bed. "There are others in the Council that will be angry over my defection."

"You didn't have to do that. You could still go to them." I wanted him to protest, to say that his place was with me, to tell me that he cared for me, but he didn't say any of those things.

"Adonijah will be back for you. That is my battle, the one I stayed in this world to fight. My brother is my responsibility." He shook his head. "I won't leave you unprotected."

So, he stayed because of his vendetta with his brother. At least I knew. "I can take care of myself," I reminded him, my voice colder than I intended it to be.

"You can," he agreed. I appreciated that he didn't bring up yesterday's incident in the cellar.

The exhaustion caused by tapping into my power combined with coming down from my adrenaline high hit me fast and I sank back onto the bed, fighting to keep my eyes open. If I closed them, I would be asleep before Jed could leave the room.

"This isn't over, is it?"

"No. You didn't let her have the upper hand and she will dwell on that. I think it has been many years since anyone defied her."

"Did you know her when you were alive?" I couldn't help myself. If she'd been one of his wives, I wanted to know.

"No," he sounded amused. "She lived in a different time than me."

"What's happening here, Jed? I think there's more than you're telling me."

He sat down next to me on his side of the bed. "I am unsure. If Christiana comes back, I hope we can have a conversation with her and find out." He handed me a blanket. "You'll get cold, and then you'll hurt."

I didn't know how I could feel cold when I had my own internal nuclear power plant. The chill was creeping across my skin, though, and shivering made my chest hurt.

"Thank you. Will they be back?"

"I don't think so. Not tonight, anyway." He stretched out next to me, braced against the headboard. "Do you want me to stay for a while, just in case?" Luna crawled out from under the bed and jumped up next to him. She wanted him to stay, too.

"Yes, please." I felt like a coward for wanting him here after he'd left earlier, but I wanted to be able to rest without worrying about what I'd wake up to. "Why did she mention my mother?"

"Are you hungry?"

"You know I am, but don't change the subject."

"Do you want me to get you something to eat?"

"No." I let silence fill the space between us.

"I know little about your mother, probably less than you do. Christiana may have been using her to anger you."

"But you know something," I insisted. If he did, he should have told me before now.

"I will tell you all I know tomorrow. Rest. Let yourself heal." He reached over me to turn off the lamp and plunged us into darkness. My sixth sense flared open in reaction to the sudden lack of visibility. I might not be able to see the walls, but I could see Jed's soul burning bright next to me.

"Why didn't you want to stay tonight? Did I do something wrong?" The darkness made me brave.

He didn't respond for long enough that I thought he might have drifted off. "I don't know what you desire," he finally spoke into the darkness.

"I could say the same." My eyes were adjusting to the change in light and I could see the outline of his face. He wasn't looking at me.

"You won't allow me to touch you. I have waited to see if you would come to me." The night he had kissed me in the barn, full of frustration and passion. I'd told him to never touch me again. "I thought you would." His voice was rough. "But when you didn't... it's difficult being here, next to you. I can't do it."

"I didn't know." It sounded lame. I knew it wasn't the right answer. "I've been too caught up in what happened to me." The bright light of his soul told me where he was and I closed the distance between us and pressed my cheek against his. "I'm sorry," I breathed into his ear, and then I found his lips and kissed him.

Jed groaned, entwining his fingers into the hair at the back of my neck and holding onto it like it was his lifeline. The world around us ceased to exist as I straddled his lap and he helped me slide my robe off my shoulders, repositioning my weight. I gasped in shock as felt him through the thin cloth of my pajamas and he answered by pulling me harder against him. A different kind of fire, long forgotten, burned through me, making me forget everything else.

"Don't ask me to stop." It was part plea, part command as one of his hands pulled my lips back to his and the other found its way up my shirt. I abandoned whatever sense of self-control I might have had when his warm hand closed over my left breast.

"I won't," I promised with my lips against his. I pulled at his shirt, needing to touch him, to feel his skin against mine. When Jed started pulling my shirt up, I had a moment of doubt.

"What's wrong?" Jed murmured against my ear when he felt me hesitate.

"My scar..."

The shirt came off and Jed rubbed his thumb over the ridge of my scar in a gentle motion that made me dizzy. He spoke with satisfaction and a hint of pride. "You are a warrior."

CHA TER THREE

THE SOUND OF A DOOR closing interrupted my dream and I resisted waking, trying to cling to the fragments of it. I felt as though something important was drifting away, but the harder I sought the memory the more elusive it became. I relaxed, focused on the darkness behind my closed eyelids, the comfort of the warm blankets. Images flashed by: a wisp of blond hair, a hand gripping my wrist. The smell of death filled my nostrils and my eyes flashed open as I remembered Christiana's voice.

"The Master will find you." Her voice had been full of danger, and when I'd asked her who the Master was, she'd said: "You will know him." She'd offered to tell him how to find me, whoever he was. She'd told him that she looked forward to watching him consume me.

That's pleasant. The conversation with Christiana had been real, but it had happened a month or two before. Why remember it now? *Maybe she's on my mind because she was in my bedroom last night. Who's the Master?*

The unexpected sound of conversation interrupted my thoughts, voices rising and falling. I rolled over, realized I wasn't wearing my pajamas, and smiled when I remembered why. I was alone in bed, and could have convinced myself it was all a dream if my body wasn't still heavy with pleasure. I was not used to the endorphin overload that accompanied lovemaking. When we were done, Jed had held me as I fell asleep, his body wrapped around mine. I'd never felt so safe. Safe, until my subconscious dug out the memories of Christiana's words. What did they mean? She hadn't mentioned this Master guy last night.

I emerged from the blankets, straining to hear the words that continued downstairs but couldn't make them out. Curiosity forced me from my bed. By the time I brushed my teeth and pulled on clothes, the conversation had calmed to a dull murmur. My best friend who was also the nurse at my clinic met me at the bottom of the stairs.

"Good morning, sunshine." Ty greeted me with a hug and held me for a little too long.

"What are you doing here?" I asked. Ty and his partner Chaz were my best friends, but they had busy lives in the city. Chaz was an attorney for a pharmaceutical firm that paid him well for the long hours he worked.

"It's Saturday. We said we might come up this weekend." I blinked in surprise. I hadn't realized it was already the weekend. Not working had me off schedule. I needed to get back to a normal routine, but my life hadn't had much opportunity for anything normal. Not since I met Jed.

"You must have left early," I noted. The drive from their house to my farm was over two hours. "Did Chaz come with you?"

"He's in the kitchen with Jed. Come with me." Ty grabbed my hand and pulled me into the small living room. We sat on the worn sofa that had been in the house since my childhood.

His eyes were red and shadows smudged the undersides of them. "What's going on? Are you guys okay?"

"It's not us; we're fine." He stared into my eyes, and my stomach sank in preparation for whatever news he was about to deliver. "Jennifer Wilson died yesterday."

"Oh, no." I felt dizzy. The self-assured paramedic and I hadn't seen eye to eye, but I'd respected her and I was to blame for her death.

"Anna, it's not your fault." He put his arm around me

"It is." Tears spilled down my cheeks. "They shouldn't have been anywhere near here. Everything that happened is my fault."

I could see Jennifer and her stoic crewmate Jones sorting through their gear in my entryway, covered in snow, as if it had happened moments ago. They'd been fearless, difficult to deal with and totally committed to their jobs. Both of them had lost their lives from the crash in my front yard. In his desire to control me, Adonijah had hurt innocent bystanders. He'd possessed Chaz and my ex-boyfriend in his quest to get close to me.

"You didn't make these ghosts come after you. You didn't choose that." He kept one comforting arm around me. "This is not your fault."

"Did she have family?"

"She had a partner, and they had a kid. That's all I know."

"I'm so sorry." More tears, for the child who'd lost a mother and the lover who was now alone. "When's the funeral?"

"I don't know yet, but I heard they're setting up a fund for the family. I'll email you the details."

"We're sending a check." I looked up at Chaz's voice and managed a smile for him.

"That's nice, Chaz. I'll send one too." It was a pretty lame thing to offer someone who had lost a loved one, but I couldn't bring her back. When it feels like blood money, it is.

Jed stepped around Chaz and knelt before me with a cup of coffee. He handed me the coffee and then cupped the side of my face with the palm that was still warm from the coffee mug, holding eye contact long enough that I almost forgot why I was crying. I blushed from the heat in his eyes, all but hearing Chaz raise his eyebrows. My relationship with Jed had changed overnight, but I didn't think it was the time to tell Ty and Chaz about it. Too late, I was pretty sure they knew now.

"Did you sleep okay?" Jed's voice was full of warmth.

Between the nighttime visitors and spending time with Jed, I wasn't sure I'd slept much, but that didn't matter. "I did. Thank you."

"Chaz, more coffee?" Jed stepped away from me and Chaz followed him, leaving Ty and me.

"Finally," Ty snorted, shaking his head. "I've never seen two people take so long to get together."

"I haven't known him that long." I wiped my tears on my sleeve.

"Maybe not but it's been electric between you two since you first met."

That was true enough that it didn't need a response. I sat back against the sofa and closed my eyes, holding the hot mug close to my chest while I tried to come to terms with my involvement in Jennifer Wilson's death.

Oncologists have high rates of depression since such a high percentage of their patients die. Surgeons survive emotionally by having a stereotypical god complex. I was just a family practice physician—the bottom of the proverbial physician food chain. I hadn't been present when people died since I was in my residency. Not that I didn't lose any of my patients, but death was usually a step removed. My little free health clinic had had its share of excitement, but thus far we'd managed to get the really sick people to the hospital or into hospice before they passed away. The true but unbearable part of being a doctor was that while we were supposed to be able to fix people, our success rate wasn't as high as we needed it to be. Life is a fatal condition.

"Anna." Ty rubbed my arm. "Come on, baby. It's not your fault. She's not the first patient you lost and she won't be the last." True words, but they didn't make me feel any better. I buried my face in the crook of his neck and let myself mourn while he rocked me and stroked my hair. I heard Chaz and Jed enter the room again, and felt Jed settle on my other side.

When my snuffling slowed, Chaz leaned close enough to hand me a tissue box.

"Thanks. Sorry for falling apart."

"No apology needed." He waited while I blew my nose. "Jed said you had some activity yesterday."

I turned to Jed in alarm, words tumbling from my mouth. "I don't—I mean, I…" *He told them about what happened between us last night?*

Jed cleared his throat in an amused rumble. "I told them about finding you in the cellar when I got back from the store."

"Of course." My blush deepened. Ty was laughing at my discomfort while Chaz politely ignored it. "It was scary." I elbowed Ty to subdue his laughter. "I would have figured out how to get out of it, but Jed came back in time to help." I tried to steer the conversation further from my embarrassment. "Did he tell you about the ghosts last night?"

"I did not."

My stomach growled, a rumble so loud it interrupted me. "We'll tell you, but I may need to eat first."

"I wasn't sure how long you would sleep, but I can cook breakfast as soon as you want it." Jed's expression, always so masked, softened when his eyes met mine. My breath stilled at the look in his eyes. Our changed relationship was an unfamiliar world and I faltered, realizing I didn't know what it meant or how to navigate it.

"I am hungry," I reiterated, deflecting further thoughts about what had happened between us.

"Bacon and eggs?" Jed offered.

"I saw some apples on the counter. If you want pancakes, I could whip some up," Chaz offered. Chaz's apple pancakes were the stuff of legend, half pancake, half apple fritter.

"Oh yes," I moaned in anticipation and Ty laughed at me.

"I'd guess our girl has been killing ghosts again?"

"It was an exciting night," I answered.

"I'll bet it was." Ty's eyebrows wiggled in exaggerated innuendo towards Jed.

"Food first, then we'll tell you about the *ghosts*." I swatted him on the arm, certain that my face was bright red.

Jedediah and Chaz kept the conversation light while they cooked, and then while we ate I told them about Christiana and her snake-like friend's visit last night. I didn't mention the bit about Jedediah asking to be released from the Council's service.

"Anna, if you go around blasting the ghosts who are supposed to be good, it'll damage your reputation." Chaz teased, but his eyes looked worried.

"They didn't seem to be on my side." I poured myself another cup of coffee. "In fact, I still think I should have released Christiana too."

"If it comes to that, it will make things more difficult for us," Jed noted.

"How so?" Ty voiced the question that had been on my mind since the night before.

"The Council may be a powerful ally or a powerful enemy. This is a choice that Anna must make." His tone was resigned as if he had given up all hope of influencing my decision on the Council.

"If they wanted to be friends they shouldn't have shown up in my bedroom in the middle of the night and threatened me. They shouldn't have tormented my dreams so that I had to take medication in order to prevent them from getting to me."

"I agree their method lacks courtesy." Jed moved our empty plates from the table to the counter.

"I didn't ask for any of this," I reminded him.

"You didn't," he agreed. "But who else will stop Adonijah? Who besides you can?"

"That's not fair," I argued.

"It is what it is." Chaz silenced my protestations. "If you hadn't been able to save me, I wouldn't be here today."

"Adonijah wouldn't have come anywhere near you if he weren't trying to get close to me." My voice was getting louder.

"It is what it is," he repeated. "You don't get to choose your path."

"I know you believe that, but I'm not sure I do."

Chaz's reply was gentle. "You cannot change this gift any more than you can change who you are."

"I'm not wild about the destiny conversation," I reminded him, turning my attention back to Jed. "What happens now? When can I go home and go back to work?" My modern condo in Kansas City seemed like it was a world away, along with my clinic and patients.

Jed gave me a look I couldn't quite read before turning back to the dishes. "They continue to target you." Now he was the teacher, trying to temper his frustration while lecturing a wayward student. "Yesterday's attack proves that they remain in the area, and that they will keep trying to hurt you."

"That's comforting." Sometimes snide commentary was all I had going for me.

"If you go back to the city, they will follow you there."

"Maybe it's time to run away, go to Canada or something," I suggested. Jed shot me another look, and this one I could read. He had tried his very best to get me out of the country as soon as all of this had happened.

"If you're going to run to another country in wintertime, you should go south. Mexico would be nice this time of year." Ty grinned at Chaz. "We should go with them. They might need us."

"Good point. Mexico it is. I'll go pack my swimsuit." I stayed put.

"But the ghosts would still be here, right?" Ty brought us back to the real world, concern coloring his voice now that he was done joking. He had been with Chaz when he was possessed, and afterward. It scared all of us that there were things that could control us so easily.

"Yes. They will continue their attempt to take over life here, no matter where Anna is."

"I'm one person." My voice trembled, and I cringed. I wasn't the kind of person who cried this much.

"There may be others with your ability, but I do not know how to find them," Jed informed us. "Only the Council knows where all of you are, and how to communicate with you."

"So, we're alone in this." I fought to keep my voice steady. "I can't stop them all."

"Seems like you are the only one who can." Chaz effectively ended the conversation with simple words. "How are you feeling now? Are those ribs that Ty broke healing?"

"I'm starting to feel better. I was pretty tired and sore for a while, but I feel much better today." I realized it was true as I said it.

"That's great. How about that cut on your chest?" Ty: the nurse who should have been a doctor.

"It healed really well." I unzipped my pullover and pulled the neckline of my shirt over so Ty could admire the top edge of the vertical red scar line overlaying my pectoral and collarbone.

"Looks good."

"Yeah, the surgeon did a nice repair."

Ty's eyes drifted up to meet mine. "I still have nightmares over how close we came to losing you."

"It was a close call," I said simply, shying away from the sweet memory of death. There was no way to tell them that until the last few days, I thought they had lost me. I didn't know how to explain how drawn I still felt to the peaceful feeling of leaving this life behind. It was easier to change the subject. "So, how long are you guys here for?"

"We could go home today." Chaz gave Ty a relaxed smile. "Unless we end up staying."

"Either way. You guys are always welcome." We all knew they'd stay over. It was too long a drive to go back to the city the same day if you didn't have to.

"We were hoping you'd say that."

"We can call Ned and Carrie, see if they want to join us for dinner," I suggested.

"You mean see if Carrie wants to come over and cook for us," Ty intoned and I grinned back at him.

"Something like that."

The phone rang and Jed reached for the handset. Ty looked surprised but I shrugged. Jed had been answering my phone since we'd come to the farm. Since it was a landline, I wasn't always close enough to grab it.

"Yes," Jed answered, and then paused to listen. "That's unfortunate. I will check with Anna." He turned to me. "Someone Ned knows may be sick. He wants to know if you'll go see them."

I held my hand out for the handset. "Hey, Ned, what's wrong?"

"Anna. Do you remember Katheryn McPherson?"

I searched my memory. "Carrie's aunt?"

"Great aunt, but close enough," he corrected me. "You met her at some point."

"Yes, I remember." I hadn't lived in the area full time since high school. When I was at the farm, I didn't spend much time socializing with people in town. There were plenty of people I didn't remember well. Carrie and Ned were the only ones I spent any significant time with. I had a vague memory of an older woman with glasses and silver hair. I probably hadn't seen her since Ned and Carrie's wedding. "What's going on with her?"

"I'm not sure. We went to visit her this morning to bring her some of Carrie's cheese, but she was acting pretty strange."

"Strange how?"

"Like she'd had a stroke or something."

"If you think she's had a stroke you need to get her to a hospital right away."

"We tried that, but she flat out refused to go. Will you come take a look at her? Maybe she'll listen to you."

"Why doesn't she want to go to the hospital?"

"I don't know, but she's acting strange, and Carrie's pretty upset."

"Of course I'll come." I wasn't above making a house call if my friends needed me to, and the last time someone had been 'acting strange' the explanation was ghost related instead of medical. "Where does she live?"

"It's out 139, up towards the state line."

I traced the route in my mind and figured it would take me half an hour to get up there. "Are you staying up that way?"

"We're going to run back to town to get some fuel. We'll meet you at the gas station."

"I'll call you when I get close."

"Thanks, Anna." The line went dead.

"Anybody up for a drive?" None of my guests looked very excited at the prospect.

"Do you need our help?" Ty whispered through his yawn.

"No. I can't imagine I'll be gone more than a couple of hours. Why don't you guys get some rest? I'll be back in time for lunch."

"I'd like to come with you," Jed informed me. I'd assumed he would, but his answer made me grin.

"You can drive," I offered and he gave me a nod of agreement. No one would ever accuse him of being effusive but I still felt the flush across my cheeks.

"I'll just grab my medical kit." I tried to rally from my embarrassment since I was acting like a hormonal teenager with her first crush. *Get a grip, Anna. There's a sick, elderly woman who needs your help. Focus.* "Just in case." If Katheryn really had stroke symptoms, I'd be trying to convince her to go to the hospital. There wasn't anything magical in my bag that would help that particular condition, but I did have a blood pressure cuff and a few other things that might be useful. I liked to be prepared.

My Subaru managed the snow-packed drive to the main road with ease and the paved roads were dry enough they didn't present any problems for us. Jed driving was a habit leftover from the days right after my injury that had stayed with us. A heavy blanket of snow still covered the ground even though it hadn't snowed in a couple of weeks. When the sun shone, the ground glittered like a field of diamonds, but recently the skies had been filled with stubborn clouds day after day. At least with the ground frozen, we weren't dealing with mud, but the perpetual lack of sunshine was depressing. I wasn't sure which was worse.

Winter had a stark beauty, but this had been a cold one. I was looking forward to the hope of spring, to seeing green buds on the trees and the early purple crocuses peeking through last year's dead grass.

While I loved living in the city, with its vibrant arts scene and great restaurants, I was still a country girl. The simple beauty of the rolling, wood-covered hills in northern Missouri was in my blood, at least on my mother's side. I didn't know who my father was, and my mother had left me with her sister before she died. My aunt and uncle hadn't been able to have children of their own, so I guessed it had worked out for them as well as it had for me.

"Why did Christiana bring my mother up? Was she just trying to annoy me, or does she really know something?" I clung to this one point, unwilling to let it go.

Jed shrugged one shoulder. "Perhaps to annoy you, in part." He glanced over at me. "But I imagine Christiana knew her."

"How would she?"

"Your mother had the power to release ghosts, just as you do."

I took a moment to absorb that, remembering the night I'd met Jed. "You said my mother might know about me once, that the ability can run in families, but you didn't say she could banish them. How did you know?"

"I know that Eva worked with the Council."

"You knew her?" My voice cracked in a rush of anger and pain.

"No, I never knew her." He rushed to defend himself. "I've just heard of her."

"If you knew this much, why didn't you tell me before now?"

He gave me a guilty glance before turning his eyes back to the road. "I should have, and I meant to. There hasn't been a convenient time."

Maybe there wasn't ever a convenient time to tell someone that you knew things about their dead parent that they didn't, but Jed had too many secrets. "That's no excuse. What else is there that you *should* have told me?"

"I am sorry." It wasn't an answer but the hard edge to his words said I wouldn't get more out of him. Why was he keeping things from me?

"What do you mean she worked with the Council?"

"If she hadn't died, I assume she would have raised you so that you knew about your gifts, and the Council."

"She was doing missionary work in Guatemala, she wasn't chasing ghosts."

"She was there on behalf of the Council. Something went wrong."

"She died in an accident. That's what went wrong." If they had done an autopsy, we'd never gotten the report, and they'd buried her there. Inter-country communication at that time hadn't been very good and we'd never learned much.

I did know her ghost was gone. I'd thought I was having a

nightmare when she'd come to me, her skin incandescent. Even in my five-year-old mind, I knew it wasn't possible for her to be there. I reached out to her, wanting her to put her arms around me. My hand had breezed through her skin with a rush of cold air, and my chest burned as I released some energy from my core. Just like that, she was gone. I'd released her without even knowing what I was doing. My throat clenched with frustration and regret. If I hadn't released her, what would she have told me?

"I don't know exactly what caused her death but the Council sent her there, Anna. I'm not certain if it was an accident."

"You think it was a ghost?"

"She wouldn't have been there at all, were there not a threat they needed her to banish. Maybe it was greater than she could overcome."

"She left me. She cared more about whatever was going on there than she did her own daughter." I tasted the bitter words, felt the reality of them lurking inside me.

Snow topped electrical poles and barren trees flashed by outside my window. A red-tailed hawk, unaffected by the bitter cold, drifted, watching the ground for his next meal.

"Maybe she went because she wanted to protect you."

"I needed a mother, not a knight in shining armor."

"If you had a daughter—"

"I wouldn't leave her."

"Even to protect her from someone like my brother?"

I took a deep breath because I didn't know how to answer that. "Who was she after in Guatemala?" The thought of my mother dying because she had to face someone like Adonijah made me nauseous.

"I don't know. But it might be useful information." He raised his eyebrows. "When Christiana returns…"

I exhaled in annoyance. "Fine. I'll try to be nice enough to get some information out of her."

My Aunt Ann had never indicated that there was anything special about her sister, and as far as I knew they'd been close. If she'd been aware that her sibling had an affinity for ghosts wouldn't she have talked to me about it? Watched me to see if I had any strange abilities? Could Aunt Ann see ghosts?

Maybe she had watched me. She'd been a quiet woman; kind and caring, with a quick intelligence and a good mind for business.

She'd loved gardening as much as she'd enjoyed running the financial aspects of the farm, and she understood horses better than anyone else. Maybe she'd seen me struggle with my abilities and watched as I'd turned my life to science, and decided I was better off not knowing. I wished I'd asked her.

What's different about my physiology? I asked the question again that had plagued me all my life. *If my mother had it, that adds some possibilities.*

"Is it a genetic anomaly?"

Jed shrugged. "You're the scientist. Tell me again what genes are. They're little things inside of us?" He gave me a quizzical smile and then turned his attention back to the road.

We'd had a conversation about the building blocks of human life before, but it was a lot to absorb if you were a three-thousand-year-old soul. When Jed was alive, good science involved sacrificing goats to the gods. Or so I assumed. He'd lived a few lives since then, but he'd said the last one was in the early 1900s. That was before they knew much about the tiny particles that make up life. Louis Pasteur introduced the concept of micro-organisms causing bacteria in the late 1800s and DNA had been discovered, but its role in genetics wasn't understood until the mid-1900s. Jed had picked up a lot of information in his short time living in the 21st century and had adapted amazingly well to the technology, but he had a lot to catch up on before his understanding of science reached modern day levels. I opted for a short science lesson.

"Genes are passed onto us by our parents. They determine all of our traits, from hair color to blood type, and can determine what diseases certain people get." That was as simple as I could keep it without giving him a complete lecture on the fundamentals of human life. He'd managed thus far without learning the fine details of mapping the genetic code. Visual aids would help frame the conversation, but I didn't have anything like that with me.

"Your ability does seem to run in families," he said.

If they mapped my genetic code would they find an extra marker? The ghost sensing and banishing gene. Maybe I'd win the Nobel Prize for discovering it. I chuckled at the thought. Physicians who went into research might have a chance at science's most prestigious honor. Family Practice physicians working in free health clinics did not.

"What kind of things did my mother do for the Council?"

"I didn't work with her. I just knew of her. Christiana would be able to tell us more."

"She and I didn't exactly hit it off."

"Souls who are thousands of years old do not always do well with being ordered about. You have a strong personality and she comes from a time when she would have been accorded respect merely because of who she was."

"What, she was a queen or something?" I was getting tired of dead queens influencing my life.

"No. But she was of noble blood. From an influential family. Wealthy."

"And I'm not."

"Bloodlines are unimportant in your world, but from her point of view…" He shrugged.

"And yours."

"I serve with you, Anna. I do not harbor such thoughts." He sounded annoyed but kept his focus on driving. "Do you feel as if I don't respect you?"

"No. I think you respect me." I stared out the window again. "I just wondered. You were a king, and I'm…" I wasn't sure what he would classify me as. Americans didn't think in terms of royalty. What was I? A commoner? A peasant? Something worse?

He guided the Subaru through a stretch of ice and slush covered road with skill. He'd learned a lot about driving in the wintertime in Switzerland before he'd come to find me. "You're a gifted healer, and you can banish ghosts. That is all that matters. Though bloodlines once meant something to me, the time when I worried about who is royal or not is long past."

"I don't know that I compete well with royalty." That was the understatement of the year.

"You have the gift, Anna. As far as the Council is concerned, you are all that matters."

"Christiana doesn't believe that."

"She was angry that you disagreed with her." I snorted. That was an interesting way of saying 'threatened to kill'.

"The times have changed since Christiana and I lived," Jed went on. "Queens and kings are no longer relevant."

"At least not here in the States." We pulled into Unionville and I spotted Carrie's Explorer at the gas station. "There they are." I wasn't done talking about my mother and what else Jed knew about her, but it was going to have to wait.

Carrie greeted me with a worried smile. "Thanks for coming."

"Of course. What are her symptoms?"

"She seems confused, and she's pretty cranky."

"How old is she?"

"She's in her late seventies."

"Any other medical conditions? Has she had a stroke before?"

"I probably should know, but I don't." Carrie ran a hand through her hair and sighed. "We aren't all that close. She kind of keeps to herself, but now that she's alone, we try to keep an eye on her. Check in on her now and then."

"That's nice of you." I meant it. So many of my patients didn't have anyone who cared enough to help them.

"We're family," Carrie explained.

"Will she let me take a look at her?"

"I don't know." Carrie shook her head. "Since she refuses to go to the hospital, I didn't know what to do."

I shrugged. I couldn't force someone to let me examine them, but sometimes people would respect a doctor when they wouldn't listen to their own families.

"How far is it?"

"Just ten minutes. You want to follow us?" There wasn't really room in the gas station parking area to leave a vehicle.

"Lead on." I climbed back in next to Jed and he followed the Explorer out of the parking lot. We drove past the outskirts of town and turned onto a road that went in a straight line up and down the steep hillsides like a roller coaster. Small farms and ranches dotted the landscape.

The drive we turned up was a well maintained, long winding road that someone had plowed down to the gravel surface. Tall oaks lined the way, planted in even intervals, their bare branches reaching up to the sky with desolate grace.

We pulled into two spaces off the garage that looked like they were for guests and got out for a hurried conference behind the cars.

"She was pretty mad that we came up here earlier," Ned reminded Carrie.

"She was." Carrie's brow pinched in concern. "Why don't you
guys give us a minute and Anna and I will go try to talk to her. She
might not feel like she's being ganged up on if it's just us girls."

"Whatever you think," I agreed. I fell into step beside Carrie and
we made our way around the house to the front door, admiring the
neat shrubs and rock lined flower beds along the way. I felt a pang of
guilt. I needed to spend more time at my farm in the spring, cleaning
up the neglected flower gardens that had been my aunt's pride and
joy.

"Who are you?" A rough voice jerked me out of my reverie,
the owner barely visible in the shadow of the doorway. My attention caught on the double-barreled shotgun that pointed through
the opening at us. Carrie and I froze. I tried to think of some way to
warn the guys, but was afraid to move.

"Aunt Katheryn, it's Carrie." She spoke in calm measured tones
as if the gun pointing at her was of little concern. "I was just here a
little while ago."

"I told you to go away." The tip of the gun didn't waver. For an
older adult, she had strong arms.

"Aunt Katheryn, I brought a friend to see you. This is Anna."

"I don't give a shit who she is." She lingered on the bad word,
rolled it around in her mouth like it had been a while since she said
it and liked how it felt.

Carrie sucked in her breath in shock and I guessed that Aunt
Katheryn didn't use many four-letter words.

Given the personality change, she might have an embolic stroke
in the frontal lobe that had blocked off blood flow, which wasn't
good news. The other possible option was an aneurysm, and if that
was it, she needed to have coils placed to fix the problem before it
burst and caused irreparable damage. Either way, we needed to get
her to a major medical center. I didn't think there was any place with
a neuro-interventionalist who could treat this kind of problem closer
than Kansas City, Des Moines, or St. Louis. But Unionville had a
helicopter pad, so if we could get her back there then there was hope
that it could be fixed.

There was a third diagnosis that came to mind, but it involved ghosts and I couldn't fathom why one would be out here, with Aunt Katheryn, in the middle of nowhere. My sixth sense wasn't picking up on anything out of the ordinary. I needed to get closer to her, but she had a shotgun pointed at me.

"My name is Dr. Anna Roberts." I held my hands out in front of me in the universal gesture of peace and spoke in loud clear tones in case she had trouble hearing. "There's no need to shoot; we won't come any closer." I didn't address her by her first name because I didn't want to piss her off more. "You might remember me. I used to go to school with Carrie's husband, Ned."

"I know who you are." She didn't sound pleased.

"Would you like us to back up?" I didn't want to do anything that would startle her, but I did want to get farther away from her gun. If she pulled the trigger, the spray at this close distance would cause major damage to both of us. I'd had my doubts about the benefits of coming back to life, but staring into the wide barrels of Aunt Katheryn's twelve-gauge drove home the fact that I wasn't ready to die again.

"You can stay right there," she growled.

It wasn't the answer I'd hoped for. The good news was that the boys hadn't come up the walk behind us. If we were lucky, they'd figure out we'd run into trouble and would call for help. Maybe Carrie and I just needed to stall for a while until assistance arrived, although I wasn't eager to be standing in the middle of a shootout between the county sheriff and a septuagenarian with a gun who'd just lost all of her social inhibitions.

I risked a glance at Carrie and saw she was as alarmed as I was. Deer do freeze when they see car headlights barreling down on them, and that exact look was reflected in her eyes. Mine too, probably.

"Ma'am, I'm sorry, how can I best address you?"

"My name is Carl," she announced in firm tones and I risked a glance at Carrie who looked confounded.

"Thank you, Carl. Your niece, Carrie, she's not looking very well. Would it be okay if she went back to the car while we talk?"

Katheryn/Carl hesitated.

"I'll stay right here," I assured her. "Carrie will just go back to the car, and wait until we are done."

"No." Her tone was final. "You think you'll—" She made a

sudden strangling noise and the tip of the shotgun jolted upwards as it discharged a spray of shot, dislodging chunks of wood and plaster as it sprayed the porch roof. I tackled Carrie and we both sprawled into the snow to the right of the front door. I scrambled to my feet, grabbing Carrie's arm as tightly as I could through her coat and dragged her around the far corner of the house where I collapsed on the ground next to her, our backs pressed against the side of the house.

"Is Aunt Katheryn always this cranky?" I whispered, glancing back around the corner to make sure she wasn't in pursuit.

"She never even cusses. She's really a sweet woman."

"I'm not sure if this is what's going on with her, but one of the options is a frontal lobe stroke, which can cause severe personality changes," I explained in a whisper. "It's treatable but we have to get her to a major hospital. Unionville can't treat this."

"What do we do?"

"We've got to get the gun out of her hand and get her to Unionville Regional. They can put her on a helicopter to KC or Des Moines."

"Anna? Carrie?" Jed's voice boomed from the front and I hoped he wasn't running across Katheryn/Carl's visual field.

"She's got a gun!" I scrambled to my feet just as Jed came barreling around the corner.

"Are you all right?" He demanded, his hands all over me as he searched my visible skin like a vet looking for defects in a horse's legs. I slapped his hands away.

"We're fine, but Katheryn has a—"

"We were coming to check on you and caught sight of the gun. We backtracked and broke in through a garage window while you were talking to her. We've got her tied up in the living room."

"Oh my God." Would the stress of being assaulted in her own home and the indignity of being tied to a chair cause a trauma reaction, and the personality manifestation to worsen? I didn't need her blood pressure any higher than it already was.

I ran as fast as I could through the crusted over snow drifts in Katheryn's front yard. It felt like running through wet concrete.

When I burst through the front door I found Ned kneeling in front of Katheryn, her long white hair disheveled. She would have been beautiful if she wasn't red with indignation, curse words streaming from her mouth in a foul river. Conscious and angry meant she was still alive. They had her tied to a sturdy looking dining room chair. I bent over and gasped for air. If I couldn't breathe, I couldn't help her. *As soon as these ribs heal it's time to get back to the gym.*

"Something's not right with her, Anna."

"Yeah, I know." I saw the shotgun carefully placed on top of an upright piano that looked like it was well loved, and knew that Ned's first act had been to get it to a place where no one would accidentally get hurt. I glanced around the rest of the living room. There was a worn couch with a distracting floral pattern tucked underneath the front windows. Built in shelves around the brick fireplace housed framed photographs from another era, many of them predating the era of color prints.

"No, I mean..." Ned sat back on his heels and evaluated the white-haired woman in front of him with the calculation of a psychiatrist. "I don't think it's her."

She was working her way through a litany of words dedicated to describing feces and incestuous acts.

"If she's had a frontal lobe stroke, this personality shift isn't abnormal, but you may be right."

"She thinks she's someone named Carl."

"Fuck you!" Katheryn yelled. "Fuck Fuck Fuck..." She tasted this word and seemed to enjoy it. "Fuck, fuck... fuck you mother fuckers!"

"Are you all right?" Ned glanced at my snow soaked jeans.

I was recovering, but my body wasn't ready for the stunt-man style moves that I'd just pulled. "I'm okay. Just haven't run in a while. Are you okay?"

Ned shrugged with a half grin. "Getting through the window wasn't the easiest thing in the world but it was the only way I could think of to get in the house without her hearing us."

"No cuts?"

"Nah, we're fine." Based on his grin I'd have bet he enjoyed the thrill of it now that he knew the threat was under control.

Jed and Carrie came through the door behind me, and Carrie let out a squeak of horror at her aunt's condition. I wondered which shocked her more, the endless string of obscenities pouring out of Katheryn's mouth, or how Ned had tied the woman to a living room chair. She looked like a trussed deer ready to be hauled out of the woods. Ned had won the calf roping competition at the state fair when we were twelve, but I hadn't realized he was able to adapt the skills to humans so easily. I gave Katheryn's wrists a speculative glance to see if they were bruised from being roped, but they seemed fine.

"You think she's possessed?" I asked Ned and he nodded. Carrie moaned. It was possible that Katheryn had a bleed, and that this personality change was just a manifestation of her internal, forbidden desire to be mean and cuss like a pirate. Despite our recent interactions with ghosts, I thought the medical explanation was more likely. What would the ghosts achieve by attacking an old woman who lived alone in the countryside?

I might be able to rule out ghost possession, though. It was the one option I might be able to rule out without access to a CT scanner. I walked closer and stood next to her, focusing my extra sense on her. There was the bright light of her soul inside her, much like that of everyone else in the room. There was something else in Aunt Katheryn, though. A second shifting of light, tethered to her own like a leech.

"I'll be damned," I muttered. "You little bastard, where did you come from?" I heard Carrie's hiss and gathered myself. Cussing at my patients was not acceptable, even when they were possessed by unexpected ghosts. "Ned, get my box out of the backseat. She's going to need fluids when we get this thing out of her." I'd added a few liter bags of lactated ringers and a few IV kits to my standard emergency medical kit after I'd come home from the hospital. Ned was already out the front door of the house.

"There's a ghost in her?" Carrie asked for confirmation, taking a step back as if her aunt's condition might be contagious.

"Yeah. I assume you want me to get rid of it?"

"Well, yes." Her eyes were wide.

"Jed, any advice on how to do this?"

"With care," Jed advised wryly, looking down on the woman. "There is some danger."

"Thanks for the help," I grumbled, eyeing my patient with trepidation. The last time I'd released a ghost that was possessing a person I'd used the buffer of a car's metal frame to temper my power. The risk Jed referred to was that I might not only release the parasitic soul but also the one that belonged there. I took a deep breath to calm myself and jumped as the door slammed and Ned stomped back in with my box and set it on the dining room table behind Katheryn.

If this didn't go well and I accidentally released both souls, I didn't have a defibrillator on hand. Not to mention that I didn't relish the thought of having to do CPR on this little old lady. She wasn't acting very frail—she had just begun experimenting with a few words I was shocked she even knew—but that didn't make me eager to crack her ribcage with compressions.

"Just do something," Ned demanded. "This is getting old."

Should I wait until we get her to the hospital? Doing it there gave her access to immediate medical care if something went wrong. Unfortunately, we were going to have a hard time getting her there without involving a lot of law enforcement personnel, and might even need a court order since she was saying she didn't want to go. Not to mention the fact that we had her tied to a chair, which the authorities would not look kindly on. *You don't have time to wait; you have to do it now, Anna.*

"Katheryn." I patted the thin, dry skin of her exposed forearm. "I think you've got a bad spirit inside of you, and I'm going to get rid of it. Is that okay?" I chuckled at the idea of getting her to sign a 'consent to treat' form. Maybe I should develop one for this situation.

Carrie glared at me. "What's so funny?"

"Sorry. I'm just nervous."

"You've gotten rid of loads of these things," Ned pointed out.

"Only one while they were possessing someone else. It complicates things."

He didn't ask for more information which was just as well. There wasn't any reason to delay. Jed nodded at me, his eyes reassuring me that I could do this. I put my hand on Katheryn's knee.

"What are you doing?" Her voice rose to a painful pitch. "Get away from me, you bitch!" I felt the muscles of her thigh tighten as either she or Carl tried to kick me. I preferred to assume it was Carl. Ned's ropes were tight enough to prevent the leg from moving much.

"Shut up, Carl," Ned ordered and Carrie smacked his arm.

"Show Aunt Katheryn some respect. It's not her fault."

"Sorry," Ned mumbled, half towards his wife and half towards Katheryn.

I took a deep breath, concentrating on the two spirits inside her. Focusing on the fainter light of Carl's soul, I slowly released a small amount of my fire, hoping I could keep my power from hurting Katheryn. My arm burned all the way down as energy threaded through it towards my hand, through my fingers, and into Katheryn's leg. It wasn't a fine science but Katheryn screamed and I saw the fainter soul inside her disintegrate in a minuscule explosion of light, the sparks from it flung from her body like invisible embers that dissipated as soon as they hit air. The other soul flickered and then stabilized again into a steady glow. I hoped that it was Carl's soul that was gone.

"Is it done?" Ned sounded impatient.

I took a deep breath to steady myself and Katheryn's body started shaking so much I worried that she might have a seizure.

"This isn't a science." My reply was curt, my fingers on her wrist as I tried to feel her pulse and couldn't. Katheryn's eyes rolled up until all I could see were the whites of her sclera. Her head lolled to one side and she passed out.

"Damn it." I reached for her neck to check for her pulse and started barking curt orders. "Carrie, support her head. Let's get her on the floor. Cut her loose, Ned."

My fingers covered the dry skin on her throat and I closed my eyes to concentrate and block out the outside noise. Finally, I felt the steady flow of blood, pulsing through her carotids. Her heart was still beating. I released the breath I'd been holding.

Eagle Scout that he was, Ned had the knots undone in moments and we were able to lay her on the carpet with a pillow under her legs. If she had the low back problems that plagued many older adults, I didn't want to be responsible for making her pain worse.

"Carrie, call 911," I requested while I listened to Katheryn's heart and lungs with my stethoscope. Her heart beat was faster than I liked, but strong. "I don't want to risk transporting her ourselves. They've got better equipment in the ambulance."

"I'm calling." Carrie extracted her cell phone from her pocket and stepped into the kitchen.

"Perhaps we should clean up the ropes," I suggested. "I don't think we want the paramedics to see this."

Jed started gathering the excess rope up. "I'm going to lift this chair over you," he warned me. I grunted assent and ducked so he wouldn't clobber me in the head with it.

I pulled up the sleeves on Katheryn's shirt and discovered that she had paper thin skin and bad veins, which meant that getting a needle in her was going to be challenging. I ran through my options. We were close enough to Unionville that I could wait for the ambulance to get her to the ER if I had to. If Ty were here… well, he was a nurse and he stuck needles in people a lot more than I did.

I assumed she was going to have the same physical reaction to ghost possession that the rest of us had. She'd feel like three shades of hell when she came to. Tachycardia, dehydration, and low blood pressure. My best guess was that the energy of the ghosts caused problems with our adrenaline receptors.

The three of us who had been through it recovered, but it had taken enough steroids and fluids that there were bets over how fast I would start growing chest hair. We were all young and healthy, though. There was no guarantee that Katheryn, as old as she was, would fare as well. Which meant I couldn't afford to wait. She needed the electrolytes and fluids contained in the lactated ringers now.

"Can you tell if she's there?" Ned leaned over my shoulder while I pulled a liter of fluids and an IV kit out of my box. Considering her small, fragile veins, I chose a smaller gauge 22 Jelco needle in hopes of improving my chances of getting access. I elbowed Ned back out of my surgical field.

"Not yet, and get back. Right now we need to get her stabilized. Her body will probably have the same reaction that the rest of us had, so we don't have a lot of time."

"What if it isn't her?" He sounded like a research scientist getting ready to pull out a clipboard and take notes.

"I can't let her die, either way," I reminded him.

Using a simple rubber tourniquet just below her right elbow, I watched with satisfaction as the cephalic vein popped out on her forearm. I wiped the site down with iodine and then rubbed the brown substance off with an alcohol pad which helped the vein pop up more. Connecting the bag of ringers to the IV kit tubing with a quick twist, I ran a few drops through the needle before placing my thumb on the lower end of the cephalic vein, just above the head of her radius. I took a deep breath, put traction on the vein and slid the needle and catheter in, pleased by the little flashback of blood into the catheter. I removed the tourniquet, anchored everything with tape and silently cheered myself for being able to get it on the first try. Putting needles into veins wasn't something I did much anymore, and there is an art to it.

Carrie brought a blanket and covered Katheryn at the same time that Jed and Ned finished cleaning up the evidence from their break in. She'd feel cold when she woke since I had the fluids going at a brisk rate.

"Ambulance is on the way," Carrie informed us.

"What's our story here?" Ned asked.

"Good question," Carrie said.

"We can't just say we found her like this?" Jed asked.

"I'd like to give them information that doesn't send them down the wrong diagnosis path," I inserted. "She doesn't need a bunch of CTs to see if she hurt herself falling when we know she didn't fall. What she does need are fluids and steroids."

"So just tell them she has whatever you and Chaz had."

"It doesn't fit the pattern of any known disease, so it's hard to convince anyone that it's a virus. The three of us who were affected haven't been anywhere near Katheryn, so I can't explain how she contracted it."

"Must be going around," Ned noted with accuracy. "What the hell was this thing doing in her, anyway?"

"It may be a leftover spirit from the battle a few weeks ago." Jed had a gift for stating the obvious with sincerity.

"And it just happened on Aunt Katheryn? There are lots of people closer to our house. Why her?" Carrie sounded angry.

"It may have been seeking out a malleable host," Jed suggested. That was a chilling thought.

"I thought you said only the strongest spirits can take over a human?"

Jed nodded. "That is true, but a weaker spirit could hold someone for a time, before all of its energy is expended."

"And they can't all make bodies, like Christiana?" I asked.

"No. That is a rare ability."

"That's encouraging." No one missed the sarcasm in Ned's voice. "So, what's the story with our dear auntie? They should be here soon."

"We were in the area and came to check on her, which is true. She opened the door and told us she hadn't been feeling well. Anna examined her and diagnosed her with the ghost virus and then she passed out." Carrie's explanation kept our breaking and entering and ghosts out of the story, but Aunt Katheryn was still going to get a head CT for her bout of unexplained unconsciousness.

I wished I could save her the hefty radiation dose but there wasn't any way around that. If we told the truth it wouldn't go well for me and I wasn't interested in losing my medical license just because the scientific community didn't know about ghosts.

"Well, we shouldn't call it the ghost virus," was all I added.

Carrie smiled. "I'll let you handle that part."

"That's them." The faint wail of a siren echoed in the distance. "Carrie, I'd like to go to the hospital with her, try to make sure everything goes well." I had no reason to be there if I wasn't accompanying Katheryn's niece.

"Yeah, of course. Ned—" she started but he interrupted her.

"Go with Anna. I'll board up the window we broke and make sure the animals are taken care of."

"She has animals?" I asked.

"Yeah. A couple goats in the shed and some chickens. She's got a barn cat. If I take care of them now they should be fine until tomorrow."

"She may be in for a few days," I warned him and he nodded.

"I figured. I can run back up here tomorrow again, it's not a big deal. I think the next-door neighbor will help too."

That was the nice thing about the countryside. Neighbors were almost always willing to help out. In midtown Kansas City, where I lived, there were people on my street that I'd never met. That might have been my fault, though. I wasn't very social. At any rate, there wasn't anyone that I could ask to feed my cat for me.

The sirens shrieked to a stop outside and Ned jumped up.

"I'll go."

"You did hide the gun, didn't you?" I asked and Ned looked at me like it was the dumbest thing I'd ever asked.

"Of course I did. It's on the top shelf of her linen closet."

"Thank you."

Katheryn still wasn't conscious but she didn't look distressed.

Her skin color had turned from angry red to a pale ivory, and a web of fine lines crisscrossed her forehead, mouth, and eyes, telling the truth about how much she smiled. I hoped she would be okay. Her breathing was even, but her heart rate was still rapid. A moment later a tow-headed man in his forties bent over her.

"Give us some room please, ma'am."

I stepped back. "I'm Dr. Anna Roberts."

He paused when he heard my title and waited while I produced the wallet sized copy of my medical license.

"I'm Steve. Paramedic here in Unionville."

"Dr. Roberts, I'm Jeff." Steve's partner looked like he was fresh out of high school, where he could have been the football team linebacker, based on his size. I couldn't help but think of the last paramedics I'd met and hoped that these two wouldn't die because they'd come across me.

"What do we have going on here, Dr. Roberts?"

"I'm not quite sure. My guess is she's got a virus."

"It's going around. Symptoms?"

"Said she wasn't feeling well. Tachycardic, appears dehydrated. I'd guess she's got low blood pressure based on her loss of consciousness."

"Were you here when she lost consciousness?"

"Yes. Ned caught her and got her to the ground safely."

"So she didn't hit her head?"

"No."

"She's lucky you were here, then. Good timing." Steve turned back to his patient and I resisted the urge to snort.

"Her temp is 97.6 degrees," Jeff cataloged while the blood pressure cuff beeped that it was done. The digital display showed 100 over 70 which validated my thoughts on her blood pressure. He pinched the skin on her hand and it stayed upright, like the stiff whip on a bowl of cream.

"Definitely looks dehydrated. Good job on the IV start, Dr. Roberts. Why'd you decide to start it?" He trailed off, waiting for me to explain.

"When we got here she was pretty resistant to going to the hospital. When she passed out and I saw how dehydrated she was, I thought I'd go ahead and at least get some fluids in her, in case she tries to go AMA on you later.

"We'll certainly try to prevent that." People who needed medical care but didn't want it were an everyday challenge for ambulance and ER medical professionals. They were pretty good at convincing people to stay if they needed to, but it gave me a plausible reason for getting an IV going. "Any other medical conditions?" Steve asked me and I glanced up at Carrie, who shook her head.

"Not that I know of. She goes to the clinic there in Unionville, though. I'd assume you can access her records."

"Is there anyone who would know more about her history?" Steve asked and Carrie shook her head.

"Just me. She doesn't have anyone else."

"What's your relationship?"

"I'm her great niece."

"Do you know her resuscitation status?" Jeff inquired and Carrie looked confused.

"Her what?"

"Does she have a living will?" He clarified. "Anything to direct us on how much end-of-life care she may want or who can make decisions on her behalf?"

"I don't know. I'm sorry. She hasn't discussed any of this with me."

Too many older people wound up having medical interventions that they didn't want or didn't understand because they hadn't had the conversations with family members and their physicians. Sometimes extending your life span wasn't the best thing, but I hoped it wouldn't be something we had to worry about with Katheryn.

"If you all can give us a few minutes we'll finish our evaluation and then take her into Unionville. Will you be coming to the hospital, ma'am?" He asked Carrie.

"Yes, of course."

"If you check in at the desk in the emergency room they'll bring you back to her."

"Thank you." Carrie turned to me, arms crossed tightly in front of her.

"We should find Katheryn's purse before we head to the hospital," I suggested and she looked relieved to have something to focus on.

"I think I saw it in the kitchen. I'll grab it."

I joined Jed and Ned in the living room, out of the way of the paramedics who were positioning Katheryn on their stretcher.

"Are you all right?" Jed brushed my cheek with one finger and it somehow seemed more intimate than if he'd embraced me.

"I'm fine," I assured him, adding Ned to the list of people who now knew that Jed's relationship with me had moved to a new level.

"Good. I believe I should stay with Ned," he offered.

He was right. Ned could be in danger if there were other ghosts around. Even though I didn't sense any, Aunt Katheryn and her guest Carl were proof that some of Adonijah's cronies were still active in the area.

"Good idea. I'll be at the hospital with Carrie." I turned to go but Jed's hand gripped my arm.

His words were low and urgent. "Be careful, Anna. These people need you."

I walked to the truck, shaking my head. Which was more important to him? Me, or his need for me to save the world?

CHAPTER FOUR

"**S**OMETHING'S CHANGED between you two."

We were two miles down the road when Carrie started talking and I wondered if Ned was having the same conversation with Jed. Was this a separate and interrogate situation?

"It has." I felt cautious about discussing something that was undefined but I wasn't surprised Carrie had noticed. She was pretty perceptive.

"Is that good?"

"I don't know what it means." I stared out at the piles of dirty snow piled up on the shoulders of the road. "Sometimes I think he just wants me to kill ghosts for him." I felt strange voicing my fears to Carrie, but we'd grown a lot closer in the last month.

"Is that what he said?"

"He hasn't said." *You can't expect declarations of love when you aren't ready to give them,* my sarcastic self was quick to remind me.

"He's just scared."

"Jedediah? Afraid?" I snorted. "He's been around for a few thousand years. He was a king and his lover was the Queen of Sheba. He's been on this earth for so long he's in the Bible." *She knows this already. Stop rehashing your insecurities.* Carrie turned the corner and caught a glimpse of the ambulance cresting a hill well ahead of us. They were running lights but they weren't driving very fast. It was a good indicator that Katheryn was stable.

"He may have been around for a while but that doesn't mean he knows what relationship today can be. When he was alive, powerful men had multiple wives and marriage was used to consolidate kingdoms. It didn't have anything to do with love."

"That's probably true," I admitted. Apparently, I wasn't the only one who'd been brushing up on ancient middle eastern history.

"From what I've read about Sheba," Carrie continued, "they

were lovers but she returned to her own country and ruled it instead of staying with him."

"Modern day Ethiopia, Yemen, and Somalia. She had quite a kingdom." Africa, where Jed and Sheba's descendants supposedly still ruled. I'd spent a little of my convalescent time researching Jedediah's first life, though what I'd learned had done little to enlighten me on the man he was now. Regarded as a saint in the Eastern Orthodox Church, a prophet and messenger of God in the Islamic faith, and a mere king in Judaism, I didn't see many similarities in the Jedediah I knew and the Solomon revered in those faiths.

Jed's bearing and his prowess with a sword was enough to make me believe he'd been a warrior, but our history books were distorted depending on who was recording the story. Jed never seemed eager to discuss the past and I'd been too tired in recent weeks to push him for more information.

"Don't tell me you're intimidated by a woman who's been dead for that long," Carrie teased, interrupting my thoughts.

"Don't tell me you wouldn't be," I retorted.

"At least she's dead. I had you."

I glanced over at her. "What?

Carrie smiled but kept her eyes on the road. "You're the only other woman Ned was ever with."

"That was a long time ago, Carrie."

"Not compared to Sheba," she pointed out. "You and Ned were inseparable for something like 15 years."

"We were kids for most of that," I reminded her, feeling a little guilty.

"Then you got into medical school when you were 18. That's pretty amazing."

"Well, it was just the University of Missouri in KC," I protested. "It's not that big of a deal." The combined medical school college program in Kansas City was one of the few in the country where you could get your undergraduate and your medical school degrees in six years, which made it much less expensive than the traditional eight-year track.

"It is a big deal. You're really smart, you're a doctor, you're pretty, and you ride a horse better than I can. It's just lucky for me that you wanted to live in the city, and Ned wanted to be out here." She kept her tone light but I could hear the truth behind it.

I was floored. Carrie had been jealous of me. "You have to know that Ned is crazy about you," I stammered.

"Ned and I know our truth." She said it simply. I wondered if she knew how rare that was. "I'm just saying it's easy to be intimidated by you."

"I was pretty jealous of you too," I admitted and Carrie wrinkled her nose.

"Really?"

"Of course. You're so comfortable with yourself. You're this pure spirit. I was determined not to like you when Ned first told me about you, and then the moment I met you I knew that wasn't going to work out. You're so nice I couldn't help myself." I shrugged. "I could go on but the bottom line is, I'm lucky to have you as my friend."

Carrie fanned her face with one hand. "You're making me cry. Stop that."

I laughed. "Sorry."

"It's okay. I think my hormones are going crazy with the baby."

"That's pretty normal." Carrie was four months pregnant but you couldn't tell yet.

"I'm scared, bringing a baby into this."

I wanted to tell her that it would be okay, but I didn't know that. "I'd be nervous too," I admitted. "You might be safer away from me."

"Aunt Katheryn didn't have anything to do with you and she wasn't safe. This could be happening in other places and I'm not sure we'd know about it."

I pondered the indicators for widespread ghost possession. Would there be increases in violent crime? Petty aggression? Wanton spending or alcohol abuse? Katheryn had been possessed and had just stayed at home, as far as we could tell. Maybe she hadn't been as easy to control as Chaz had been. He'd gone out and bought a massive new SUV while he was possessed. It could also be that Katheryn's ghost wasn't as strong as Adonijah.

"You might be right." I added it to my mental list of things to talk to Jed about when we had time. Houses and businesses flashed by as we entered the town, and Carrie slowed down to accommodate the decrease in speed limit.

"We're nearly there." She turned left, following the blue hospital sign, and then pulled into the small county hospital and selected a parking space for visitors with family.

"You've been here before," I observed.

"Yeah, my grandparents were here a few times for different things."

"Let's get in there and see if we can get the hospital staff to put Katheryn on steroids and fluids." It wouldn't be the first treatment option that came to mind and I'd have a difficult time convincing them to do it. If they didn't act fast enough, Katheryn could die of the electrolyte imbalance while they tried to figure out what was wrong with her.

We had to wait in the hallway while they got Katheryn settled, but we could see into the room thanks to an emergency department that had been renovated with glass walls. The new format made it easier for the nursing staff to keep an eye on their patients since they could see them from the central workstation.

I leaned back against the wall and resigned myself to a long wait. It takes longer than you'd think to do the initial evaluation of a patient, especially one that isn't conscious and can't tell you what's wrong. I wanted to intervene, get her on the right mix of steroids and electrolytes right away, but this wasn't my hospital and Katheryn wasn't my patient. I stood next to Carrie and kept quiet while the nursing team hooked Katheryn up to the machines that would track her heart rate and rhythm, as well as her blood pressure, temperature, and oxygen saturation levels.

There was a lengthy conversation about the existing IV line, with both nurses evaluating it. They left it in place. Everyone had their own protocols for lines, but this one was working so they were leaving it. I was glad Katheryn didn't have to get stuck with another needle since it would just cause her more pain. She'd been through enough.

"Anna Roberts?" I turned towards the unfamiliar voice to find an African-American man in his late thirties walking towards me. The stethoscope tucked haphazardly into the pocket of his scrubs pegged him as a clinician. His head was shaved and the stubble on his face gave him a rugged look that paired well with remarkable blue eyes. His ears had holes in them for absent earrings and a thin chain around his neck held a simple gold cross. I was sure I'd met him before but his name wasn't coming to mind. I started cataloging through my medical contacts to try to identify him but he stuck out his hand before I got to his name.

"I thought it was you. John Fowler. I was two years behind you at UMKC."

"Goose." I remembered the nickname that he'd earned in the Air Force before he went to medical school with a grin, relaxing a notch. "Sorry, I didn't recognize you."

"It's okay." He gave me a rueful grin. "It's the hair. I mean, I had hair when we were in med school." We'd had friends who were friends, and it was a small school. I remembered him being calm and level-headed when things were stressful. "I might not have recognized you either, except you were in the news a few weeks ago, when that medevac helicopter crashed in your yard. That must have been pretty awful." I didn't know what to say to that. It hadn't just made the local news; we'd been on CNN and the front page of USA Today.

"You went into emergency medicine," I stated the obvious to change the topic and he smiled.

"Yes. I joined KC Regional Emergency Physicians after my fellowship. We cover this hospital." I was familiar with the group name, though I didn't know much about it. The only emergency room doctors I worked with were at the local teaching hospital that my clinic partnered with.

"Do you live out here?" I wouldn't have pegged him as a small-town guy but I hadn't known him that well.

"No. I've got a loft near the Power & Light District. I stay at a hotel here when it's my week to cover Unionville." He gave me a smile. "What about you?"

"I run a free clinic in Midtown."

His eyebrows rose a notch. "Who do you practice with?"

"No one, it's just me."

"Solo? That's got to be hard."

"Well, the Family Practice residency program backs me up."

"That's good then. What are you doing up here?" His tone was gentle, aware of the fact that we were probably here to visit someone close to us.

"This is my friend, Carrie Joules. Katheryn Wilkinson is her aunt." I gestured to the room across from us.

John shook hands with Carrie, his expression switching from friendly to one of clinical distance.

"I'll get a look at her once they finish settling her in. I talked to the ambulance crew on the way in. They said she wasn't feeling well and then passed out?"

"That's pretty much it." Carrie glanced at me.

"She didn't hit her head because we were able to get her to the floor without any damage," I expanded on the situation, still hoping she wouldn't have to get a CT.

"Had she demonstrated any personality changes in the past few days?" John asked, his blue eyes examining Carrie and me.

"Interesting question," I remarked since we hadn't told the ambulance crew about Katheryn's personality change. Carrie looked at me to answer and I decided to tell a watered-down version of the truth. "She seemed pretty aggressive, which apparently isn't normal for her. That's why Carrie asked me to go take a look at her." It was a nice segue into why I was there. "Why do you ask?"

"We've had a bit of an epidemic here the last two weeks." He shook his head. "Quite a few people with sudden personality changes, often followed by heart irregularities and dehydration. Some have had syncopal episodes, like your aunt." Bile filled the back of my throat. I swallowed it down as I opened my second sight and watched for the spirits of the dead, but all I saw was the bustle of a building full of souls, the normal pulse of the living. I concentrated and then I caught it, the underlying shimmer of something more, like white noise in the background. The spirits of the dead were here too, but their light seemed muted as if they were being dampened somehow. Maybe because they were inside living people, and not wandering free.

The nurses came out of Katheryn's room and a short plump blond gave us a polite nod. "She's ready for you, Dr. Fowler."

He thanked them and gestured to Carrie. "Go on in. I'll be there in just a minute." He touched my arm, indicating that we weren't done talking.

"So far your friend's aunt fits the profile I've seen with my other patients. I hope she doesn't have it, but I want to be honest with you. We've lost a few of them."

My stomach churned but I wasn't surprised to hear it. Without the steroid support, I might have lost Chaz, too. "How many have you had?"

"She'll be the twenty-third in the hospital. All our beds are full. I'm expecting the state health department to be out here today, and I notified the CDC. I've taken a couple extra shifts out here so that I don't carry it back to the other hospitals we work at." He shrugged. "I've already been exposed to whatever it is, and we don't know how it's transmitted."

A one-man quarantine wasn't the answer, but it was nice that he'd thought of it. I was overwhelmed by the number of patients he had with the symptoms of someone possessed by a ghost, but I tried to stay focused on the clinical conversation. Maybe there was a way for me to help.

"What do you think it is?" I asked and he ran his hand over his head in frustration.

"I don't know. It's got to be a virus, right? Only I don't know of any that cause psychosis. None of them show signs of strokes, though brain waves on the EEG are a bit overactive."

"What about Functional MRI?" I hadn't thought of it before, but the brain activity monitoring MRI technology was a fascinating option. What would Jed's look like?

John shook his head. "We don't have one here." Of course they didn't. Unionville was too small a town to support that highly specialized piece of equipment.

"Have you tried steroids?" I asked, and he gave me a curious look. "No. Why?"

"I think I had it a few weeks ago. Your virus." I turned towards Katheryn's room, where Carrie was bent over her aunt. "There were three of us at Truman West just a few weeks ago with the same symptoms you describe here. Our electrolytes were seriously out of balance. They pumped us full of steroids, electrolytes, and fluids and we all got better."

Of course, if any of John's patients still had their ghost in residence, no amount of prednisone would help. I needed to get him to let me evaluate them, but since I wasn't on staff here that wasn't an option. At a minimum, it took weeks to get through a hospital's privileging department since they had to validate each practitioner's credentials.

"That's an unusual treatment regimen." John pointed out the obvious without discounting it, and my respect for him rose a few more notches. "Why do you think it worked?"

"I think the virus causes an adrenergic instability. A regimen of high-dose steroids, as well as resolving the electrolyte imbalance is what worked for me. I needed a bunch of glucose and sodium too."

"I've never heard of a virus causing that kind of reaction." His tone was flat but I didn't think it was because he doubted me, he just couldn't make scientific sense out of it.

"I hadn't either. You can call and get my records if you think the comparison will be useful," I offered and he nodded.

"I'd like to, if you don't mind."

"Like to what?" Ned rounded the hospital corridor with Jed close on his heels. In the hospital hallway, Jed looked even larger than normal. He took up a territorial spot by my side. John's gaze flipped back and forth between the three of us while he tried to figure out who belonged to whom. I took pity on him.

"John, this is Carrie's husband Ned, and this is Jed Peters. John Fowler was in medical school with me. He's Katheryn's physician today."

John's glance slid casually across my left hand as he reached out to shake Jed's. He wasn't wearing a band either but doctors often didn't, at least not while they were working. Too many things they could get caught on, and no one wants their finger ripped off. Still, warmth spread through me just knowing that he had checked to see if I was wearing any telltale sign of attachment. It had been so long since anyone had acted like they were interested in me, other than Jed. He had given me plenty of confusing signals before last night.

"We were just talking about the mystery virus." John's voice brought me back to the conversation at hand. "Anna said that she was one of a few people who recently had similar symptoms to some patients here."

"We're going to give Dr. Fowler my records from my hospital stay," I informed them. I hoped that my recent medical history of cardiac arrest didn't derail his thoughts on treating the people here possessed by ghosts. "He's got a bunch of patients with symptoms similar to Katheryn's. Just like I had."

I let Ned and Jed absorb the implications of that while I followed

John into Katheryn's exam room. Convincing him to give her steroids would be a hard sell, and I still needed to figure out how to check in on the other twenty-two patients to make sure that they weren't harboring a fugitive ghost. Based on what my senses were telling me, some of them certainly were.

"Did you have the symptoms of psychosis as well?" John asked as he checked Katheryn's eyes. She was still unresponsive.

"I experienced a brief personality change." I shrugged at Carrie when she glanced up at me. What was I supposed to say?

"That must have been very disorienting. I can only imagine." John had a good bedside manner, very sympathetic. I liked how his hands were respectful as he examined Katheryn. He acted like he remembered that she was a person and not just another patient. Some physicians had a hard time holding onto a sense of empathy, partly out of a need for self-preservation. John seemed to have that balance figured out.

"It's very possible that your aunt has this virus that we're seeing." He addressed Carrie without making me feel like I was excluded from the conversation. "Unfortunately, this is so new that I don't have a test to run that can prove it. She could have suffered a stroke or have any number of other problems going on. Since we can't talk to her, we need to rule out some of these other conditions. It's critical that we know what's going on so that we can treat her properly. I'm going to order some bloodwork, and I think we should get a CT of her head to be sure she isn't suffering from anything else."

John's explanation made sense, and since we couldn't tell him what was really happening, we didn't have much choice but to agree with that course of treatment. When Carrie looked at me for help I nodded my agreement.

"In the meantime, we'll keep giving her fluids. She seems stable right now, so let's find out what's going on with her before we go any further. I don't want to make things worse." He gave me a warm smile. "It's nice to see you, Anna. I'll have the paperwork brought down so we can get the medical records from your hospital stay. I've got some other patients to see but maybe we can talk again in half an hour or so? I'd like to hear more about your experience with this virus."

As soon as the glass door slid shut behind him, Ned, Carrie, and Jed peppered me with questions. I waved them to silence. "Give me a second and I'll tell you everything I know." Since each of them had heard different pieces of the story, I told them everything from the beginning.

"Twenty-three people?" Ned asked when I was done.

"Those are the ones that are here," I told him.

"What do you mean by that?" Ned sounded irritated but I knew it was just stress talking.

Jed answered for me in his normal verbose style. "There are more victims."

"If there are twenty-three here at the hospital, how many more are there that haven't made it to the hospital yet?" I elaborated. "We have no way of knowing how many people in this town are possessed by ghosts."

"Can you feel them? Here in the hospital?" Carrie asked.

I nodded. "Yeah. It's like a buzzing... less distinct than when they are roaming free, but I can tell there are ghosts here."

"Let's go find them," Jed suggested, and his right hand closed as if he felt the hilt of the sword in his hand.

"No stabbing people." Carrie stepped between Jed and her aunt.

"Of course not." He looked affronted as if the thought had never crossed his mind.

"I agree, we need to help everyone affected by this," I told them. "But we can't just go walking into people's hospital rooms."

"You could tell your handsome doctor friend what's going on and have him take you to them," Carrie suggested.

"I don't think that's a good idea, babe. If we didn't believe Anna at first, what chance is there that other people will?"

"I believed her," Carrie reminded Ned.

"For now, just stay here with Katheryn," I suggested. "I'll think of something. I'm going to go find a cup of coffee. Do you guys want anything?"

"I'd take a cup." Ned settled into one of the two chairs next to Katheryn's bed.

"Herbal tea?" Carrie asked and I gave her a sympathetic smile. She had chosen the 'no caffeine' route to pregnancy, but giving the stimulant up was harder than it sounded.

"I'll see what they have." I didn't know if Unionville stocked herbal selections or if everything would be plain black tea. "I'll bring you water if they don't have decaf tea."

"Perfect, thank you."

"I'll come with you." Jed's offer sounded more like a command but I didn't mind.

The cafeteria was small and didn't have many options, but the coffee was hot and they did have chamomile tea bags. I set two Styrofoam cups on a table and dipped the tea bag into the one with hot water and sat to wait for it to finish steeping. The room bustled with conversation and the tables were too close to avoid overhearing the conversation at the table next to me. A priest, distinguishable by the clerical collar with his long sleeve black shirt, sat at a table with a woman whose back was to me. Her over processed blond hair was pulled up in a limp ponytail, and the tired set of her shoulders said she'd been at the hospital for a while.

"I know the church believes in possession by demons, Tracy, but it's not something I've ever seen. The doctors say this is a virus. Give them time."

"He's not himself, Father," she insisted. I took a closer look at the pair while Jed paid for our beverages. She was Caucasian, maybe ten pounds overweight. I couldn't tell how old she was without seeing her face, but the skin on her hands was smooth, free of the fine network of lines that come with age.

"It also may be that he has a mental illness. Schizophrenia and bipolar disorder are things that the church once interpreted as someone possessed by a demon, but we now know that these are substantiated mental illnesses." His face was full of sympathy and sadness. The white eyebrows and creases on his face led me to think he was in his sixties, and I guessed that this wasn't the first time he'd had a family deal with the tragedy of a severe mental illness. Based on what she was saying, though, this woman was probably closer to the right answer than the priest was.

"He's only nine," she said. "He's been saying words he doesn't even know. I know this sounds crazy, Father, but it's not him."

"He could have learned them on TV or at school, Tracy." He glanced past her and our eyes met.

I looked away, embarrassed to be caught eavesdropping. I

couldn't help but suspect she was right, though. Her little boy was possessed. I knew well how a ghost could seem like a demon.

"Just come see him, then tell me what you think."

"Of course." He patted her on the arm. "I'm ready if you are." She gathered her purse and he followed her away from the table.

"We have to go after them," I informed Jed as he walked up to the table. Handing him my coffee cup and grabbing Carrie's cup of tea, I pushed the door open with my hip, dumping the tea bag in the trash next to the door as I passed through. The priest was tall and thin making him easy to spot as he turned left down the far hallway. We got there just in time to see them step into a room. I noted the room number and then turned around to find Jed right behind me.

"Shit," I cursed as a little of Carrie's hot tea sloshed onto my hand.

"Now where are you going?" Jed stopped in front of me.

"We need to drop off the coffee, then I can come back. There's a little boy in that room who's possessed."

"What is it you plan to do, Anna?"

"I don't have a clue."

"Ah. Good." Sarcasm carried through in his tone.

Katheryn had gone for her CT scan and John was nowhere in sight when we got back. Ned had his jacket on.

"I'm going for sandwiches. There's a deli down on Main Street, locally owned, does a great job."

I raised one eyebrow in disbelief. "Great sandwiches in a small town?" Ned laughed at me.

"Don't be such a snob, Anna. Hipsters are everywhere, even Unionville."

"This great couple runs the place," Carrie clarified. "They make everything themselves. They even raise the turkeys and pigs that supply their meat."

"Sounds great." I was impressed. I had a hard time getting that complete package in Kansas City, and it had a pretty good reputation for its farm-to-table food scene.

"I'll just bring back a variety of stuff if that's okay." He disappeared out the door without waiting for an answer.

"I hope it's okay that I sent Ned for food."

"You know I'm hungry," I assured Carrie and she laughed.

"I can always count on that," she admitted. "I am too, these days."

"Any change with Katheryn?" I asked and she shook her head. "Okay. There's a kid that's a patient here, and I need to go help him. We'll be back in a little bit." Carrie looked confused, and I explained. "I overheard his mom talking to a priest. She thinks he's possessed by a demon."

Carrie's expression of confusion intensified and Jed stepped forward. "The child may be possessed by a ghost."

"No, that's awful!" Her hands folded over her abdomen.

"Yeah," I agreed. "We'll be back as soon as we're done." I left Carrie with her chamomile tea.

"What *do* you plan to do?" Jed asked again as we headed back towards the wing where we'd last seen the priest.

"I don't know." I tried not to think about how I could lose my medical license by getting caught in a patient's room that I shouldn't be in, but it was a hard thought to dismiss. Was the risk worth it? I didn't have a choice. I didn't know what to do about the other twenty-some people in the hospital that John thought had the virus, but this child I could help right now. I wished I could bottle my energy, or somehow contaminate the water supply with it, but I didn't think that was possible.

The priest and the boy's mother were in the hallway when Jed and I rounded the corner. The priest's face was tinged gray. He put his arm around the woman and guided her up the hallway. I looked at Jed when they passed.

"I've never performed an exorcism, Tracy. It's not something to be taken lightly."

"But you see what I mean, Father? About how he's different? You saw them sedate him." Their voices trailed off as they rounded the corner.

Jed and I were left alone in the hallway, and I seized the opportunity to step into the boy's room. It smelled like stale pre-pubescent sweat and urine. The child was asleep, thanks to whatever drugs he'd been given, but I didn't know how long he'd stay that way. It depended on how much he'd been given, so I didn't waste any time. His forearm was clammy under my hand.

I could see the second soul in him, a distortion of energy that lay on top of his own spirit. I concentrated, pulling on a tiny thread of my power which arced from my skin into his and it was done. He moaned and his eyes fluttered. I checked the various monitors hanging over his bed, watching as his vital signs reacted to the absence of the spirit. His blood pressure dropped and his heart rate accelerated. The monitors over his bed reacted to the sudden change and started beeping.

"Anna, let's go." Jed's voice was an urgent whisper.

He was right, I'd done all I could for the boy. I hurried for the door, rubbing at the ribbon of fire that ran from my chest down my arm. It still hurt, but at least I could walk. A nurse stopped short on her way in, alarm marring her features. This was a minor child's room and she didn't recognize us.

"What are you—" she started, and I gave her an embarrassed smile.

"Wrong room. I thought they said 16 East but it must have been 16 West."

"You shouldn't be in here." She sounded alarmed, but the boy's monitors were calling for her attention. "The West Wing is that way." She gestured down the hall and then closed the door behind us with a definitive thud. I turned to go and flushed as I met the priest's inquisitive gaze. He'd come back and was standing in the hallway watching the commotion we'd caused.

"This way, Anna." Jed pulled me around the tall figure in the middle of the hallway and ushered me around the corner.

"Are you all right?" He murmured as he hustled me from the scene of the crime.

"I'm okay." I rubbed my hand up and down my jeans, still trying to ease the sting. "It's easier than it used to be."

"Using your power will always take a toll but as you learn to control it, you can lessen the impact." He looked me over with a critical eye. "You need to eat." As he said it, hunger gnawed at my stomach.

"I do," I agreed, leaning into the comfort of his body. I'd released two ghosts in as many hours, and touching him was a welcome distraction from the discomfort. "Do you think Ned is back yet?"

"He should be soon. This is a small town. It can't take long to get sandwiches from a deli."

True to his word, Ned brought back a variety. I took one with turkey, topped with red onion, sprouts, cream cheese, and raspberry mustard. I finished it off, along with a small cup of pasta salad before any of the others were done with their first halves.

Ned gave me a mock look of admonition. "You're eating like you haven't seen food before, Anna. Even faster than my pregnant wife." Carrie elbowed him and he rolled his eyes.

"She freed the child. The spirit is gone," Jed informed them.

"Thank you," Carrie breathed. "I was afraid to ask." Her right hand again went to her abdomen.

"So, what, that leaves us with twenty something more to go here at the hospital?" Ned, always the optimist.

"Yeah."

"What's your plan for them?"

"I don't have one." My tone was testy, but I was tired of the automatic assumption that I was somehow going to make all of the bad ghosts go away. I was one person, and there were a lot of them.

"You can't just leave everyone like that." Ned sounded affronted.

"I know that, Ned." I tossed the plastic pasta salad cup into the trash with more vigor than was necessary. "But I can't break into all of their rooms. I'll get arrested and lose my medical license!" I pulled the door to the hallway open. "How about you figure out how to make it happen instead of telling me what I already know." I stormed out with as much finesse as a petulant pre-teen and felt instant remorse as I headed down the hallway. "Get a grip, Anna," I muttered to myself. "You're an adult, not a child."

I glanced away from a patient lying in his bed in the hallway as I walked past. It was a common sight in hospitals. He might be waiting for transport to take him to another room, or to radiology for a test. When his hand snaked out and grasped my arm with enough force to knock me off balance, I shrieked, more from the shock than in pain.

"It's you," he bellowed, hauling himself upright in the bed while yanking me back towards him. My feet followed the force of my arm in an instinctive attempt to keep my shoulder in one piece. A nurse noticed the commotion at the far end of the hallway and started running towards us. I heard doors opening, voices shouting. It felt like time slowed as I sensed the presence of the second spirit inside his body. I looked into his blue eyes.

"You shouldn't have touched me," I whispered, unfurling another thread of the fire inside me and letting it flow into him through the connection of our skin. It got easier every time, to control how much of my power I used. The man screamed like a scared child and collapsed. His eyes rolled up into his head and the hallway filled with more people. I stepped back from him as nurses clustered around.

John pulled me away from the unconscious man and examined my arm. "Are you all right?"

"I'm fine." I rubbed the red imprint of the man's fingers and acknowledged to myself that ninety percent of the pain I felt was due to me banishing the ghost, not from being grabbed. Glancing over John's shoulder, I noticed the priest, leaning against the wall, watching me with interest. I avoided his eyes.

"You're sure you're okay?"

"I am. Thanks for your help," I murmured, turning away from him.

"Where are you going?" John sounded protective and I had to stop myself from snorting. He was just being kind, but John couldn't save me from ghosts.

"I was just going to get something from my car," I lied.

"I'll walk you," he offered.

"No, I'm really fine." I gave the blue-eyed doctor a pointed look. "Your patient needs you."

He ran his hand across his shaved head as if he was used to running his fingers through his hair. "He's another one of our virus cases."

"Load him up on steroids," I recommended, again turning down the hallway. "I'll be back in a few." The priest hadn't moved, and I had to walk past him to get to the lobby. I didn't mean to look at him but couldn't stop myself from glancing up as I walked by.

Eyes that were a surprising shade of gray appraised me underneath eyebrows bushy enough to get him an honorable mention in an Albert Einstein look-alike contest. He was probably six feet tall and lean, like a runner. He carried himself with a sort of humility that made me think he took his vow to serve others to heart. It wasn't too far from what I had chosen to do with my life, minus the religion part. I'd never considered that I might have anything in common with a priest, but maybe I did.

"Do you believe in God?" His question took me by surprise and I stopped walking.

"I don't know," I admitted out loud. "I'm a doctor," I added as if that explained something, which it didn't. Most of the physicians that I knew were believers, whether they were Christian, Jewish, Hindu, or Muslim.

His lips turned up at the sides in the beginning of a smile. "There are days when I don't know if I do either." The fact that a priest had shared his doubts with me made me hesitate, and I thought about that sweet indescribable moment after I'd died.

"For what it's worth, I don't know about God, but there is something. I know there is." I hadn't spent much time contemplating the fact that I couldn't be classified as an atheist anymore. Religion, or the lack of it, hadn't been an important piece of my identity, but the reality was that something changed the night I died.

I didn't know what it meant, but I didn't feel the need to discuss it with a priest. I gave the man in the white collar a polite smile and started to walk away from him but he fell into step beside me.

"That's what they call faith," he informed me. I shrugged, wondering why I'd allowed myself to fall into conversation with this man. He'd seen too much.

"I don't believe in faith. I just know what I know," I replied, stepping in front of the door sensors so the automatic doors slid open. The cold air on my skin was a relief.

"The boy is better now, after you were in his room." The priest spoke in a practiced tone, low enough that he wouldn't be overheard. I stepped back into the warmth of the entryway, far enough from the sensor to let the door shut again.

"I don't know what you're talking about," I denied. I was happy to hear that the boy seemed better. It might be hard to get his electrolytes balanced, though. I hoped someone realized that he needed steroids before it was too late.

"And that man just now... He'll be better too, now that you touched him?"

"He grabbed me," I protested. The man in black just watched me. I had the unsettling feeling that he could see far more than I wanted him to. "I don't know anything about that patient." I was trying to ignore the fact that it didn't feel right to lie to a priest, even if I didn't follow his religion.

"I've never done the rites of exorcism." The sudden topic change surprised me into paying closer attention to him. I thought he sounded a little embarrassed, and I guessed this topic wasn't one that came up often in conversation for him, even among those he kept near and dear.

"After I saw the child today, I thought I might have to do them." he paused. "His name is Aiden. I was leaving to call my bishop, and to pray about it." His eyes were intent on me, full of curiosity. I feared what he would see in me and looked out to the cold wasteland that Missouri became in the wintertime, that fertile soil hidden under blankets of snow waiting for spring.

"I left my planner in Aiden's room," he continued. "When I came back for it, you were just coming out, weren't you." It wasn't a question.

"I was lost," I told him.

He made a non-committal noise to acknowledge my lie before he continued. "Aiden woke up while I was there. He spoke to me, asked if he could have a soda. He said he was glad he didn't hurt anymore. He said that it was just him now, that the thing inside him was gone."

I knew that the priest was trying to gauge my reaction, but I was used to masking my thoughts. That poor boy, though, it was such an awful pain to have the ghost inside of you controlling you. I hoped that this one hadn't hurt him the way Adonijah had me. I suppressed a shudder and forced myself to give the priest a level stare.

"I'm glad to hear the child is doing better. This virus that's going around causes quite a few changes in personality." I could feel myself stuttering over my words, and my cheeks heated. "Hopefully he's through the worst of it now."

"Doctor ..." His pause invited me to introduce myself, and I offered him my hand with a sigh.

"Roberts. Anna Roberts."

"Grayson Harwell." He enveloped my hand in both of his so that his dry skin warmed my cold fingers. "Dr. Roberts, I've been a priest for forty years. It teaches you something about human behavior. I'm pretty good at distinguishing between fact and fiction."

I extracted my hand. "Is there something I can do to help you, Father?"

"I think we will need each other's help, Dr. Roberts, before this is through."

What the hell did that mean? My inner conscience chastised me for cussing in front of a priest, even if I hadn't said it out loud. "I don't think I understand what you mean by that, Father Harwell."

"There are too many people at risk for games, Dr. Roberts, and you and I are too old to be playing them."

"All right." There should be mathematical algorithms for figuring out how to negotiate this kind of conversation with grace, but I didn't know of any. "Say I agreed with your statement, then what?"

"Why don't you tell me what you think is going on around here?" He transformed his face with a friendly smile. "I don't mean the story about the virus."

I was losing the linguistic battle. "Let's pretend that I know something you don't." He gave me an encouraging smile. This was a game he was willing to play. "Why would I tell you?"

"If we are dealing with what I think we are, I may be of use." What did he think we were up against? Demons? I doubted the truth had crossed his mind.

"I don't mean to offend you, Father, but how could you help?"

"Let's just say that it might be an area that I have some expertise in."

I stepped out of the way of a woman hurrying into the hospital, and sighed. One of these days I was going to tell this story to the wrong person, but the priest was right. We needed all the help we could get.

"How much time do you have, Grayson?" I didn't think that the titles were a formality that we needed, and it seemed that the priest agreed.

"However long we need, Anna."

"I could use another cup of coffee, and the coffee here isn't bad."

"The cafeteria, then." He agreed and extended his arm to indicate that I should go first. I turned and a jolt of electric energy rushed through me as I realized Jed was leaning against the wall of the lobby, his face devoid of expression. Of course he'd followed me. I narrowed my eyes in a glare but since I didn't have any other option, I stopped in front of him.

"Jed, this is Father Grayson Harwell. Grayson, this is Jedediah Peters."

Jed raised an eyebrow when I combined his full given name with that of his body donor, but I didn't know how else to introduce him in modern company. Maybe they didn't use last names three thousand years ago, but it was weird to not have one in the twenty-first century.

"Jed's involved." I offered in explanation to Grayson while the two men shook hands. Jed raised an eyebrow at the implication that the priest was in on our little secret. He wasn't yet, but he was about to be.

"Grayson believes that he may be able to assist us," I explained.

"That he might," Jed said as he appraised Grayson. Jed thought the priest could help us? Interesting.

"I'm going to talk to Grayson for a few minutes. I'll be back in a bit."

Jed blinked at the dismissal but didn't let it deter him. "I'll come with you." It was a statement, not an offer.

"That's not necessary," I informed him and his eyes narrowed.

"It is. I can't protect you when you aren't with me."

"I don't need protecting,"

"Why do you fight me?" He gave an exasperated sigh.

"Because I'm not used to being ordered around," I reminded him. He gave me his half bow. It felt sarcastic and I glared at him.

"I wouldn't have to give orders if you took more care." He looked taut with irritation.

I sucked in a breath and let it out again to give myself time to calm down. "I didn't ask for any of this."

Jed's expression softened a notch. "Anna Roberts, if you would allow me to accompany you, I would be most grateful." He managed the sentence with less sarcasm than I'd expected.

I glanced at the priest and saw he was watching our childish argument with amusement. I'd been frustrated by the exchange with Ned, flustered by the patient/ghost grabbing me in the hallway, then engaged in a verbal test of strength with the priest, none of which was Jed's fault.

"Of course," I told Jed, trying to make it sound like the apology it was. "I'd like it very much if you'd come with us."

The cafeteria was mercifully empty this time around. I bought a massive peanut butter cookie to go with my coffee as the after effects of a third release had sunk into my bones in a deep ache. If I was going to stay upright, much less do twenty more of these, I would need lots of calories.

I sat across from the man in the white collar and got to the point. "So, what is it you think is going on, Grayson, if it's not a virus?"

"I could ask you the same question." His expression was unreadable.

"I could lose my job for saying out loud some of the things that I know are true." I wouldn't lose my medical license for believing in ghosts, just for thinking that I could heal sick people by laying my hands on them. "Correct me if I'm wrong, but I don't think you have as much to lose." He raised his eyebrows at my directness and gave me a thoughtful nod.

"That's fair." He took a sip of his coffee. "I'm one of the on call ecumenical ministers for the hospital, and I've counseled more than one family in the last few weeks affected by this 'virus.' I've wondered if there was something in our water supply, a toxin of some sort causing psychosis. It's been like something out of a movie.

"Aiden, though, was the one that made me understand. His mother was right. It was so obvious that something other than Aiden was speaking." He paused and took a sip of his coffee while he appraised our reactions. "If I were to tell anyone else this, they might think I had the virus myself, but you two aren't at all surprised."

"Go on," I encouraged him in between sweet bites of crispy peanut butter.

"I always thought demons were a metaphor for evil, but after seeing Aiden, I think it was a demon. I don't know what else it could be," he murmured. His bushy gray eyebrows scrunched together. "After you were in his room, it was gone. Aiden woke up and seemed like a normal child who had been ill." He made eye contact with me. "My experience has taught me that every now and then something happens that can't be explained by our modern world. I think you cured Aiden, and for that I'm grateful. I don't understand what's happening, but I think you do. There are more people that are sick. I'd like you to tell me what you know so that I can try to help you."

It was time to tell Grayson what the demons were. I glanced at Jed for confirmation and he nodded his agreement. Or was he giving me permission? Perhaps I needed it. I was too used to not telling people about the ghosts.

"They aren't demons." I kept my tone low and as matter-of-fact as I could. After what he'd just told me I was certain he wouldn't laugh at me. "They're ghosts." I waited a moment but he didn't register surprise, as if this was in the realm of answers that he expected. "They want to return to life, and the stronger ones have started to possess people."

"A ghost was inside of Aiden?" Grayson asked and I nodded. Grayson inclined his head for a moment and I didn't know if it was in prayer or just deep thought. "How did you come to be involved?"

"I've always been able to see ghosts." I took a breath. The second part was more difficult to explain. "I can release them. I can send the spirits on to wherever they are supposed to go when they die."

His eyebrows rose. "That's what you did to the one inside Aiden?" I nodded in answer to his question.

"That is a rare gift, Anna. God chose you for a reason."

"I don't believe in God," I answered automatically.

"What you told me was that you know something else exists, but you don't know what it is."

"I didn't say it was God." For some reason, it was important to me that he understood that.

"Whether you believe or not does not change the fact that you have been blessed."

I shrugged. There was no point in non-Christians and Christians debating whether God did or did not exist, and in what form. "It's not much of a blessing. Every ghost in the state, and then some, has been trying to kill me."

"The patient in the hallway," the priest murmured. Jed looked down at the remains of my cookie with suspicion.

"You banished another one?"

"A man on a stretcher grabbed her arm as she was walking by," Grayson explained. "I don't know what happened, but he screamed when he touched her."

"I released the ghost that was inside him," I explained.

"It was clear to me that you did something to him."

"Did he harm you?" Jed's voice was stormy. "You should have waited for me."

"I'm okay. Nothing bad happened."

"It could have." His expression was cold.

"Do you also have this gift?" Grayson turned his attention to Jed.

"I have others," Jed told him and Grayson nodded acceptance as if he was used to hearing extraordinary tales.

The priest's attention shifted back to me. "There are other people in this hospital that need your help, Anna."

"I know. I can feel them," I admitted. "But I can't just walk into their rooms."

"I can." Grayson smiled. "You could come with me." I considered the priest with newfound appreciation. Hospital privacy rules were strict but Grayson might be able to help me gain access.

"I'm not letting her go alone. It could be dangerous for her."

"Do you believe in God, Jedediah?"

"I do." Jed didn't mention his prominence in the Bible, his history as a man-of-God turned worshipper-of-idols who after his death had again become a devout believer in one God. I suspected that our new friend would find his history fascinating. I did, and I hadn't spent my life studying the Bible. Maybe someday we would be able to tell him.

"Good." The priest scooted back from the table and stood with a satisfied smile. "We will offer to pray for them." He wiggled his eyebrows at me. "It's a very effective way to get access to patients' rooms. I have an employee badge." He pulled the hospital ID out of his pocket and strung it around his neck while he led the way out of the cafeteria.

"Badge or not, we can't just waltz into patient rooms and offer to pray for them," I protested.

"I bring seminary students with me all the time. Trust me, most of these patients' families won't mind." He was right. We were in a rural town in the Midwest, not far from the Bible Belt. The vast majority of the population here were Christians. As long as we were with the priest, we weren't likely to be questioned.

Grayson stopped outside a closed door and knocked. The door had a sign on it warning us to sanitize our hands when entering or leaving the room. I guessed that was John's attempt to stop the contagion from spreading the only way he knew how.

"I visited this patient earlier today. He and his wife are members of my congregation. I'll see if they are willing to have you come in with me."

Jed and I waited in the hallway in awkward silence. Trying to be inconspicuous with Jed was impossible. Between his large frame and his leather overcoat, he didn't look like he belonged in the hallways of a small-town hospital, and people noticed him. He ignored the overt admiration of the female nursing staff and the sideways glances that men threw his way as they hurried by. I admired him for his indifference to it.

The door opened and Grayson admitted us to the room. Inside, there was a tall, middle-aged woman in blue jeans and a sweatshirt. She looked drawn as if it wasn't just her husband's illness that weighed on her.

"This is Laurel and her husband Richard. Laurel, these are the people I've brought to pray for Richard."

I was surprised she didn't question Jed's and my presence, but people tend to trust their priests, and her full attention was on her husband. Richard was tied to the bed rails by cloth bands around each wrist. He must have been either a danger to himself or others to earn that treatment. They weren't necessary right now as he was unconscious, facial muscles lax, mouth open.

"Will you join us in prayer, Laurel?" Grayson asked and she reached for his hand.

Laurel offered us a distracted nod and I thought that even though she was tired, her dark eyes looked kind. Jed folded his hands in front of him, closing his eyes and lowering his head in contemplation while Grayson began.

"Let us pray." It should have seemed awkward, praying over a stranger's bed, but Grayson made it feel normal.

Bracing one hand on the bedframe, I focused on Richard and saw the two souls inside him. Like in the others, one soul was brighter and the other adhered to it like a leech. Releasing a trickle of my energy into him, I concentrated on the parasite and watched in satisfaction as it disintegrated in a brilliant shower of sparks that only I could see. Richard's soul didn't change, and he didn't move, but the numbers on his monitors started ticking as his blood pressure dropped and his heart rate sped up.

"Through Christ our Lord, Amen." Grayson finished in practiced tones as Laurel switched her attention to the monitors I was watching.

"What's happening?" She asked.

"He looks a little tachycardic," I told her. "He might be dehydrated." That was as far as I dared go.

"I'll call the nurse." She pressed the button while we wished her good night.

"I'll check in on you tomorrow, Laurel," Grayson promised before closing the door behind us.

"Did you get it?" He asked me.

"I got rid of it."

"When will we know if he's better?"

"As soon as he wakes up, I'd imagine."

"She said they had to sedate him."

"A few hours then, for the drugs to wear off."

Grayson nodded with determination. "The next one is a few doors down."

CHAPTER FIVE

"**K**ATHERYN." The priest's voice was filled with kindness, but something else too. Was it longing I saw in his expression? She stared at him for a long moment and then reached a hand out to him. He crossed to her bedside, embracing her hand in both of his, just as he had done with me. "Are you all right?" He asked her.

"I'm better now." She gave him a smile that looked like a mix of fondness and regret.

I snuggled back into the plastic wingback chair next to her bed and tried to distract myself from my burning pain by wondering what had happened between Father Grayson and Aunt Katheryn before he went to seminary. Or after. My mind filled with thoughts of improbable scandalous liaisons while their conversation continued.

"You're the one who helped me." Katheryn was still holding Grayson's hand, but she was staring at me through the side rails in her bed as if her green eyes could see through me.

I was too tired to lie anymore. "Yes."

"Was it the devil?" Katheryn asked and Carrie patted her arm.

"No, Aunt Katheryn, it wasn't the devil. You had a ghost inside you." Carrie explained. Ned looked surprised that she told Katheryn the truth, but I agreed with her. Anyone who'd been through possession deserved to know what had happened to them. Deserved to know that they weren't crazy.

"Nasty thing. Felt like the devil," Katheryn muttered into the bed frame, making me smile.

"Katheryn, this is our friend Anna Roberts. We've talked about her before." Carrie said. "She owns the land next to us."

"I know who she is. We've met. She's the doctor," Katheryn noted with clarity. Carrie smiled through a sheen of tears. I hadn't realized she cared this much for her great aunt, but I could see why she did. Katheryn Wilkinson seemed like a remarkable woman.

"That's right. The doctor." Carrie beamed with relief.

Jed walked into the room and handed me a fresh Styrofoam cup of coffee loaded with sugar, and started unwrapping a packet of peanut butter crackers. Ned glared at Jed as if he were drugging me instead of feeding me.

"She looks like hell," Ned spoke quietly in deference to the hospital environment, but he sounded mad. "What happened?"

"With Father Grayson's help she banished four more ghosts," Jed explained as he handed me the first cracker.

"I took her to see some of the people here who are sick," the priest said.

Ned ignored the priest, saving his wrath for Jed. "That's too many for her. She'll run out again. You're supposed to take care of her." Ned wasn't wrong, I'd depleted my energy more than I should have, even though I'd been trying to be careful about how much I used at once. I needed time to recharge.

"You are the one who pointed out that she needs to help these people. After all, they're innocent." Jed used the argument Ned had earlier, and I would have laughed if I'd had the energy to.

"It's too much for her. I didn't mean she should do them all at once."

"I'm fine, boys," I mumbled around a bit of crumbling peanut cracker. "If I can help people, you know I have to." My voice sounded weak.

"Let him do some of the work, Anna." I rolled my eyes at Ned's flippant remark but didn't have enough energy to respond. Jed didn't have the same limitation.

"My way has other consequences," Jed reminded him. I thought of the blade slicing into my chest and releasing that magical fire. I had to suppress the shudder of revulsion because it hurt to move. Using the sword on another human being wasn't an option.

"You've got to know someone else who can help with this." Ned's voice was steely.

"Perhaps Father Harwell can help." Jed nodded towards Grayson who was now leaning against the wall with the ease of someone used to standing for long periods of time.

"What did you have in mind?" Grayson asked.

The door swung open and John strode in. He acknowledged the

priest with a nod and then turned his attention to the tall woman curled up in bed.

"Katheryn, we got your scan results back and everything is normal. Based on your symptoms and blood work, my best guess is that you have the virus that's been going around. I'm going to admit you for observation."

"Are you going to give her the steroids that Anna recommended?" Carrie asked. John looked cautious. He hadn't bought into my treatment recommendation, which wasn't good news for everyone else who was inpatient.

"I'm not sure if that's the best action. There are a lot of potential side effects."

"Dr. Anna said I should get them?" Katheryn's voice rang out strong from the bed.

"Yes, ma'am." John faltered under her tone of authority and then regained his footing. "But there are risks to those drugs. We don't give them lightly. They also aren't typically used in the treatment of a virus of this sort."

"Do you have a better treatment option?" She demanded and John gave a small sigh. Discounting her because of her age was a mistake. She contained an indomitable spirit.

"Anti-virals." He tried to rally.

"Are those working for your other patients?" For a woman in a hospital gown, she managed a feisty tone. I decided I liked Aunt Katheryn very much.

"It takes time for them to work." John defended his treatment choice, but he was already defeated.

"I'd like you to treat me according to Dr. Anna's recommendations." She hadn't sat up but her voice brooked no arguments. When it came down to it, though, John didn't have any reason not to try it. His anti-virals weren't doing a bit of good and he knew it. He raised a questioning eyebrow at me.

I did a quick mental calculation of drug dose for Katheryn's body weight. "4 mg of Decadron three times a day for five days," I suggested.

John raised his eyebrows at the high dose but acquiesced with a defeated shrug. "I'll order it, but if we don't see improvement in 24 hours, or if you get worse, then I'm switching you to the anti-virals."

He was speaking to her but staring at me. I acceded with a nod. "Katheryn, I'll get you moved to your room in a few minutes." He gave the rest of us a steady look. "She needs rest. Once she's settled you should go home or move to the family lounge for a while."

We nodded our agreement but Katheryn had different thoughts. "I'd like someone to stay with me." Her voice wavered a bit and I empathized with her fear. I was scared too, whenever I thought about Adonijah and what he had done to me.

"I'll stay with you," Carrie reassured her and John nodded.

"The chair in here converts into a bed of sorts. Just make sure she gets some rest," he ordered before walking out.

Jed convinced me to move to a couch in the family waiting room, which despite the full hospital was empty except for us. I needed some time to recover, and there were still a lot of people with ghosts in them. We'd visited one woman who appeared to have the 'virus' symptoms and was no longer possessed. Was she so sick that the soul gave up on the body, or had she been able to drive him out? If there were other ways to force a ghost out of a body, I needed to know what they were.

Father Grayson pulled a small tablet out of his satchel and settled at a table, a look of firm concentration on his weathered face.

"I'm going out to the car for my laptop. You'll stay with her?" Jed interrupted him.

Grayson looked surprised. "Of course. I'll be here if she needs anything."

"Thank you." Jed nodded so deeply it involved most of his chest. After he left Grayson spoke.

"He's very protective of you." The priest's eyes stayed focused on his screen.

"Yes."

"Is there a reason for that?"

"I keep getting attacked by ghosts. He's trying to watch out for me."

"Can they do anything to you?"

I paused. "Yes," I admitted. It didn't feel good to confess my weakness to someone I didn't know well. Father Grayson's tablet was forgotten. He was watching me now as if he could see inside my soul.

"They have already hurt you," he observed.

I squirmed like a school girl under the gaze of a strict teacher. I wasn't used to spending time with people who were so insightful.

"I don't really want to talk about it."

"Maybe you should." He folded his hands, indicating that his attention was on me and not the device in front of him. "Sometimes it helps to talk about these things."

"I'm afraid to." I bit my lip. That was a bit more honest than I'd planned on being.

"What's the worst that could happen?" His voice was low, raspy, and sincere.

"I'd have to admit to being weak."

"Weakness is not a sin, Anna. We are all weak in different ways and at different times."

"It's not something I allow myself to be," I explained and he nodded. Weakness, insecurity, and doubt weren't allowed in my career. Confidence was required. It was something I needed to work on because they were all traits inherent to being human. I was learning how much my own humanity meant to me.

"That may be. For right now it's just the two of us, so no one else will know. I am used to keeping conversations confidential."

"You carry a lot of secrets for people."

"As do you," he acknowledged.

"You should have been a therapist."

He smiled. "Most clergy are therapists, just with slightly different training."

"Doctors too."

"Yes, I've thought as much." He shifted his position, giving me a moment to think it over. "So, then it's just the two of us, both part-time therapists. It's your choice, Anna, if you don't want to talk about it, that's okay. But if you do, you can tell me and I won't think any less of you."

He made it feel easy. I propped my head up with my arm and started talking.

"I was possessed, too, just like the people here. The ghost that was in me was old and strong. I couldn't fight him."

"Your power?"

"I'd run out. When I use it a bunch it takes a while to recharge."

The priest straightened in concern. I'd just banished five ghosts in front of him, and two more before that. "Are you okay?"

"I'll be all right but that's why I need to rest for a while." I was pretty low on whatever my ghost banishing energy was, but I wasn't going to be careless enough to use it all at once. Not ever again. Maybe I shouldn't have done the last one, but there wasn't any way I could have said, 'Hey, I'll come back later and get that thing out of you. I don't feel up to it right now.'

"If you couldn't fight him, it must have been a terrible violation."

I stared, because he'd been able to describe what I'd been feeling but hadn't been able to put to words. "You can't imagine," I told him. When he replied, it was in a tone that forgave my insensitivity.

"The situation was different, and it was long ago, but I have felt violated. I imagine that the feeling may be similar." He was calm but I could see that he understood too well. Somewhere along the way, my new friend had been hurt. My heart ached in empathy for him, and my tone changed. Our conversation shifted from one between professional part-time therapists and became one between two injured souls.

"I can't describe the pain." I took a breath and waited for words to come that I hadn't allowed myself to say, hadn't even let myself think. "I've never been so helpless. At first, I couldn't fight him at all. He just overwhelmed me. Then when I tried to resist him he hurt me. I don't know what he did, but it was like a terrible cutting pain. I couldn't even think through it." I closed my eyes, lost in that moment when Adonijah had controlled me. I finished in a whisper. "He enjoyed hurting me. I could tell that he did."

"You must be very strong, to have survived that." Grayson broke the memory, reminding me at the same time that it was in the past.

"I'm not." I shook my head, thinking of the boy that morning that I'd freed from his own private hell. "No stronger than anyone else."

"I'm not sure that's true, Anna. There are many people with strength but many more that are too afraid of failing to tap into it."

The door clicked open and Jed ended our conversation.

"Anna, your doctor friend would like to speak with you." His face was expressionless but I caught an edge of concern in his tone.

"All right." I stood, holding onto the edge of the sofa in case I got wobbly, but my legs held me.

"Are you sure you're okay?" Grayson asked.

"Yeah." I heard the tone of surprise in my voice. "I think I'm better now." It wasn't much, but a small weight had been lifted from me now that I'd been able to say aloud what had happened to me. My world was a touch brighter than it had been since I'd met Jed. I reached a grateful hand out to Grayson and he covered it in his. "Thank you for listening."

"It was my pleasure," he said. Jed gave us both a curious glance but didn't say anything.

"Where's John?" I asked.

"Waiting for you near the lobby. There's another man with him. I'll go with you."

John stood in the front hallway with a wispy man in a tired navy suit who looked like he was in his late fifties. He'd grown his thinning gray hair long, gelled it, and combed it in a circle around the bald spot on top. I sent silent kudos to John for his decision to shave his head.

"Anna, let me introduce you to Leonard Chambers from the State Health Department." Leonard gave my hand a brief shake and then gestured to a closed door behind him.

"If you'll come this way, I'd like to talk with you."

John opened the door and held it for me, and I followed Leonard into a small conference room, Jed on my heels. His size made the room feel smaller.

"Mr..." Chambers started towards Jed and then paused as he realized Jed was almost a foot taller than he was.

"Peters. Jedediah Peters." Jed shook his hand and I hid my smile.

"Ms. Roberts will be with you again shortly." His attempt at dismissal didn't faze Jed.

"Dr. Roberts." Jed pulled out the leather chair at the head of the table and the one around the corner next to it. He seated me first and then took off his long coat, which I knew had the sword in it. He sat down and draped his coat over one knee. It didn't fold due to the concealed length of steel, but was hidden beneath the table.

"Mr. Peters, you aren't needed in this interview." He was flustered and it showed.

Jed leaned back in his chair and crossed his leg over his knee.

"I'm gathering information on a potential public health issue, which does not concern you." I had to give Chambers his due, he wasn't backing down even though Jed had thrown him off his game.

"Mr. Chambers," I inserted. "I think we can proceed with Mr. Peters present."

Leonard Chambers didn't appreciate my suggestion. "This is a health department matter and it's my jurisdiction." He paced along the other side of the table.

"If you want to speak with me I'd suggest you start. My time today is limited."

"I could get a police order, Dr. Roberts."

I gave him a polite smile. "That would lose you a great deal of time in your investigation, Mr. Chambers, as well as my willing co-operation. We all have the same goal. Let's talk."

"If Mr. Peters is a distraction he'll have to leave," he growled as he sat opposite Jed.

John settled into the seat on my other side as Chambers pulled a manila folder out of his briefcase and spread it in front of him.

"Dr. Roberts, you were hospitalized several weeks ago at Truman Medical Center in Kansas City, Missouri, were you not?"

"Yes." He waited for me to expand on that but I left it to him to ask another question.

"Dr. Fowler has suggested that your hospitalization was due to an illness that he thinks may have also infected several people in this facility."

"I also believe that is the case," I agreed.

Chambers directed a stern look at both John and me. "I am charged with investigating possible contagious epidemics in the state of Missouri, Dr. Roberts. In all my years here, we've never had a new virus appear that has the contagious capability that Dr. Fowler is suggesting this one has." His condescending tone rankled. "I wouldn't have a job, though, if physicians such as yourself didn't leap to these conclusions based on the small sample of patients you are seeing."

I choked back a scathing retort when John tapped my foot with his under the table. Chambers stayed focused on the paperwork in front of him, rubbing his nose as if he was planning on pushing up his glasses but had forgotten that he didn't have them on.

"Dr. Fowler provided me with the medical records from your hospital stay, Dr. Roberts. It appears that you were hospitalized for complications due to a helicopter crash." I was surprised that John had shared them without my permission, but legally he could since this was an issue that affected public health.

"I was injured by a piece of debris from the helicopter. I also had a number of the symptoms shared by Dr. Fowler's patients. Adrenergic instability and electrolyte imbalances that were only corrected after several days of steroids and fluids."

"The patients here have additional symptoms, I am told."

"Yes, the personality change. I experienced that as well."

Leonard flipped through the papers in front of him and settled on my discharge note with a shake of his head. "There isn't anything here that mentions that."

"I'd recovered from that aspect of it by the time I reached the hospital. I had other more pressing injuries, as you may be able to tell from the records there. Having been in cardiac arrest took precedence. We may have forgotten to mention it." We hadn't mentioned it, I knew.

"I see." He used the tone of an overworked high school counselor talking to a troublemaker. "That does shed some doubt on whether you had the same condition."

"John, did you have a chance to look at my records?"

He shook his head. "No, I was busy so I passed them on to Mr. Chambers as soon as he arrived."

"I'd be interested in knowing if Dr. Fowler believes that my blood profiles and other symptoms are consistent with what he's seeing in this facility."

Chambers hesitated.

"The treatment plan that the Truman staff used with me, and with the other two patients worked. By withholding this information from Dr. Fowler, you are risking the health of most of the patients in this hospital. As I understand it, people are dying. It would make for some interesting headlines later."

"Are you threatening me, Dr. Roberts?" Chambers sounded affronted and I was pleased that I'd gotten under his skin since he was trying so hard to be difficult.

"As a physician, the health of these people is my primary concern, Mr. Chambers. I would think that as a member of the health department you have the same goal." He blinked.

"Of course it is." He sounded annoyed but slid the manila folder over to John.

There were photos of my chest wound from the ER, close up and from a variety of angles. They'd taken them as evidence in case it turned out that a crime had been committed.

John flashed me a look as he flipped through them. "That's quite a laceration."

I shrugged and tried to not feel embarrassed about the fact that all three men in the room had just seen glossy photos that included my bare breasts, albeit covered with blood and fresh bruises.

John shuffled the pictures to the back of the paperwork stack and sifted through until he found my lab profiles from the emergency department.

"Here's the metabolic profile from when you were admitted." He ran his finger down the row of indicators that were flagged as being abnormal. "This is very much in line with what we are seeing in the patients here, Leonard."

"Take a look at the lab profile from my last day there," I recommended. "You'll see the improvement after several days of steroids."

"This isn't Africa, Dr. Fowler," Chambers intoned while he readjusted his imaginary glasses. "We don't have a jungle for strange new diseases to crawl out of." My breath hissed out at the racist overtones.

"First of all, Mr. Chambers," I said, my voice full of my contempt for his ignorance. "Africa doesn't have much in the way of jungles, so I'd recommend that you discontinue that particular stereotype as it makes you sound obtuse and some people might believe it was a racist statement." My tone made it clear to him that I was one of those people. Chambers flushed with anger but I kept talking. "Second of all, new diseases are discovered all the time, in this country as well as in others. As a scientist, you should know that." John tapped my foot under the table again, telling me to shut up. I ignored him. "I'm sorry, you must be a political appointee. I assumed you had a scientific background. Maybe the health department should send someone more qualified to handle this medical emergency."

Chambers was purple now, flushed through his neck and ears. Jed's intimidating presence may have been the only thing that kept him in his chair.

"I think you should consider the possibility that she may be right, Chambers." John kept his tone polite, but he'd lost any pretense at friendliness. He tucked my medical records back into the folder as his phone started beeping. He glanced at the screen and stood. "Three more patients have come in while we've been in here talking. You tell me that you aren't getting reports from other facilities around the state. That tells me that it's either locally contagious, or that the source of infection is here. Like the water supply or some other environmental contaminant."

Chambers snorted, which didn't match well with his current shade of mauve. I almost felt sorry for him. John and I weren't giving him much of a chance.

"That's very unlikely. You haven't given me any definitive proof that this is the same disease."

"Millville didn't think they had a problem with their water either, and it was full of lead," I reminded him and earned another glare. I knew it wasn't the water but John's explanation sounded more believable than the truth.

"There's no way to prove it's a virus unless we can identify the viral markers, and between Dr. Roberts records and the patients we have here, we can identify them and use them to evaluate new cases."

"You don't know that she had the same thing."

"We don't have any way to test for it, but I'm giving the steroids that helped Dr. Roberts improve to a couple of patients here. We should know in a few hours if they are helping." John tucked my records under his arm. "I need these for comparison with the patients we have in-house. Excuse me. I have patients to attend to." He walked out, letting the door slam shut behind him.

"I'm very concerned that there are other cases. This being isolated to Unionville is unlikely." I spoke into the silence that followed John's departure. I was thinking about those walls of ghosts, hundreds and thousands of them. I'd released many of them, but others had just left when Adonijah's leadership failed them. How many of those had sought their own host in the areas near my home? It was an epidemic, but not the sort that either John or Chambers imagined.

"I haven't received any other reports of contagious epidemics from strange new viruses." Chambers tone was subdued despite the sarcastic string of words.

"Perhaps they don't have as many cases as we have here." I tried to make it a gentle suggestion and Chambers shrugged.

"I'm not sending out a statewide bulletin on this." His tone was adamant.

"I didn't ask you to." I wished he would because I needed to know how widespread the ghosts were. Telling him that, though, wouldn't garner any cooperation from him, and I'd done too much to anger him. "Maybe just make a few phone calls to nearby hospitals? Just in order to be certain that this is an isolated incident."

"I'm sure it is." His words were argumentative, but his eyes darted back to the map on the table and I thought he was wavering.

"Just to verify," I encouraged. I rose to leave and Jed followed me, waiting to speak until we had cleared the lobby.

"How are you feeling?"

"I'm better. We should see if Grayson wants to go visit a few more people."

"You cannot cure everyone today, Anna."

"I know, but I can't leave them like this."

"There could be hundreds of them."

"Or more."

"Yes," he agreed.

"I have to help them if I can."

"We need to find Adonijah. It may be the only way to stop this."

A shiver of revulsion and fear ran through me at the mention of his name. "How do we find him?"

"The Council holds our best hope for locating him."

"I'll check my email to see if Christiana's reached out." It was good to know my snarky side was intact. If I could be snide, I could pretend that I wasn't scared.

He ignored me. "It's evening. We'll go home. Perhaps she'll contact you tonight."

"I'm not going to sleep in the hopes that I'll wake up with that crazy bitch in my bedroom," I spoke with too much force and the nurse walking by looked up at me in alarm. She evaluated both of us with a level stare that told us to keep it down and then continued on her way.

Jed lowered his voice. "We need their help but I will not let them harm you." He said with confidence I wasn't sure he felt.

"Haven't you been working with the Council for the last thousand years?" I shook my head. "Would you really choose me over them, if it came down to that?"

"I have done all I can to protect you."

Had he? Would Adonijah have been able to find me if Jed hadn't located me first? "I'm just saying that you must feel loyalty to them too."

"I told Christiana that I wish to be released from my duties so there would be no doubt in her mind that you are my priority, but I am capable of both fulfilling my obligation to you and assisting the Council in their goals. They are more closely aligned than you realize." I heard the frustration in his voice.

"I don't want to be an obligation of yours." It came out with a note of vehemence and was closer to the truth than I meant to get.

Jed's expression turned stony. "You are not an obligation."

Not exactly a declaration of love. My internal voice never cut me any slack. Part of me needed to pursue the question of what he wanted our relationship to be, but the conversation had the potential to go someplace we weren't ready to go. Never mind that the middle of a hospital hallway wasn't the right place for a relationship talk.

I reverted back to the original topic. "What will you do when your duty comes into conflict with your current posting?"

"I believe our goal and those of the Council are aligned." He reiterated with icy finality, but I wasn't done.

"I don't know that they are and I'd like to know for sure which side you'll be on when it happens."

"What is it that you think will happen?"

I leaned back against the concrete block walls of the hospital and shook my head. "I don't know, but I don't trust your Council." They hadn't given me any reason to and I didn't understand Jed's faith in them. "If Christiana shows up I'm going to shoot first and ask questions second."

"Shoot? You have a gun?" Jed's eyebrows rose in sudden confusion and I sighed. I'd forgotten about Jed's lack of modern day cultural exposure.

"It's an expression. It means I'm not going to give her the chance to be creepy, weird, and dangerous. I'm just going to release her." I ignored the other part of his question because we were in a public place. I did have guns, safely locked in a closet gun cabinet. I'd grown up on a farm; of course I had guns, and knew how to use them. It was unfortunate that ghosts weren't susceptible to bullets, unless perhaps Christiana was, in her physical form.

"I realize that she didn't come across very well last night, but it would be better if you would show restraint. She might have valuable information. Information we need."

"I'll take that under advisement."

"Thank you," Jed responded to my overt sarcasm as if I'd spoken with sincerity. He bowed and then gestured down the hallway as if we were taking a garden stroll and not arguing in the middle of an institutional corridor. I stifled my frustration and allowed him to guide me back to the visitor waiting room.

Grayson wasn't alone. Ty and Chaz perched on the sofa I'd sat on earlier. Three bulging plastic grocery bags adorned the small table and I perked up at the sight of a bag of chips sticking out.

"Hey guys. Is that food?"

"Yeah. Jed called me and said you guys would be up here a while so we brought supper."

I flopped onto the sofa next to Chaz. "You've met Grayson?"

The priest glanced up from his tablet. "I didn't realize they were part of your group."

I introduced them to each other. "Grayson is helping us. He knows about the ghosts."

"That's interesting." Ty's tone invited more details but the door opened and Ned walked in before I could tell him the story of how Grayson and I happened to be discussing ghosts.

"How's Katheryn?" Grayson asked before I could get the words out.

"She seems a bit better. She's resting. Carrie's staying with her."

"Good." He relaxed into his chair.

"What's the situation here?" Chaz inserted the question like the former military man that he was. He was an attorney now but when he was younger he'd been in the Marines.

"Well, we've got a lot of sick people with ghosts in them." I updated them all as concisely as I could. Chaz's skin turned a shade of gray.

"Oh." He'd had Adonijah in him a lot longer than I had. I

knew how awful it had been for me in the few minutes I'd had to deal with him. I'd tried to bring it up early on with Chaz, but he hadn't wanted to talk about it. Since then I'd been afraid to ask too many questions.

"How many are a lot?" Ty, always the practical one.

"There may still be twenty or so. And that's just the ones that have come to the hospital."

Chaz was regaining his normal skin tone. "What are we talking about? An invasion?"

"There's no evidence that they're that well-organized." Jed settled at the table next to Grayson.

"They may be leftovers that scattered after the helicopter crash," Ned suggested.

"Do we know it's not more than that?"

"That is a possibility that we must consider," Jed admitted.

I hesitated before I asked because I hated to say his name. "Adonijah?"

"Maybe," Jed said and the room silenced. "He should not be strong enough yet, but it is possible he has rallied again."

"If the Council knows how to find him, why haven't they gone after him before this?" I asked. Jed answered with silence and I suppressed the urge to scream at him. "Well, I need food." I didn't know what else to say and I did need to eat. My energy reserves had taken a hit and there were still a lot of people who needed my help. "Who else wants a sandwich?" I spread the contents of the grocery sacks out on the table with more vigor than was necessary. It wasn't going to be a gourmet dinner but we had basic sandwich makings and tubs of deli coleslaw and potato salad.

"What do we do about the ghosts?" Chaz asked.

"I'm trying to get to everyone but releasing them one at a time is going to take a while."

"What does the hospital think?" Ty asked.

"The emergency department doctor is a guy I went to medical school with. He thinks it's a virus of some sort. He's called in the state health department because it's something he's never seen before and based on the case volume he's afraid it's contagious."

"That could get complicated." Ty waited for me to finish making a plate before he stepped up to the table.

"It already has. I just got out of an interview with the inspector from the state health department."

"And?" Ned prompted.

"He's a pompous jerk who doesn't believe that there's a new virus."

"He's right though, isn't he? This isn't a virus," Grayson inserted.

"No, it isn't, but it is an epidemic of sorts. The people who are affected need urgent treatment with steroids and fluids. If the health department believes it's a virus, we could get some communication from other hospitals in the state to see if they have any patients with similar issues."

"And get all patients treated with the right drug cocktail after you get rid of their ghosts," Ty added.

"John told me that they've had a few people die," I explained.

"You don't think it's just here?" Ned asked.

"I didn't know it was here at all," I reminded him. "I have no idea how widespread this is."

"How many of them could there be?" Grayson asked.

"There are many spirits of the dead that have stayed on this world," Jed explained. "Maybe enough to populate it several times over. Most of them are neither organized enough nor strong enough to take over a human."

"How do you know?" Grayson inquired, his bright gaze turned on Jed.

Jed hesitated, but Grayson wasn't exactly a stereotypical priest. I thought he could handle the truth. "Jed's a ghost. He took over a body without a soul in it." At this point, it was easiest to just say it. We could explain more when we had more time.

Grayson's eyebrows shot up. "How did he find a body without a soul?"

"The man was medically brain dead and on a ventilator," I explained. "He couldn't have ever come back. Jed's on our side. He's been helping us fight them."

"That's incredible." He looked Jed over like he was on exhibition in a museum. "Why aren't you sick like the others?"

"I'm stronger than they are, and this body didn't have a soul that I have to control."

"Does that make the process easier?"

"I believe it does."

"Could you possess someone and control them?"

Jed looked as if he found the priest's questions amusing. "I think it's likely that I could, if I was willing to give this body up."

I'd been reckless, thinking that everyone who was possessed was actively ill. Jed was living proof that a body didn't always have a physical adverse reaction to being possessed. Chaz hadn't demonstrated any signs of illness either, until after Adonijah left him.

"What's it like to die?"

"It depends on the method of death. I have lived several lives after my first one, in bodies like this one. To die of old age after a full life is not a bad thing. To die with certain regrets is terrible. I lapsed in my faith and died without it. I believe that is why I stayed here."

"Fascinating," Grayson murmured. He wasn't the only one who was mesmerized, we were all paying attention. It wasn't often that Jed talked about himself in any detail, but maybe we hadn't asked the right questions. "Were you Catholic?"

Jed gave Grayson a level stare. "My death preceded the formation of that church."

"How old are you?" Grayson asked and I intervened before the conversation got as far as Jedediah's life as King Solomon. If we started that conversation with the priest we could be sidetracked for hours. Although if that conversation did ever occur, I wanted to be there for it.

"Jed, how does a ghost take over a person? What would make them leave? Is there any other weakness that we can exploit, something that would force a ghost out without me having to release each one?" There wasn't enough of my power to go around, that much was clear.

"The ghost has to be stronger than the host in order to take control." Jed shifted his weight and his chair squeaked in protest. "When Adonijah took Chaz, he was able to suppress the host spirit and control all of the body's actions, was he not?"

Chaz looked uncomfortable at the implication that he was weak, but I understood.

"There wasn't anything I could do against him when he was in me," I admitted so that Chaz didn't have to.

"It may be that in these cases, the ghost has tried to take over a host but is unable to fully integrate. The host spirit is strong, and the ghost is too weak to take full control."

"Thus the personality changes we've seen here. It looks like a psychotic break." Ty looked at me.

"That describes what Carrie's Aunt Katheryn was like when I got there." Was ghost possession the cause behind mental illnesses? Had some of the patients we had cared for over the years with schizophrenia, depression, OCD and Bipolar disorder actually been victims of ghost possession? Would I have noticed the parasitic spirit if I'd looked? I'd never had any reason to look for one inside human being before. If I'd had the ability to cure them and just not known to do it…I felt queasy and set my half-eaten sandwich aside.

"It can seem like they have something wrong with them." Jed continued.

"Are all mental illnesses caused by ghosts?" I blurted out.

"You think every crazy person is possessed?" Ned sounded like he thought I was joking.

"Mentally ill," I corrected him with a glare that said, 'mind your manners.'

"I don't believe they are, but I don't know." Jed shrugged.

"I am sure they are not." Grayson allayed my fears with his calm denial. "I have known many people with these illnesses and there are no similarities to what we are seeing here. If this had been going on all along, your virus would have been noticed sooner."

"You're right, it would have," I breathed in relief. "Thank you. So, if the ghost has to be stronger, you think the cases we are seeing here are people whose ghost wasn't quite strong enough?" Jed nodded. "There may be a lot more people, people whose ghosts are in fact strong enough to control them and the body they are in, without immediate symptoms."

"That may be," Jed agreed. I sank further into my chair. It made sense but I'd been hoping that most everyone who was possessed was so obviously ill that they'd eventually make it to the hospital.

"After my experience with Adoni, that isn't much of a surprise," Chaz noted. Ty had known he was acting strange, but he wasn't far enough out of character to make Ty believe he wasn't himself. "Is there anything else that will force a ghost out?" Chaz prompted. "I mean, aside from Anna doing her thing?"

"If the host is sick enough, or about to die, then the ghost might abandon the host body," Jed noted.

"Can they be reasoned with?" Grayson asked and we all looked at him with surprise. "I mean, what if we talked to them, told them they had to leave?"

"I don't believe there is much chance that you will convince them to depart." Jed sounded doubtful.

"Even if they knew they would be destroyed if they didn't abandon the host?" Grayson persisted.

"I have a few problems with that scenario. First of all, If I don't banish them, and they leave the body they are in, what's to keep them from going out and finding another person to attack? One that's farther away from me?"

"We could make them promise?" Ty suggested and I couldn't help but smile.

"No way." I was adamant. "If they've shown that they're willing to possess someone, they should be sent to the next world."

"It puts you in the role of being judge, jury, and executioner." Chaz's lips pressed into a thin line. "Absolute power is dangerous."

"Do you have another method, Chaz, to detain them and hold them for trial? Is there ever an instance where they would be in the right and be allowed to keep the body they've taken?" I asked.

"Not in any other situation than Jed," he agreed, "but it's a dangerous path when you take that power into your own hands."

"I was given this power. I didn't ask for it."

"I know, chica. Be careful with it."

"There may be another way," Jed offered.

"Something that doesn't involve your sword?" Ty asked.

"I believe Father Grayson knows what I am referring to."

"The Rites of Exorcism." Grayson's brow furrowed with concern. "Yes."

"Would they work for this?" Grayson asked.

"I believe they can be effective. They can force the invading spirit from the host, much like my sword does," Jed informed us.

"I thought exorcism was for demons," I protested.

"What do you think a demon is, if not an evil spirit looking to torment the living world?"

"Oh." I let that sink in. I had thought they were some sort of mythical beasts from another dimension.

"I've never performed the Rites of Exorcism." Grayson held his hands up in a helpless gesture. "I've never even seen it done. This isn't something I thought I'd have a need for until today."

"Do you speak Latin?" Ty asked in curiosity and Grayson gave him a forgiving smile.

"Well enough, but the Rites are available in English."

"Oh. Sorry. I'm not Catholic." Ty gave him an apologetic shrug.

"None of us are perfect." Grayson smiled and Ty couldn't help but respond with a chuckle.

"Can you do it?" I asked. If he could, I needed the help.

"I would need time to prepare. I have to speak with the bishop and get his permission. Each family and the doctors would have to agree before I could proceed."

"We don't have that much time." Jed reminded him and Grayson shrugged.

"That may be, but that is what would need to happen before I could take that course of action."

"Aside from the fact that no one would believe you, Grayson, you run the risk of losing your place here." I was risking my profession too. If any of us stood up and said that these people were possessed by ghosts we'd be the laughingstocks of the year. We had to fight them, though, or we would lose our world to them. There had to be a way.

"If it will help these people, I will do whatever I can. I need to think about the best way to go about it." Grayson's tone said he was done discussing it, so I shifted the conversation away from him.

"Anything else, Jed?" I asked. "Any other weaknesses?"

"We have covered all of the options I am aware of."

"Well, you are our resident expert." I was acutely aware of how valuable Jed was to our cause. Would anything happen because of the stance Jed took with the Council? He'd worked with them for too long to renounce his allegiance to them without a second thought, yet that was what it seemed like he'd done. What were the ramifications of my actions? Christiana deserved the poor reception I gave her, but if there were members of the Council who might help, I may have damaged that relationship. Then again, they'd sent Christiana as their messenger. The real question was whether or not they knew about and agreed with her ideals.

"So, we have three things." Ned leaned against the wall, one long blue jean clad leg crossed over the other. He'd been standing there for a while but he made it look comfortable. "Anna can zap them, the priest can do this exorcism thing, or we have to get the person close enough to death that the ghost wants to leave."

Jed shrugged and nodded as if to indicate that while he might not have put it the same way, he agreed with the essence of what Ned had said.

"Are there any times of day that they are weaker? During the day, maybe?" Chaz, looking for a strategic way to get the upper hand.

Jed gave him a level stare. "These are ghosts, Chaz. I believe you are thinking of a creature called the vampire."

"Vampires don't exist, do they?" Ty asked as if he'd been worrying about it.

"Not that I'm aware of," Jed answered with poise but it looked like he was trying to stifle his amusement.

"So, garlic is out, then. Damn," Ned added, making us all laugh.

"How many people have these things in them right now?" Chaz asked.

"Around eighteen or so, that we know of," I answered. I'd been trying to keep a running tally of the number we'd started with, minus the five I'd released, plus the three I knew of that had come in since then.

"And how many can you take care of, Anna?"

"At a time? It seems like I can do three or four and then I have to rest for a while. It might take me a few days to get to all of them." That was if more cases didn't show up. "I'm afraid of letting my reserves get too low."

Chaz nodded. "Okay. We don't know if Father Grayson can do the exorcism, or if it will work. What about medically?"

"You're asking if we can trick a ghost into thinking that the host is so sick they should abandon the body?" I asked.

"Would that work?"

A few things had crossed my mind, like medically induced comas and general anesthesia, but it wasn't without substantial risk to the patient. Not to mention the fact that I couldn't just start experimenting on people to see what the ghosts would react to. Taking someone's body to the edge of death was too dangerous.

"Not ethically, morally, or realistically," I said simply.

"So, we spend a few days here and Anna zaps them all. It takes time but it's the best way." Ned shifted against the wall and re-crossed his boot clad feet.

"While I agree that freeing the people here is important, there are other stakes to consider," Jed informed us.

"What do you mean?" Ty asked.

"Earlier when Chaz asked if this was organized—"

"You said it wasn't," Chaz interrupted.

"I said we had no evidence that it is," Jed rebutted. "It is possible though, that Adonijah, and whoever he follows, is behind this."

"Do you know who he's working for?" I asked. During one of the nights that Christiana had been tormenting me, she'd hinted at a ghost that Adonijah might work for called the Master. If there was some terrible ghost that the Council knew about, why hadn't Jed mentioned him?

"I don't know," Jed answered but he was looking away from me. I had the uncomfortable feeling that he wasn't telling me everything he knew.

"Who is this Adonijah you keep talking about?" Grayson asked and I realized we hadn't filled him in on the whole story.

"Adonijah," Ned shifted away from the wall, "is the ghost that crashed a helicopter in our field about a month ago. He's the one that hurt Anna."

Chaz nodded, looking grim.

"He's the ghost that possessed both Chaz and me," I told Grayson. "He was Jed's brother back when they were living, and he seems to think that hurting me is a way to get back at his brother. I'd used up all my energy that night, or I would have been able to release him once he was in me. Jed has a sword, though, that has similar power. That got Adonijah out of my body, since I didn't have any power left." Grayson raised one bushy eyebrow but didn't reply.

"Didn't you say Adonijah would be too weak to cause us any trouble?" Ned asked, an edge to his voice.

Chaz was a little on the gray side again. I was scared too.

"The power of the sword should have weakened him, but he may be stronger than I realized." Jed avoided making eye contact with me.

"How do we find him?" I asked, trepidation making my voice shake.

"Perhaps I can speak with some of the spirits here, before Anna releases them," Jed suggested. "Maybe I can find out why they are here."

"That's not going to be easy if the patients' relatives are around," I pointed out.

"Maybe we'll find someone who's alone," Jed mused. He had a determined look that worried me. I couldn't imagine what acceptable interrogation techniques were like when he was alive, but whatever they were, I hoped he wasn't considering using them.

"It's getting late." Grayson gave his wrist watch a pointed glance. "After eight we'll have a harder time accessing patient rooms since visiting hours are over. It will be more difficult for me to get you in." We needed the relative's permission to pray over their loved ones. If the clock on the wall was right, it was a little after six.

"If we hurry now, I could banish a few more tonight. Then tomorrow we can work on the rest."

"Shall we go and pray, Father?" If I'd said it, it would have sounded insincere, but Jed was resolute. He'd pray for them with the priest, and then he'd try to intimidate a ghost into giving us information before I released it. Ruthlessness and faith intertwined.

John caught us coming out of the second patient's room. I had one hand braced against the wall to help hold me up. Nine banishments in one day was an incredible amount for me, but I was getting better at using a small amount of it at a time. My body felt fevered from the energy I'd released and I wasn't holding up very well. There was still enough left, though. My inner core glowed with a few more sparks of the strange energy that affected souls.

"Anna?" He looked from me to Grayson. "Father. I didn't realize that you two know each other."

Grayson folded his hands in front of him and gave a gentle nod. "These good people joined me in prayer for this woman, Dr. Fowler." John's eyebrows skyrocketed and Grayson rushed to reassure him. "Her family gave their permission, of course. Are you familiar with the benefits of prayer for people who are ill?"

I tried for a thoughtful expression and hoped I didn't look disingenuous.

"There is anecdotal evidence," John admitted. "Nothing that's been proven in clinical trials." His eyes were evaluating me with curiosity. "I myself am a Christian." He faltered, his fingers reaching for the cross around his neck and when he spoke again his voice dropped with raw honesty. "I'm sorry for my surprise. Physicians don't usually promote prayer as part of our treatment regimens, but perhaps we should."

"Even doctors can believe in the power of prayer," Grayson informed him.

John nodded with vehemence. "Yes, of course we can. I do." He gave us a smile now that he'd dropped his professional demeanor. "I'm not in the habit of discussing religion with my patients. It's a county hospital, after all."

"In many countries caring for the spiritual side of things is just as important as caring for the physical body," Jed said. I felt like an imposter.

"Since I can't help in my role as a clinician, I accepted Father Grayson's invitation to follow him on his rounds." I smiled at John and Grayson, looking for a graceful end to the topic. "I think we brought a little bit of peace to a few people today." I managed the final sentence with sincerity.

Jed snorted under his breath. I'd banished two more ghosts, but we hadn't been successful in getting any of the intelligence that Jed was looking for. Both patient's family members had been willing enough to allow us to say a prayer over their loved ones and hadn't been concerned when I'd laid my hand on the ill patient, but there was no chance of questioning the ghost in their presence.

"It's very generous of you." John's tone was full of admiration. "It is too easy for physicians to forget about the importance of caring for the spirit. Thank you for reminding me."

"It was kind of Father Harwell to invite us on his rounds." That much was true but I was pretty sure that if God did exist, he was busy preparing a special spot in hell for me for the lies I'd just told.

"Will you join me again tomorrow?" Grayson made a show of inquiring in front of John.

"We'd be happy to. I'm sure we'll be here."

"I almost forgot why I was looking for you." John gave his head a shake and again donned his public persona. "May I have a minute of your time, Anna? Leonard Chambers wants to meet with us again."

I failed to prevent the expression of dislike from showing. John laughed, transforming his serious features with an attractive smile that made it to his deep blue eyes.

"There's strength in numbers. Will you come with me?"

"Sure." I let go of my wall and threw Jed a glance. "I'll just be a few minutes. You don't have to come with us."

His eyes narrowed. "I intend to come with you."

"It's not necessary," I hissed, embarrassed to be having this conversation in front of John.

"I disagree."

"All right, all right." I caved rather than fight about it in front of everyone. He wasn't going to leave me alone when I was weak. I forced my legs in the direction John was going. With any luck, I wouldn't collapse in front of him. Jed followed several steps behind me as if he were a bodyguard, or an overprotective boyfriend. If we'd been alone I might have let him support me, but if I admitted how weak I was, it would earn me a spot in John Fowler's emergency room.

"I apologize again for my reaction. I don't know why I was surprised by your faith." John slowed his pace as he realized that I wasn't walking as fast as he was.

I searched for an appropriate reply as we strolled down the hallway, one that wouldn't add to the lies I'd told. "Mine isn't as strong as it could be."

"I admire your ability to be honest about that, but I think everyone feels that way. I do, at least." He stopped and looked at me, ignoring Jed. I couldn't help but notice that he was standing a step closer to me than was necessary. "Most people are afraid to admit to their doubts."

"Sometimes it feels like I'm the only one with doubts," I admitted. John was staring at me like I was a new species of colorful bird he'd just discovered. Was John Fowler flirting with me? "But I've never really talked about it with anyone." I started walking again, acutely aware of Jed's towering presence behind me.

"Are you Catholic?" He inquired, determined to continue the conversation. I guessed it was a fair question since I'd been praying with the priest.

"No, I'm not. Father Grayson doesn't seem to mind, though."

"Do you have a church?"

I shook my head. I was having a hard time forcing myself to continue the charade, but I needed to keep it up for a few more days. Lying was bad enough, lying to John about religion when he was being sincere felt worse. "It's difficult to find the time."

"I understand. It's hard for me, too." He opened the conference room door for us. "I just try to keep in mind that even when I'm not participating in a Christian community, I'm still capable of being a spiritual person."

"That's a nice way to look at it." It was nice. He was nice. It was refreshing to meet someone who seemed to be practicing the values that they espoused, even if I didn't share his faith.

Having known about ghosts since childhood, I'd grown up aware there was more to the universe than what science could explain. I'd never felt that the presence of ghosts in this world equaled the existence of God, but after my brush with death, I was certain that there was more to the universe than I'd been willing to admit. Whether it was God or not, I didn't know. I hadn't had the opportunity to figure out for myself what it meant to me.

Chambers didn't appear to have left his seat in the conference room. A cup of stale coffee perched dangerously close to a leaning pile of binders. Paperwork surrounded him, printouts of labs and a map of the county. He was typing on a laptop keyboard using his index fingers with methodical determination.

"Dr. Fowler, Dr. Roberts." He nodded towards the seats on either side of him and we took our places. "I've sent a few inquiries to nearby hospitals." Chambers glanced up and realized that Jed was in the room too. He glared at him for a moment but decided not to say anything about it. "I don't have reports back from all of them, but this one…" He pulled out a piece of paper that had a small state map on it and circled a town to the south, near the interstate that bisected our state, "seems to have a few patients with similar symptoms."

John, looking excited that his theory might be correct, leaned forward to look at the map.

"How many?" I asked, swallowing back a fresh surge of nausea.

Chambers shrugged as if this was unimportant information. "More than one. While I still believe this is a very remote possibility, Dr. Fowler, it is possible that you are correct. We need to understand

what this illness is. I've instructed the local health department repre-
sentatives to research Dr. Robert's case and the cases of the other two
patients that were hospitalized with the same symptoms at the same
time she was.

"There were more than one of you?" John sounded reproachful
as if I'd been withholding information from him.

"Two others," I reminded him.

"Which leads me to wonder, Dr. Roberts, how the three of you
became infected." He'd found his reading glasses and was staring at
me over the rims. I wondered when he'd realized he wasn't wearing
them. "Any thoughts on that?"

"It's not something I've thought about." It was the truth. I knew
what had caused my symptoms so hadn't needed to question it.

"Well, you might spend some time on that endeavor, if you can
spare it."

I didn't appreciate his patronizing tone. "I'll let you know if
anything comes to mind." I used my clinical tone of voice which
disguised personal feelings and might remind him that I was an MD.
If I'd hoped to generate some tone of respect in him, though, it was
in vain.

"Be sure that you do. I expect I'll see you tomorrow, Dr. Fowler.
Dr. Roberts, call me if you think of anything pertinent." He handed
me a business card and I walked out of the room, feeling again like
I'd been dismissed from the principal's office.

"What a jerk," John muttered and I choked back a laugh as the
door closed behind us.

"He is a peach," I agreed.

"So, three of you had this virus?" John asked.

"Yes."

"I'm just trying to figure out where it started. Did you all have
contact prior to becoming ill?"

"Not before we started to show signs of infection. Chaz and I
did, but not the third." My ex-boyfriend Eric had definitely already
been possessed by a ghost when he came to the farm to find me.

"Who's Chaz?"

"He's a friend of mine. He's here today. He and his partner are
staying with me at my farm this weekend."

"And the third party? Was that anyone you know?"

"Sort of. Eric Steinman. You might remember him. He went to medical school with us too."

"The cardiologist. Yeah, I know him." He paused as if assessing how close Jed and I were standing to each other. I could almost feel the heat from Jed's body on my backside. "So, you guys aren't still in touch?"

I didn't want to get into the details of my failed relationship with Eric Steinman. "No, not since we were in residency." My voice was devoid of emotion and I was happy to realize that it didn't bother me anymore.

Jed stepped away to the men's room, giving me the opportunity to lean against the wall again. My legs felt like they had filled with molten lead through the day, each drop making them heavier.

"When's the last time you saw him?" His tone was conversational as if we were just chatting, but I was cautious. It was possible to relax too much, to get too close to the truth. I didn't think that John Fowler would be as accepting of the reality of the ghosts as the priest was.

"At the hospital, the day we were all discharged."

"You hadn't seen him before that?" John shook his head. "There's got to be a link if you three are the first known patients with this virus."

"He came out to my farm and lost consciousness, because of the virus, I assume. He's the patient that I was having evacuated out on that helicopter that crashed."

"What was he doing out here?"

"I don't know." Another lie.

"Oh." John's tone told me he didn't believe me. "Was he hurt, too?"

"Not much. He was strapped in on the stretcher. He was the only one who wasn't injured."

"Somebody died in that, didn't they?"

"Two people." My voice cracked. "They were both paramedics." With kids, and families, and people who loved them.

John's hand was on my upper arm. I could feel the warmth of it through my sweatshirt. His touch caused pain in my skin, which still burned from releasing ghosts, but it felt so good to be touched.

"Are you all right? That had to be really hard to deal with." He was staring into my eyes and I worried for a moment that he would try to hug me. I might start crying if he did.

"Yeah, I'm fine." *Tell yourself that, Anna, if it makes you feel better.*

The bathroom door opened and Jed walked out, his eyes meeting mine over John's shoulder. John pulled back as if he sensed danger behind him.

"I didn't mean to upset you." He spoke as if he were reassuring a child who'd dropped her ice cream. "I was just trying to figure out the etiology of the virus. It's very interesting that you were all in the same place before you fell ill."

He had no idea how interesting it was. "Eric was already sick when he got there, and it's okay. I don't mind talking about it." I tried for nonchalance. I did mind, but I didn't think it would be polite to tell him that.

Jed stepped up to my side, and I could feel his concern. He'd stood next to me with each ghost, watching me as I used my energy, burning myself out. If I showed too much weakness he'd pick me up and carry me to the car. I forced myself to give up the wall and stand upright, proving to both of us that I was strong enough. It was harder than it should have been.

I gestured to Jed. "We should get going. I think I'm tired."

"So am I. These fifteen-hour days are killing me." John rubbed his face with a groan.

"Kind of what we signed up for, isn't it?" I reminded him and he rewarded me with a deep chuckle.

"Yeah. It wasn't very smart of us." He had a point. The reality of being a physician was a far cry from the fantasy I'd had when I'd been applying to medical school. John must feel the same way. We'd thought we'd just be helping people. Instead, we spent much of our time on administrative duties, checking the boxes that the government required.

"Will you be back tomorrow?"

"I'm sure we'll come by to see how Katheryn is."

"Can we talk again then?" John asked me. "I'd like to know more about what happened in the days before you got sick. Maybe it will help us identify the source of the illness."

There are ghosts, John. Evil nasty ghosts who want to take over the world. I couldn't say that out loud, of course, so I gave him a cautious nod instead. "Sure. I'll be here." We rounded the corner and found Ty and Chaz waiting for us outside Katheryn's room.

"Ready to go?" Ty asked, his eyes bright with concern.

"I am." I gave John a brief wave goodbye and Jed offered me his arm in one of those chivalric gestures he made that didn't fit in with modern society.

I surprised myself by taking it.

CHAPTER SIX

I **WAS RELIEVED** when we crested the hill and navigated the slick descent into the small valley that sheltered my cottage. I'd had my sixth sense on full alert and didn't sense any ghostly presence, other than Marnie, who looked like a small star in the valley beyond my home. She was the spirit of a young girl who stayed in the ruins of the cabin she had lived in. She was my friend, and she'd helped save me the night that I'd died and come back to life again.

"I'll go get the horses in and feed them." Jed stepped into the snow and skirted around the house, disappearing into the darkness. We'd kept both of Ned's mares in at night for the last couple of weeks. Charlotte was pregnant and I was glad that we were able to keep her in the barn instead of the pasture. Horses were outside animals, and in theory, they could handle the winter weather fine, but it made me feel better to keep them in.

Chaz pulled up behind me in the circular drive, parking his A6 behind my Subaru. Before Adonijah, they'd been planning to buy a Prius. Ty hadn't understood why Chaz had changed his mind. I was afraid that I knew why.

The Audi was a sporty car and had sexy performance. The Prius was an environmentally-conscious social statement. The Audi was a compromise between the massive SUV that Adonijah had favored and the Prius that a pre-possession Chaz had decided on. I was afraid that having Adonijah's spirit inside of us had changed us both, and that it might be a while before we understood how much impact he'd made on us.

I questioned every emotion I had out of fear that Adonijah was somehow behind it. Was I quicker to anger than before he'd been in me? Less caring, more stubborn? The thought that I might have incorporated some of Adonijah's evil spirit into my own persona was terrifying. I needed to talk to Chaz about it, but I hadn't yet. The topic was one I was afraid to give voice to, as if speaking of it would make it more real.

"Sorry about today," I said to Ty as I unlocked the front door.

"What are you sorry for?"

"You guys came up here to visit and all we've done is spend our time at the hospital dealing with ghosts."

"You know it sounds weird when you say it like that, but I'm getting used to it."

I stuck my tongue out at him before I plopped down at the kitchen table.

"It is weird," Chaz reminded us. "We shouldn't get used to this."

"I guess it's a little easier for me since I've always known that ghosts existed, though I never imagined anything like this would happen." I'd spent too much time avoiding my dreams. Maybe the Council could have warned me if Christiana hadn't been terrorizing me so much that I'd had to take drugs to avoid dreaming for the better part of two decades.

"So now what, Anna?" Chaz settled next to me, as at home in my farmhouse kitchen as I was.

"We brought wine," Ty announced, pulling a bottle of red out of a grocery sack on the counter. "I have a new rule. I don't talk about ghosts if I can't drink while I do it."

"The way things are going," Chaz spoke in an exaggerated whisper, "he'll need a new liver."

Ty wiggled his eyebrows suggestively. "Do you want some?"

"Yes, please." I sounded a little more emphatic than I'd meant to.

"Don't worry, we brought more." Ty was quick to reassure me as he poured three glasses and set them in front of each place at the table. He slid into a chair next to Chaz and leaned against his partner. Chaz kissed the top of his head and I gave them a smile.

"How's the clinic?" I asked Ty, skirting Chaz's original question about what we should do about the ghosts. He gave me a look that told me he hadn't forgotten it.

"Roz says I'm supposed to tell you that everything is fine and that you should take all the time you need."

"And the reality is?"

"Those residents are driving me crazy. They don't work as fast as you do and they don't know our patients like you do, Anna. You have to come back."

Guilt tugged at me. I'd made the practice my life, telling myself that the patients needed me. In reality, I'd used work as a way to avoid relationships. It was a distraction I used to keep myself from getting hurt again. If I ever got to go back, I'd still take care of my patients, but I needed to make time for my own life too.

The back door opened in a rush of cold air as Jed entered, as though I had summoned him by thinking about him. There were thumps from the mud room as he discarded his boots and coat.

"Do you want a glass of wine?" Ty called and Jed didn't waste time answering.

"Yes, thank you." Shod in a pair of heavy wool socks, Jed settled in the chair to my right as Ty poured him a glass and handed it across the table.

"Are you well?" Jed asked me.

I wanted to lean against him and breathe in his scents of sunshine and forest but I stayed where I was. "I'm better. The wine is helping."

"Are you getting your power back?" Chaz asked.

"It's getting there. I'll be recharged by morning."

"What does it feel like?" Ty's eyes were bright with curiosity.

"It's like I have a nuclear core of some sort. I deplete it a little bit every time I release a ghost, and then it regenerates again." The energy that had been burning in my bones was resettling itself deep inside me. The feeling was painful, but the more I used it, the more comfortable I was with it. Like an unused muscle that was getting regular exercise.

"That must feel pretty strange."

"I guess I don't know what it's like to not have it," I admitted.

"Do you have some extra organ?" Ty was suddenly eyeing me as if he'd just figured out that I was an alien species. I'd never had an MRI of my abdomen and pelvis to find out what was inside of me. Did I look like everyone else or was there something different about me?

"I don't know." It was a bit unsettling but I couldn't ask someone to do a scan on me just to find out. Whatever they found would be hard to explain. *Maybe you are an alien.* My snarky inner voice was less than comforting. "Are you guys seeing anyone at the office that might be possessed?" I asked to distract the conversation from how abnormal I was.

"I don't think so, but we have plenty of mental health issues going through the office on a good day so it's a little hard to tell." Severe mental illness was a common problem among the homeless population in Kansas City that we worked with.

"So, what's with the sudden round of possessions?" Chaz asked. "I asked earlier and I haven't gotten a full answer."

"I don't know," I told him. "It could be just leftover spirits, or it could be something more organized. A new way to attack us."

"Jed?" Chaz was direct as ever.

"I've told you everything I know," Jed replied with a shrug.

"Have you?" Chaz's tone was mild but his eyes indicated skepticism.

"Of course," Jed said. "We're on the same side."

"Of course we are." Chaz gave him a broad smile that suggested the matter was put to rest. I doubted it was. Something was on his mind. "I have a feeling that the ghosts have a plan, but Adonijah doesn't know the whole thing. He wasn't calling all of the shots." He'd had Adonijah in him for a long time, so he knew more than the rest of us did. Except maybe Jed.

"I'm almost certain he was working for someone else," I agreed.

"My brother was never one to bow to the authority of others. If he is working on behalf of another ghost, it's only because their goals are aligned for now."

"What other bad ghost is out there that's running this thing?" Ty asked.

"I don't know. He didn't tell me that." Chaz shook his head in confusion. "He didn't exactly tell me anything, I just learned a few things from him. Almost through osmosis."

"You were sharing your body, so that makes sense." I agreed. "Maybe he couldn't shield all of his thoughts and some of them filtered through to you." The only thoughts Adonijah had shared with me were his desires to control me and use my power to kill his brother.

"That helps me feel less crazy." Chaz took a sip of wine before continuing. "I know Adoni wants Anna. He needs her power so he can get rid of Jed and anyone else who he thinks stands in his way."

"And to keep her from killing him," Ty added.

"It's not murder if they're already dead," I clarified. "Call it releasing."

"I refer to it as banishment," Jed added.

Ty laughed. "You can't kill the dead. Got it."

"Any other tidbits you learned from him?" I didn't like to say his name out of an irrational and superstitious fear that it would somehow bring him to me.

"He really hates Jed."

Jed gave a dismissive chuckle that resonated through my small kitchen. "I murdered him. We lived a long time ago but I think it's clear that he has not forgotten."

"Understatement of the year," Ty intoned.

"How did he recognize you?" It was one of those questions I had meant to ask but hadn't gotten around to because I hadn't been ready to talk about Adoni and what happened to me. "I'm sure you don't look the same now as you did then."

"I don't know," Jed admitted. "I've wondered the same thing."

"He knew who you were when he got here. He talked about your old girlfriend and mentioned something about a murder." Ty had been paying close attention.

"Alleged murder," Chaz added.

"Alleged? No, I killed him." Jed gave a chilling smile and Chaz buried his head in his hands in mock dismay.

"Jed, never, ever admit to killing someone," Chaz instructed. "I don't care if you're found with their body and have the weapon in your hand."

"You can take the attorney out of the courtroom..." Ty whispered loud enough for everyone to hear.

"There are times that I don't understand your world," Jed admitted and Chaz gave a quick barking laugh.

"It's okay Jed. I don't think we can try you for something that happened that long ago. Just advice for the future, in case there are any other people you plan to murder."

"There are men that should not be permitted to live. Adonijah was one such..." He paused. "He planned to murder me for the throne. The commander of my guard would have killed him, but I wouldn't ask another man to take a life for me."

"Fair enough." Chaz nodded as if he'd been looking to take Jed's measure and felt that he'd learned something useful about his character. The fact that Chaz and I both had personal experience with Adonijah helped us disregard the fact that we were hanging out at the dining room table with a self-professed murderer. There was no doubt in my mind that Jed had made the right decision.

"It was long ago," Jed reminded us. "The world was very different."

"I can't imagine." I couldn't. What had it been like three thousand years ago? Did they have running water where Jed was? Italy had built their aqueducts, but Jedediah's ancient world was far from there. No electricity, no hot baths, no toilet paper...I was spoiled.

"Someday, if you wish, I will tell you more about what life was like then. When we have more time. When we aren't in the middle of this." He gestured towards the three of us but I knew what he meant. We had ghosts to deal with.

"I need to free more of those people at the hospital tomorrow. I may not be able to do them all in one day, but maybe if we start early I could get through half of them."

"We need to take a more strategic view, Anna," Chaz advised me. "If you don't find Adonijah and whoever he's working with, you'll spend the rest of your life trying to deal with these things one at a time. You're treating the symptoms rather than the cause."

"That's a very depressing thought." Ty took another sip of his wine. It was a depressing thought, one I'd had often in the last eight hours.

"I take it Adonijah wasn't at the hospital today," Chaz stated and Jed was quick to agree.

"Not that we are aware of."

"So how do we find him?" Chaz asked.

"Anna doesn't want to hear this but the Council is our best hope. I know of no one else who can tell us how to find my brother." Jed gave me a cautious glance.

"No way," I was adamant. "That bitch is insane."

"I agree she can be hostile. Being dead doesn't lend itself to maintaining one's manners."

"I don't trust them."

"I'm not asking you to trust them." I glared at Jed but he kept going. "You don't have to invite her into your room. Just go to sleep and talk to her. See if you can get her to share what she knows. This is how it's supposed to work." His voice had a patronizing tone that I objected to. He wasn't the one who had to deal with her, and he didn't seem to believe how she'd been behaving.

"Don't try to make this sound like some sort of natural thing, Jed, because it's not." I didn't try to keep the angry edge out of my voice. I didn't appreciate being told I'd overreacted.

"You were made this way, Anna." His tone mirrored mine. "God gave you this gift."

"I don't believe in God," I argued, but I'd lost that point. He was right. Whatever my strange gift was, I'd been born with it. It was indeed a natural element of my being. "I have a bad feeling about Christiana." I tried to salvage my end of the discussion. "She hasn't been forthcoming, and quite frankly, she's done nothing but try to scare me for years."

"I'm sure it was frightening to have ghosts in your dreams trying to communicate with you." I could hear the frustration in Jed's voice. "I don't believe she was intentionally trying to frighten you."

"It's definitely intentional." Annoyance that he was defending Christiana bloomed in my voice. "If she's so dedicated to the Council, and if the Council needs me to help them fight the bad ghosts, why has every action of hers been to alienate me?" I paused in case he wanted to reply, but he kept quiet. "Either the Council isn't all good, or Christiana isn't. It doesn't matter. After our little exchange last night, she isn't going to be very inclined to talk to me anyway."

"You didn't tell us everything about that earlier," Ty prompted.

"She threatened me, I threatened her, she thought I was bluffing and her friend attacked us, so I released her friend. Now she knows I'll use my power against her," I summarized.

"You also told her that they can't enter your dreams," Jed reminded me.

"Yeah, well, I guess I'll check my email," I retorted, my voice thick with sarcasm. "Maybe they've written." I didn't actually think that Christiana would listen to my instructions, but it would be nice to be able to sleep again without worrying about her joining me.

"You don't have to wait for the Council to come to you. You could go to them, once you are asleep."

I sucked my breath in and then exhaled before speaking. Why hadn't he explained this to me before? "I can make it happen?"

"You have the ability to control this."

A shiver of fear raced down my back. "I don't think that's a good idea."

"Can they hurt her?" I shot Ty a look of thanks for asking a question that had been weighing on my mind.

"I don't believe so." If Jed's response was meant to be encouraging, I didn't take it that way.

"Maybe we'd better figure out the answer to that before we risk our Anna." Chaz gave Jed a level stare. "She appears to be our only asset in this situation."

Jed stiffened. "I won't allow anything to happen to her. I'm here to protect her."

"How can you protect me from something in my dreams? You're not there." My voice wavered a little bit. I'd taken a hard line with Christiana, but she scared me. She haunted my dreams where my power didn't seem to work and then showed up in my room when I was sleeping.

"They will not harm you, Anna. They need you."

"So you've said." My retort was quick as my anger flared again. "But I don't believe that. They haven't exactly given me any reason to trust them. I don't feel safe when Christiana is around."

"We cannot do this alone, Anna." Jed ran his hands through his thick curls, smoothing them back as he gathered his thoughts. "We may win this battle, and the next, but at some point they will overwhelm us."

Trying to temper my frustration, I spoke in carefully measured tones. "I agree that we have limited resources. I don't know what to do about it, but I am telling you that Christiana is not interested in helping us."

"I've known the Council for more than a thousand years, Anna."

"I don't care." I punctuated each word with disdain.

"It is your duty."

"You are choosing *her* over me."

"You are being unreasonable."

"Damn it, I am not." I rose to my feet in a rush of indignation. "She threatened me. She said she was going to tell some ghost named the Master how to find me—"

"What?" Jed roared, gripping my upper arms and pulling me towards him as he towered over me. I hadn't seen him stand.

I tried to withdraw from the force of his rage, but his grip on my arms prevented me from moving. My heart raced, fury coursing through my veins.

"Do you have any idea what this means?" He gave me a shake and I looked into Jed's dark eyes.

"Let go of me," I ordered.

"Jed. You need to sit down." Chaz spoke from behind me and his hands settled on my shoulders.

Jed glanced at Chaz and chose to ignore him. "Why didn't you tell me this before now?"

"Stand down, Jed." Chaz's words were cool and full of command. Had everyone forgotten that I could take care of myself?

"Back off, Chaz," I ordered. "I don't need your help." His hands fell from my shoulders but he didn't step away. Jed still gripped my arms while he glared down at me.

"Sit down," I commanded and he squeezed my arm a little tighter. I relaxed a little. I wouldn't get far in a physical fight with him.

"I'm not telling you anything while you're like this," I informed him, keeping my voice calm and he seemed to realize he'd gone too far. He released his hold on me and stepped back.

"I apologize for my anger." His tone was controlled again but I noticed that he didn't apologize for grabbing me, just for getting angry. Chaz didn't step away from me until Jed was settled back in the chair at the other side of the table. I stayed on my feet.

"What the hell was that?" Ty exploded now that the situation had started to calm down.

"Leave us," Jed dismissed Ty and Chaz like the king he had once been, but he wasn't their ruler.

"I'm not going anywhere," Chaz responded in a surly tone. He was a lot smaller than Jed was, but he could be formidable. He wasn't someone you wanted to mess with, in the courtroom or on the street.

"Jed's right," I told him. "You two should go to bed." I hoped my heartbeat would slow down. It felt like it would explode out of my broken sternum and flop onto the table in front of me.

"He could hurt you," Chaz argued.

"He won't."

Chaz stood behind Ty. "Maybe you should stay somewhere else tonight, Jed. We'll be here with Anna."

"Anna is safest with me." Jed's voice sounded like danger. "I would never hurt her."

"Your word isn't feeling very solid right now, Jed. You must see that." Chaz was a natural negotiator, someone who could talk to criminals, and juries, and judges with persuasion and tact. Instead of responding to him, Jed turned his attention to me. I understood the message in his eyes. We needed some time alone.

"Can I talk to you two for a minute?" I tipped my head in the direction of the dining room beyond Ty and Chaz.

"Sure." Chaz stared at Jed for a moment longer and then walked out, with Ty and I trailing him.

Chaz stopped in the small library beyond the living room. It was as far as we could get from the kitchen and still be in the house.

"I get that you two need to talk," Ty started in, "but you were both pretty angry there. Has he ever hit you?"

"He has not. And I haven't been beating him either. This is just an argument. It's not the end of the world but he and I do need to talk."

"He could hurt you," Chaz said again.

"He could if he wanted to, but he doesn't, and he won't." My conviction increased in strength with my words.

"What if this is how it starts?" Ty asked. He'd seen domestic violence growing up, so I understood his concern.

"It's not," I reassured him with a gentle shake of my head.

"How can you be sure?"

"I'll be careful, Ty, but don't tell me that you and Chaz haven't ever had a fight and hurled dishes at each other, because I'm the one that stitched him up." I reminded them and Chaz gave me a sheepish grin while Ty flushed.

"We'll be upstairs if you two need anything," Chaz informed me. "But if I hear so much as the bedsprings squeaking I'm coming in there to check on you."

I glared at him. "My bed doesn't squeak."

"Goodnight." Ty winked. If it were anyone else I might be mad at them for interfering, but Ty and Chaz were my family.

"Goodnight."

Jed was still at the table, looking relaxed as if we hadn't been arguing. "When did this happen, this conversation about the Master?"

"A month ago, maybe? Not long after we met."

"Why did you not tell me of this conversation before now?" His tone was steady now; matter of fact. The Jed I knew. The Jed I thought I loved. I took the chair next to him again.

I shrugged. "We were probably busy fighting ghosts when it happened. I remembered it this morning. You haven't been very open to the possibility that Christiana isn't on my side, though."

He placed his elbows on the table and leaned forward to demonstrate how prepared he was to listen to me. "I will believe you."

"Why now?"

"She should not have mentioned that name to you. As a member of the Council, she shouldn't have anything to do with him. Will you tell me what happened?"

I gauged his body language and decided he seemed sincere.

"I'll tell you as much as I can remember. I was sleeping, and she showed up."

"When was this?" He kept his tone even.

"I think it was right after we first came to the farm."

He looked thoughtful as if he was calculating the days in his mind, counting back that month. "What did she say?"

"I don't remember word for word, but she said that the Master would find me. I asked who that was and she said that I'd know him when I met him."

"Is there more?" He prompted.

"She didn't make it sound like he was someone I wanted to meet. She called the Council a bunch of fools, or something like that." Jed's breath hissed out but he didn't interrupt me. "Then she grabbed my arm and squeezed it." I rubbed my fingers over my wrist as I remembered the tight claw of her hand. "She said that she wanted to watch the Master consume me."

"Is that it?"

"No. She threatened to tell him where to find me."

"I see." Jed rubbed the bridge of his nose between his fingers as if he was trying to figure something out. "Is there anything else?"

"Not that I remember."

"I may have placed too much faith in the Council, and in Christiana as their representative. I wanted you to talk to them, and my desire for you to do so has placed you in danger." He raised his eyes to meet mine. "There is a door in your mind that you control. You can keep Christiana, or anyone else, from coming to you when you sleep by keeping it closed. And you can open the door if you want to find the Council."

"I don't know how to do that," I reminded him.

"This is one of many things about your gift that your mother would have shown you."

"I don't suppose you can teach me how to control it."

"I cannot." Jed shrugged. "Perhaps knowing that the door exists, and that you have the power to use it, will help you determine its location in your mind."

I took a sip of wine, savoring the tart flavor. How was I supposed to find a door and figure out how to use it in a brain that didn't have doors? It had to be a metaphor but it wasn't one that correlated to the convoluted folds of the cerebellum.

"You know who this Master is?"

"He's more of a legend. Said to be an old spirit, one of the strongest. There are many rumors. I've heard speculation that he was cast out of heaven with the original Council but that he chose a less righteous path.

He may have made a habit of taking over bodies and living their lives, and he has been credited with starting wars and ruling empires." Jed took a breath as if he needed to be careful about how he phrased whatever it was that came next. "He was never a benevolent ruler, slaughtering entire nations."

"Are you sure he's not in the Council?" I asked.

"He is not." Jed was emphatic. "The Council do not speak of him."

"And you didn't know that Christiana was connected to him?"

"I promise you, if she is, I had no knowledge of it. It is possible…"

"What?"

"That she was trying to frighten you, for sport perhaps." I glared at him in response. "Did she say that Adonijah was working with the Master?"

"She might have implied it. Why didn't you tell me about this Master guy? I shouldn't have to learn about such a big threat from them."

Jed shifted in his chair like a scolded schoolboy. "He is like a myth. The Council does not speak of him at all, and the stories are always secondhand."

"So, this mythological ghost is just as bad as Adonijah?"

"If even a small portion of what I've heard is true..." Jed's voice trailed off.

"Then he may be worse," I finished for Jed.

"This is great cause for concern," Jed admitted.

"And Christiana knows him. You trusted her?" My voice slid up, incredulous.

"She is in the Council." Jed's right shoulder lifted. "I believed that our objectives were similar. Until now I had no reason to doubt her."

"And you want me to believe that the rest of the Council is on your side?" I could see the doubt in his eyes.

"I believe they are, mostly, on the side of good, Anna. I have not misrepresented myself to you. Even if Christiana has fallen from the path, there are others on the Council who I am certain are above reproach." It sounded like he was struggling to rationalize what I'd told him with his previous beliefs. "We will have to question the motives of everyone on the Council until we can be sure of where their loyalties lie."

I didn't point out that I'd done nothing but question them since Jed first told me what the Council was.

"What did Christiana have to gain by telling me about her relationship with the Master?"

"That is what we must find out," Jed answered. "I don't know what her motives are but they are suspect."

"She could be crazy. Maybe she's been dead for too long." It slipped out before I realized what I was saying. I snuck an embarrassed glance at Jed. He was staring at me, expressionless. The silence hung between us.

"I have had some time to contemplate the nature of the dead." His tone held the weight of his three thousand years.

I was relieved he spoke first, and tried to lighten the tension. "That you have."

"I have come to the conclusion that souls that are unstable were also afflicted when they were living."

Oh.

"Who was Christiana when she was alive?" I squeaked out.

Jed's shrug seemed both regal and dismissive. "A minor lord's wife, I think."

I raised my eyebrows in mock disbelief. "She wasn't a queen? A princess? Some wealthy and influential person that's in the history books?"

Jed's expression shifted to one of amusement. "She had royal blood, but she did not have much of it. Why do you ask?"

"I just thought that all of the dead people you hang out with were famous. Like royalty."

"I see." He didn't look as if he caught the joke. "However unremarkable she may have been in life, she has made up for in her death."

"She didn't fall from heaven?" I tried to keep the skepticism from my tone and failed.

"Christiana is not one of the original Council. She joined them later, as did I."

"How many are there, in the Council?"

Jed raised an eyebrow. "I guess scores of them. I don't know them all."

"You worked with them for a thousand years and you don't know them all?"

Jed sighed in a way that said I didn't understand how complicated it was to be a ghost. "They are not always together."

"I guess that makes sense." I changed topics to a question that had been on my mind for a while. "How did Christiana recreate an actual body? It was a body, wasn't it?"

"It did look realistic," Jed agreed.

"Except her tits," I spoke with certainty and Jed chuckled at my use of the word. "Those were definitely fake. I never thought I'd see a ghost with silicon breasts." Jed looked like he was trying to keep from laughing. "Not that I had the opportunity to examine them close up," I admitted, "But they couldn't be real." Jed's eyebrows rose. Women in his era probably hadn't discussed breast proportions, at least not around him. "I want to know how she made that body."

"It's not a power that I had witnessed prior to last night, but some spirits are stronger than others."

"She had to be creating matter and then when she was done it disintegrated. From a physics perspective, it's not possible." Clearly, this was a question that I wasn't going to get an answer to anytime soon. I'd taken a few physics classes in school, but theoretical physics wasn't my forte. "Why do you think she didn't try to make clothes too?" I asked, but Jed didn't answer. "I think she was trying to intimidate me and make me jealous."

"Jealous?" Jed looked amused.

"By insinuating that you two were an item."

"She wanted to anger you." He looked a little too pleased that it had worked. "She is nothing to me, other than a member of the Council."

"It's none of my business what your relationship with her was." My tone was curt, and he objected to it with a sudden arc of his eyebrows. His expression darkened.

"Isn't it, Anna?" His inquiry was a low whisper that sent a shiver through me and I didn't know how to respond. "Knowing what I want isn't an issue," Jed began as if continuing a conversation we'd been having, his tone a low murmur.

"It's not?" I folded my arms against the intensity of his expression and settled into my chair.

"I am pledged to protect you, not take advantage of you."

"You don't take advantage of me."

"I have." His eyes sought the shadows of the kitchen, avoiding my gaze. "I fear that last night I again overstepped the bounds of our relationship."

"How so?"

"It's easy for me to forget what you've been through, the upheaval I have brought to your life."

"It's not your fault." I didn't sound like I believed it.

"I am sorry that I became irate earlier."

"I'm sorry too." I wasn't sure where he was going with this.

"I shouldn't have allowed the situation last night to escalate. I don't want you to resent me." Didn't guys usually wait a little longer before they started to break up with you?

"You think we shouldn't have made love last night?" He'd seemed enthusiastic at the time.

"It wasn't right." He switched his focus from the corners of my dark kitchen back to me.

"I know the intensity of the situation last night contributed to us having sex. I don't understand why you think that was wrong."

"In my day I would marry a woman before I took her to my bed." If the little bit of history I'd read on him was right, he'd married quite a few of them so that he could sleep with them.

"This isn't your era, and things have changed in the last few centuries," I noted. "And it was my bed we were in, not yours."

His upper lip twitched with a repressed smile and he relaxed a notch. "Your world is very different than the one I lived in. I am trying to learn your ways, but I may never fully adapt." He took a deep breath. "I want you to come to me again, but you should wait until you are certain that I am what you want."

"What if I already know?"

Jed stood, towering over me. "You don't," he informed me, and then bent down, brushing his lips against my temple. "Allow me to see you to your bedroom."

I planted my hand on his chest and he stopped. "You don't get to choose what's best for me. You can choose for yourself, but you can't make those decisions for me." My neck felt strained from looking up at him but I wanted him to see my resolve.

"You aren't sure." His lips twitched with amusement.

We'd only known each other for a month, but with all we'd been through, it felt longer. "I'm certain enough," I told him.

His smile faded. "Very well."

CHAPTER SEVEN

JED AND I GOT READY for bed in companionable silence, trying to be quiet for the sake of our houseguests. It wasn't the first time he and I had taken turns in the bathroom and brushed our teeth together, but with our relationship changing, it felt like it. I tried to pretend it was normal which made me feel more awkward.

"It's quite late. You need to rest," he whispered, turning off his bedside lamp and moving the cat from in front of his pillow to the foot of the bed. She stared at me as if calculating how long she had to wait before she could take over half of my pillow without being evicted.

"I am tired." I crawled into my side of the bed, plunging us into darkness when I turned off my light. When Jed's arm wrapped around me I stiffened, and he shifted back to his side of the bed.

"No, please, it's nice. You just surprised me," I told him.

I scooted towards the middle of the bed until I found him. I settled my back against his front, and his legs curved behind mine, warming me with the length of his body. I relaxed back into him as if I belonged there and he again tucked his arm around me, his palm spreading over my belly.

"Goodnight, Anna." His voice was a rough whisper and I felt the brush of his lips against my hair. I squeezed his hand in reply.

I drifted so deeply into sleep that the sound of the strange voice felt like a distant dream.

"Why are you being difficult, child?"

The words resonated through my head and I woke enough to realize I was sitting cross-legged on what must be the solid floor of that horrible closed-in cave that Christiana always took me to, still in the same lightweight sweatpants and t-shirt that I'd gone to sleep in. The voice wasn't Christiana's, though.

They'd entered my head again, while I slept. I saw the bright orb of the ghost's energy with my sixth sense. I didn't want to be here. I scrambled to my feet, anger flaring in a rush of warmth that surged through me. The stone floor beneath me rippled into a carpet of lush soft grass and as the cavern ceiling dissolved I saw stars in the open sky above me. The ghost hissed as if I'd angered him by changing the scenery. I didn't care if I had. The scent of earth and green things filled my lungs in a rush of comfort and I knew that I had made the space around us change, though I wasn't sure how I'd done it. By wanting it? Willing it? Was this place that easy to alter?

"You are strong," the voice noted. It was still too dark for me to see much more than the dim glow of the spirit, but this was my dream and I was tired of not being in control.

I concentrated on the sky and my desire to see. Nothing happened at first, but then a soft orb of light began to gather in the distance. I bit my lip in concentration and the orb brightened in gradual stages until a sun blazed overhead. The walls of the cave were intact, sloping upwards in slick gray rock that surrounded us with twenty-foot tall cliff walls. The ghost hadn't taken form but now seemed to glow as hot as the star I'd created above us.

"You didn't like the dark?" It queried.

"Why are you hiding?" I countered.

"Perhaps I'm not as strong as you are."

I couldn't tell from the voice if it was male or female and found it a little unnerving that I couldn't place it into either of these predefined societal roles.

"Maybe I'm wrong, but I don't think you'd be able to show up while I was sleeping if you were weak."

It didn't deny the truth of my statement. "You show spirit for one so new to this form of communication."

"I know what my power can do." That was all bravado talking, but I'd found the best way to deal with ghosts was to act like they didn't frighten me. So far, this one hadn't threatened me, but I wasn't going to make the mistake of appearing weak. Maybe it just hadn't gotten around to being scary.

"Your power to banish the dead doesn't work in this realm," it informed me.

"Are you sure? I destroyed the cave and I'm the one who created that sun." It met my challenge with silence which made me think that it wasn't certain. I hoped it didn't call my bluff because last time I'd tried to use my power in this realm it hadn't worked. I hadn't known then I could change our environment, though, so maybe I could banish a ghost if I needed to. What else could I do in this dreamlike realm? It would be interesting to find out what my limits were. If I was going to keep coming here, I needed to find out for my own safety. My first concern, though, was to figure out if this was one of Christiana's friends or one of Jed's. Or maybe it had some new agenda.

"As long as you don't threaten me or the people I care about, I won't release you right now," I offered.

"You grant me safety."

"I'm just laying down the ground rules."

It spoke without hesitation. "I agree to your terms." That was easy. Too easy?

"Are you going to stay like that?" I was surprised it wasn't showing me more of its form, like Christiana and her friends had.

"Does it bother you?"

"No, I'm just curious."

"I can take a shape if you'd like."

"Any shape, or your own?" I was interested to know what it could do. How strong was it?

"If there is something that would please you, I would attempt to comply." It moved closer to me and I stepped back.

"You don't have to do anything on my account, except behave yourself."

"Have I misbehaved?"

"Not yet, but I have good reason to be suspicious."

"I will keep my word, Anna." It sounded affronted. Maybe I was being rude. Maybe I didn't care if I was.

"It's not fair that you know my name and I don't know yours."

"I've been dead for so long I don't know if I have a name anymore."

I decided to interpret that as a joke and chuckled. "You had to have had a name at some point, didn't you?"

"In actuality, I have lived many lives, each with a different name." I wondered if he meant through possession and shivered with revulsion while I tried to come up with a polite response.

"Well, pick one. What do your friends call you?" The cloud of energy swirled in silence and then a figure stepped out of it. Not a flesh and blood form, nor the ghastly skeletal remains that I sometimes saw, this one struck me by how normal looking it was. *Normal for a ghost.*

Though the light of the sun shone through it, I could make out the draping of some sort of red tunic, and feet clad in leather thong sandals, though I still couldn't see its features.

Its hand gestured to the soft grass beneath us. "Be seated, and I will join you." It settled on the ground cross-legged with the red cloth of its skirt covering its knees, so I sat across from it. Now that it was closer I could see that the tunic was clipped at the shoulder with a brooch in the shape of an elephant's head that looked like it was carved from ivory, with red jewels for eyes. The spirit turned opaque in gradual waves. It didn't have a living body like Christiana had, but as it solidified further, it appeared to be male.

His skin tone was a shade lighter than Jedediah's olive complexion and I could see the flat slope of a nose set between wide cheekbones. A high forehead balanced the cheekbones in a proportionate fit. His entire face was lean and harsh as if he had lived a difficult life. Maybe death, too, had been hard for him. He now looked as solid as Christiana had when she'd come to my bedroom, his thick curly hair was pulled back into a low ponytail. Long delicate hands with fingers made for flowing over the keys of a piano settled onto his knees. Would my hand go through his arm, if I reached out to touch it?

"You may call me Scipio. Scipio Africanus," he announced and I nodded, unsure of the protocol. Was I supposed to offer to shake his hand? I'd seen a lot of ghosts and had conversations with a few of them, but this was the first time I'd gotten such a formal introduction. I didn't want to find out what would happen if I touched him, and he might think I was threatening him with my power if I offered to. I kept my hands in my lap.

"I'm Anna," I offered unnecessarily.

He was looking me over like someone evaluating horses at auction. "You are a beautiful woman." He leaned forward and I leaned back to keep some distance between us. "Such pale skin," he murmured as if he'd forgotten I could hear him.

"Scipio…Is that name the one you were born with?"

"Scipio Africanus. You do not know me?" He arched his shoulders back and I could see I had offended him. I had to stop myself from laughing. These ghosts, they all thought I should know who they were, but at least he wasn't staring at me anymore.

"I'm sorry, I don't." I tried to make my tone conciliatory but it was difficult. "Should I?"

"I led a most auspicious life," he informed me, lifting his head to the sun as if he were posing. "I was the greatest general of the Roman Empire."

Okay, Mr. Ghostly. That was a hell of a long time ago. His name seemed familiar from some long forgotten high school textbook, but my condensed college and medical school program hadn't left a lot of room for the liberal arts. I decided to bluff and forced a look of astonishment onto my face as if the light bulb in my head had just gone off.

"Of course you were. I can't believe I didn't recognize you from your portraits." The great General Scipio had some portraits drawn of him, surely? He leaned forward, satisfied now that he thought he'd been recognized for the important persona he'd once had.

"There are several of my portraits at the Louvre," he offered and I nodded with vigor as if I knew what he was referring to.

"Of course there are. But I've never had the fortune to go there."

"That is a pity."

"Yes, I hope to go someday."

"I will take you," he announced and I had to smile. This ghost was going to take me to France?

"That's a very generous offer. Right this minute, I'm afraid I'm pretty occupied with some ghosts that are causing all sorts of trouble. I don't suppose you know anything about that, do you, Scipio?"

"I am aware of your difficulties."

"And which side are you on?" I was so tired of playing games.

"I believe you have met Christiana," he offered up and I recoiled.

"I have and she is not a friend of mine. If you are with her, then this conversation is over."

"We have made a pact today, Anna, that neither of us will threaten the other."

"I wasn't threatening."

He sighed as if I was a child that he was losing patience with. "The Council is here to help you."

"You're with the Council."

"I am." He puffed his chest out, with pride or self-importance. I wasn't sure which.

"And Christiana is with the Council?"

"She is."

"Christiana has made it clear that she is not on my side and as a result, I don't trust your Council."

There was a long moment of silence while he considered my words. "She tells us your conversations were proceeding nicely, until most recently. I have come to discover why you rejected her overtures of friendship and banished her pet."

"That's clever phrasing on her part."

"You see your conversations differently?"

"I'm quite sure she means me harm." I gave Scipio a benevolent smile. "If she comes anywhere near me again I will release her." *Let's see if he considered that 'proceeding nicely.'*

"That is unfortunate." He pondered this with a slight smile and I got the feeling he wasn't disturbed by it at all.

"I warned Christiana that none of you are allowed to disturb me when I'm sleeping. Why are you here?"

"All of us are different, on the Council. Please, don't judge me by Christiana's actions."

"Do you trust her? Do you think she's loyal to your little ghost group?"

I have had my concerns about Christiana." He looked regretful.

"Have you?" I didn't manage to keep the skepticism out of my voice. "What concerns have you had?"

"Some of us have wondered if she is as devoted to our cause as she once was."

"Is she the only one you have doubts about?"

"It can be hard to know who you can trust, can't it?" It was a backhanded answer to my question that told me everything, and nothing.

"Indeed, it can," I agreed, tired of the small talk. "What do you want from me?"

"I suppose we are here so that I may earn your trust."

"Where is Christiana?"

"Location is a difficult thing to define, for spirits."

"Fair enough. Getting rid of her would be a good first step to earning my trust." One of many.

"It is beyond my power to remove her from the Council, if that is what you are asking of me. And she is already dead. You are the one with the power to release her."

I snorted in frustration. "So, what can you do?"

"I am able to be of help to you, Anna. Of great help."

"Please, be specific," I insisted and he laughed.

"How well versed are you in how to use your power?"

My eyes narrowed into slits and I answered with a threat. "Well enough."

He laughed as if he thought I was joking. "I am not being disrespectful. I'm offering to help you, to teach you."

"What makes you an expert?"

"You are not the first with this ability."

"Yes, I know. My mother had it."

"I was referring to myself."

"You?" I couldn't hide the surprise in my voice. His expression suggested he was a ghost of many talents. "Maybe I already know everything that I need to know." I tried to regain the upper hand but I'd lost much of my advantage and we both knew it.

His laughter echoed off of the rock walls around us. "There are many complexities of the soul and its attachment to the body. I could explain this to you." I waited, to see what else he could offer. "And then there is this space. You appear to have mastered some of it, but I wonder how much there is that you cannot do?"

"What is this place?" I gave myself away without even thinking about it.

"It is the place between life and death."

"I thought it was a dream," I said. "A way for the brain to process all that it has seen and done for the day, the worries and the yearnings."

"You speak of when normal people sleep, perhaps. Yes, they may have this brain processing you speak of when they dream. You, though, are different."

I tried to process the scientific implications. If he was right, there were more ways I was different than just my abdominal nuclear core. What would an MRI of my brain look like? I shivered.

"There might be one or two things I could learn from you." Starting with the doorway that I could close to keep him out of my head. "What would you want in return?"

The look he gave me was too familiar and I had to keep myself from recoiling. "My greatest hope is to develop full cooperation between you and the Council." That sounded a little too hokey.

"I need to think about it." I was going to talk to Jed before I made any agreements with ghosts.

"Very well." He stood and he leaned forward in a delicate half bow. One hand kept a firm grip on his tunic so it didn't slide off his shoulder and I had to suppress a snort of laughter. "I will come to you again soon."

"Don't go yet, please." Now that he was leaving all of the things I needed to know came to me in a rush. "What about Adonijah? Can you help me find him?"

"Adonijah's vendetta for his brother does not concern the Council."

"I thought you were supposed to keep the balance between people and ghosts. Adonijah has been possessing people, hurting them. Using ghosts to attack me. Doesn't the Council know about this?"

Scipio frowned. "He may have gone further than we realized. I will see if we have any recent news of him. Perhaps he is in league with the Traitor."

I'd heard that name before, in the same conversation where I'd learned of the Master. "Christiana mentioned the Traitor once. Who is that?" Scipio looked at me with guarded eyes. "You want me to trust you but you won't tell me what you know?" He didn't respond and I tried a difference tactic. "Do you know the Master?"

His eyes narrowed with caution. "I know of him."

"Will you help me find him?"

He considered me for a long moment before responding. "The Council will come to you. Prepare yourself for that day."

"When will that be?" My voice cracked with frustration.

"Farewell, beautiful Anna." Was his only reply.

"Scipio, I need to find the door to get back! Can you help me?" I pleaded but his form faded into translucency in gradual stages until

I could only see him using my second sight, and then that faded as well. "Goodbye, Scipio. Thanks for leaving me, asshole," I spoke into the emptiness around me. I paced the small grassy space, walled in by the canyon of rock that had once been a cave.

Awesome. I'm stuck here. At least Christiana always sent me back when she was done tormenting me. There wasn't any obvious way out, but for some reason, I was annoyed instead of being scared.

I sank back onto the thick grass, waiting for whatever came next and relishing the feel of the warm sun on my arms. The heat felt good after four months of winter. I relaxed, closing my eyes and allowing myself to enjoy the sunshine.

The smell of bacon cooking brought me to my senses again. I opened my eyes, confused by the pillows under my head instead of grass. *Oh. I'm home.* I savored a few moments of gratitude for house-guests who liked to cook. I was hungry, as if whatever I'd done in that dream place impacted my power reserves. I was alone in bed, so I didn't know if it was Jed who was cooking, or Chaz.

I followed my nose downstairs and found my kitchen full of men. Ned and Jed sat at the table, heads bent together over mugs of coffee while Ty and Chaz quibbled over how done the bacon should be. There was a large glass pan with wheat bread soaking in an egg mixture.

"I like my bacon crispy," I reminded them as I poured the last cup of coffee and claimed my spot at the table next to Jed.

"Good morning, Anna." Ned nodded to me from the end of the table.

I wasn't sure if it was a good morning yet or not. "Morning, Ned. What's the news from Unionville?"

"Katheryn and Carrie were both sleeping when I left last night and I haven't heard anything yet." He spun his phone in a circle on the tabletop. "I was getting ready to head back up there, thought I'd stop by here first and see what the plan is."

"I don't know yet. Let me drink my coffee and then we can figure it out."

"Fair enough."

"Anybody hungry?" Ty hollered over his shoulder.

"I am. It smells fantastic," I offered as encouragement and got the first piece of bacon as a reward. Ned glowered while I crunched through the salty piece of bliss.

Jed settled his hand on the back of my chair and rubbed his thumb across my shoulder blade. I grinned at him like an idiot. I'd forgotten how stupid I acted when I was in love.

"How did you sleep?" he asked.

Ned was staring at us, his eyes narrowed as he watched us and I realized that Carrie must have kept our conversation to herself. I nodded at him, answering the question he hadn't asked out loud and he nodded back at me, as if in approval.

"I had a visit from a Council member last night."

"Here?" Jed jolted upright in alarm. My nighttime adventure hadn't been noticeable enough to wake him up.

"In my dream." I took another sip of coffee and realized that the room was silent other than the bacon grease popping. Four sets of eyes watched me.

"You looked like you were just sleeping when I left. I wouldn't have left you alone, if I'd known. Was it Christiana?" Jed's voice was cold and I shook my head.

"No, this was one I hadn't met before. He called himself Scipio."

Jed leaned back in his chair. "Scipio Africanus."

"You know him."

"He has a certain reputation. Did he try to harm you?"

"No, but I'm not surprised to hear that. He didn't seem as bad as Christiana. I mean, I don't trust him, but he didn't threaten me."

"So, what happened?" Ned looked a little twitchy, like he wished he'd brought his shotgun in with him.

"He made a big deal about whoever it was he used to be."

"Scipio Africanus was the guy who defeated Hannibal Barca," Ty informed us.

"Hannibal was the guy with the elephants, wasn't he?" I was remembering Scipio's ivory broach, the dark red stones inset into the animal's eyes.

"Yes, Anna, the guy with the elephants. Hannibal led the Carthage army and defeated the Roman Empire in large part due to the elephants he brought over from Africa. He had to get them over the Alps. Don't you remember that story from high school?" Ned asked.

"I remember the thing about the elephants." I sounded more defensive than I intended but I was embarrassed that both Ned and Ty remembered their history lessons better than I did.

"It's quite well-known. I remember it," Ned offered and I glared at him.

"Well, I don't remember learning anything about Scipio Africanus." Or whatever his name was.

"As well-known as he was, that was not Scipio's first life," Jed informed us.

"He gave me the impression that he'd lived quite a few times."

"I believe that Scipio may have been his favorite life. He is not fond of being limited to the spirit world." I took a moment to ponder how often that had happened over the course of history, without any of us being any the wiser.

"I thought the Council was against ghosts taking over living people?" I grumbled.

"On a wide-scale basis, yes."

"But not for their own members?" Chaz noted. Jed shrugged as if it wasn't a matter of particular importance.

"Hypocrites." Ty sat a towering platter of nicely browned French toast and a pitcher of warm syrup in front of my plate. "Eat up."

"Yeah, they aren't giving me a warm fuzzy feeling either." I stabbed a piece of toast and passed the platter to Jed with a glare that he either didn't see or chose to ignore.

"So, this isn't a new thing." Chaz took the seat between Ty and Ned. "Ghosts taking over people." His tone held an accusatory edge as if Jed had tried to sell him a jug of sour milk.

"On the scale that we have seen these past weeks, the attacks have been unprecedented. You are correct, though. There have always been some ghosts that weren't satisfied with the life they lived, or with the fact that death was upon them."

"Are you one of those, Jed?" Chaz asked.

"I have lived other lives, but only at the behest of the Council," he answered, stiff with defense. "All of them were cases where the soul had left the body."

"Fair enough." Chaz leveled his eyes on Jed. "You can't blame me for asking."

"I understand," Jed answered with his typical reserve.

"What else did this Scipio character have to say?" Ned broke through the tension and I gave him a grateful smile.

"Well, he said he wants me to work with the Council, and I told him that I didn't trust them because of Christiana."

"What did he have to say about that bitch?" Ty asked.

"At first, he defended her, but when I pushed him, he said that he'd had his doubts about her loyalty."

"I'm starting to like this ghost." Ty grinned. "I never thought I'd say that. Present company excluded, of course." He gave Jed an apologetic smile.

"Christiana has been with the Council for a long time, as has Scipio," Jed informed us. "I find his willingness to throw her off strange. He may just be trying to gain your trust," he cautioned.

"Maybe he's more realistic about her than you were." Jed didn't react to my snide comment with anything more than a raised eyebrow. "Don't worry, Jed. I'm not ready to trust him."

"Did anything else happen?" Ned, trying to make sure I'd given out all the information I had.

"He claimed that he was like me, in one of his lives, and that he could teach me how to do more things with my power."

"What else can you do?" Ty's voice was quiet astonishment and I shook my head.

"I don't know but he implied that there was more, especially in that dream place where they like to talk to me."

"There may be truth to that." Jed turned back to his bacon.

"I was able to change some stuff in that place last night. I made the sun come up, and I changed the setting of the place we met. It's always been this dark cavern, but I changed it so it wasn't a cave at all." Somehow it all sounded less plausible when I said it out loud.

It is possible that you are insane. Is this what the beginning of a mental breakdown feels like? I suppressed my inner thoughts with a surge of annoyance. No one else seemed to know what to say either so I changed the subject.

"That was pretty much it. I guess I'll see what happens if he comes back. Maybe we could make a list of some of the things I should ask him."

"Yeah." Ned sounded doubtful. He'd been slow to believe in both ghosts and my abilities with them. Me having conversations with spirits in a dream state where I had more strange abilities pushed the boundaries of what he was willing to accept. "Anyway."

He gathered himself. "What's your plan for today? I need to get back to the hospital."

"I have to go back up there, too," I reminded him. I'd been delaying over my breakfast, but there were a lot of people there who needed my help. "I just need to take a shower and I'll be ready to go."

"We have to work tomorrow," Ty reminded me.

"Of course you do." I felt guilty since I should be at the clinic with him. The people there needed me too. "You guys are going to head home?"

"Yeah. Somebody has to keep the clinic running while you're off saving the world."

I gave him a sad smile. "I'm glad you came up." Even if it was to deliver the news that I was responsible for another person dying.

"We'll clean up the kitchen, Anna. Then we'll take off when you do."

"Thanks, guys. You're the best. Ned, we'll see you up there." I left the men to take care of the kitchen.

CHAPTER EIGHT

THE HOSPITAL PARKING LOT was a hotbed of activity. There were two news vans from Kansas City stations and one with a logo I didn't recognize, their long antennas extended above them. The parking lot was full and drivers had started to create their own parking spots on the medians, wherever they could find a place. Jed evaluated the situation for a few seconds and then pulled around the side of the building and found a lone spot near a side door.

"Let's go in here."

"It's a madhouse. What the heck is going on?" It was a rhetorical question. Unless there'd been a dramatic accident that had drawn the cameras, then I knew well what the fuss was about.

His lips set in a grim line. "I fear we will find out soon enough."

The hallways were busy, but we made it to Katheryn's room without incident. She appeared to be sleeping, long white hair spread in a smooth sheet around her face. I handed Carrie the thermos of decaf coffee I'd made her with a smile while Jed took a chair next to the window.

"Oh, thank you," she whispered, giving me a boisterous hug as if spending the night on the hard hospital visitor couch and skipping a shower hadn't bothered her in the slightest. "Ned brought me a plate of that delicious French toast earlier but all I've had to drink is tea. At least this way I can pretend that I'm getting some caffeine."

I nodded towards the still form in the bed. "How's she doing?"

"I feel better." Katheryn opened her eyes while she spoke and then closed them again. She didn't look any better but if she felt it, it was great news.

"That's good. Have your doctors been through yet?" I wanted to look at her morning lab work to see if the steroids were helping as much as we needed them to, but I needed John's help to get access to them. The days of paper charts hung over the foot of each patient's bed were long gone.

"Your friend, Dr. John, was here earlier. He said he'd be back," Katheryn informed me. I gave her arm a gentle pat, hoping John had managed to get back to his hotel to get some sleep last night.

"Get some rest, Katheryn. We'll try not to bother you. How was the night, Carrie?"

"It was pretty quiet. John said there's a lot of activity here this morning, though. He suggested you stay in here until he can talk to you. Ned's gone to find out what's up."

"There are TV crews set up out front," I told her.

She pointed up at the television in the corner behind me, showing the local news channel with the volume muted. "I know."

"What are they saying?" I asked as the door opened and Grayson slipped in. He was dressed exactly as he had been the day before. The white collar looked uncomfortable, but having a standard uniform must make it easier to get dressed in the morning. No time spent in the closet wondering what to wear.

"They've heard about the 'virus,'" Grayson informed us as he made his way towards Katheryn's bed. He settled beside her and took her hand in his as if he belonged there. They looked pretty comfortable with each other, in a way that spoke of deep affection and I wondered again what their story was. "The hospital won't let them inside, but they've been out there all morning."

"This does not make our situation any easier," Jed announced. "You shouldn't be here, Anna."

"Why not?"

"Broadcasting your coordinates on television will not help us."

"Are you telling us ghosts watch a lot of daytime TV?" Carrie asked with a chuckle.

"They are capable of watching television."

"Fair enough. I'll stay away from the reporters." I took a deep breath and got ready for an argument. "I'm not leaving anyone with a ghost in them, though." Jed stiffened in protest. "No, Jed." I made eye contact with him so he could see how important it was to me. "Don't ask me to leave when I can help them."

"There is too much risk in staying," he argued. "The situation here has changed from yesterday. I promise you, we'll find another way to help."

"It is her calling, Jedediah." Grayson inserted himself into our discussion with ease. "Just as mine is to God, hers is to ease suffering. Asking her to stop when she can help someone would be like asking you to stop protecting her."

Jed threw his hands up in defeat. "Stay out of sight of the cameras." His voice had a regal tone of command to it and I nodded.

"What's this?" Katheryn's voice was bright with interest and we all turned towards her.

"The cars," Carrie supplied helpfully pointing at the television.

The TV camera panned in on a procession of shiny black SUVs rolling to a stop at the front door of the hospital.

"I don't have a good feeling about this," Carrie murmured and I had to agree with her. The last time I'd seen SUVs that nice arrive, they'd carried Adonijah.

The doors opened and a flurry of activity ensued as figures dressed all in black except for the white of their clerical collars emerged. They gathered one occupant from the back seat of the middle car and escorted him inside.

"My heavens," Katheryn exhaled. "We've just been invaded by Catholics." She gave Grayson an apologetic smile. "Friends of yours?"

"Possibly," he admitted. Carrie turned up the television volume. "I reached out to an acquaintance of mine who happens to be the diocesan exorcist."

"The diocese has an exorcist?" I tried to mask the surprise in my voice and failed. Grayson kindly ignored it.

"It's not something that we talk about very much, but yes, every Catholic diocese has an exorcist."

"That looks to be more than one," Jed observed as Grayson's phone rang.

He pulled it out of his pocket and answered, releasing Katheryn's hand with obvious reluctance and stepping into the hallway for privacy.

On the television, the SUVs pulled away from the covered drop-off zone, their occupants having disappeared inside the building. The cameras followed them while the reporters voiced baseless speculation on the church's presence.

"I think we'd better go find out what's happening," I whispered, following Grayson into the hallway. The priest had already disappeared. I felt Jed's presence behind me as Katheryn's door clicked shut.

"Will they help us?"

"The priests? I don't know."

"If they can get rid of the ghosts, then they won't need me." A note of hope tinged my words. John rounded the corner and increased his pace when he saw us.

"I'd rather they not learn of your talents," Jed said, his voice low enough that John couldn't overhear. I agreed. I didn't think the Catholic church would be impressed with my ghost-banishing gift.

"Anna, good morning." John handed me a sheet with Katheryn's morning bloodwork. Her electrolytes were still out of balance but not as much as they were the day before. "It looks to me like the steroid dose is working."

I glanced over her numbers, smiling in relief. It was what I'd hoped for, but wasn't guaranteed. "They are helping."

"Well, I'm sorry for doubting you. For what it's worth."

"It's an unusual treatment for a virus," I admitted.

"Very. I'm adding this to the regimen for my other patients who are infected. We'll see how they do today."

"Great. Keep me posted?" I worried about how the steroids would affect the ones that were still possessed but the only way to deal with that was to get to them as quickly as possible and release their ghosts.

"I'm a man of faith, Anna, but I don't often recommend prayer in the treatment regimens of my patients." He paused while he considered his next words. "It's clear, though, that the patients you visited yesterday with Father Harwell have improved, even without the steroid dosage."

This was a conversation fraught with risk, and I proceeded with caution. "I'm glad to hear it. They'll still need the steroids, maybe more than you realize."

"I've already ordered the steroid regimen for them. It's quite remarkable, though, how much the ones you prayed for have improved," John insisted. "I've never seen anything like it." There was a fanatic glow to his eyes that worried me.

"Did you see the cars that arrived?" I changed the subject.

"No. Why?"

"Just something I saw on TV," I said, hoping Grayson would return soon.

"I know I shouldn't ask this, but would you be willing to visit the rest?"

"The rest?"

"The rest of the patients that are sick. I thought maybe you three could offer to pray for them? It's entirely up to the patients and their families, of course, but we've got a few that are critical."

We needed help getting access to all of the patient's rooms, and here John was, offering me his personal assistance in the matter. "Of course, thank you. We'll help any way we can."

"I've seen people using prayer as part of their treatment before," John mused, "but I've never seen consistently measurable results." He paused as if expecting a response. When I stayed silent he went on. "Why do you think that is, Anna?"

"It may be coincidence." My scientific mind intervened, saving me from the truth. "The virus may just be running its normal course."

John evaluated me as if he knew I was withholding something. When he spoke, his voice was flat. I'd irritated him by being evasive. "Based on my experience here the last two weeks, I don't believe that's the case." He took a step to move past me, to get on with his day. I sought words that I could say with sincerity. John deserved whatever honesty I could give him, even if it wasn't the whole truth.

"I told you yesterday that my faith isn't as strong as it could be." He paused, his back still turned to me, but his head cocked at an angle to listen. "But if there's anything we've learned, it's that science doesn't have all the answers. It's a piece of the puzzle, not the whole part of it." He turned back towards me, giving me hope. "Who am I to explain what may help?"

"Father Harwell is a very devout man," Jed intervened. "If the power of prayer is helping it would be him you should look to."

"He is a good man," John agreed, "but he has been praying with patients at this hospital for years and we've never seen a miracle before you two got here."

"Miracle is an awfully strong word, John," I objected.

Grayson came around the corner and I listed him as my own personal savior for rescuing me from the conversation with John. Jed wasn't done, though.

"Perhaps the miracles have been occurring, John, but you weren't willing to recognize them for what they were. Sometimes the lack of ability to see God's grace resides in the observer's lack of faith, not in a lack of miracles." He didn't wait for a reply. "There is Father Harwell now, Anna, looking for us. Good day, John." He put his arm around me and guided me around John, who looked as if he was giving Jed's words earnest thought. I was sorry that he had to deal with this strange intersection of faith and science. The spiritual world was wreaking havoc on us all.

Grayson seemed too calm. "The bishop has come," he informed us in low tones while we walked.

"The bishop?" I was confused

"Of the Diocese of Western Missouri. My colleague appears to have told the bishop of our struggles, and now he's here." Grayson shrugged with the demeanor of one who has long since learned to accept acts beyond his control. "He comes with an entourage."

"This complicates matters." Jed prickled and I wondered what he was holding back. Irritation? Anger?

"It does," Grayson admitted. "But they are stalled right now with the hospital administration. We could continue our prayers for the suffering."

"We should," I agreed. I had a feeling that things were about to get a lot more difficult. I wanted to finish my work here and move on.

"Anna," Jed cautioned, "there is too much attention."

"We may not have much time, Jed. Let me banish as many as I can."

He held his reply while a frazzled nursing assistant trotted down the hallway. She locked onto us and increased her pace. Jed touched my arm in warning, but I could tell she wasn't possessed. She had the look of someone worried, and her soul's beacon wasn't polluted with another.

"Father Harwell?" She sounded out of breath.

"Yes?"

"I've got a patient in sixteen West. She's not doing well this morning and I heard that a couple patients got better yesterday after you prayed for them. The family asked if you will come?"

I was already moving, pulling Grayson and Jed with me. "We'll come," I told her.

"Oh good!" She babbled details she shouldn't share while she escorted us to the patient's door, my brain cataloging the pertinent information. The patient's sodium and magnesium were dangerously low, and up until this morning, she'd been ranting like a lunatic. Now she was unconscious.

We crowded into the room and I was surprised to see that she was younger than I expected given the nurse's description of her lab work. She was in her early twenties with long blond hair that was streaked with sweat and oil. Her skin had a yellowish tinge under the harsh fluorescent lights. Was she jaundiced? They'd used a lot of tape around her IV in order to make it difficult to pull out, and she was in four-point restraints, though they weren't needed now that she was unconscious. An older woman, her mother I assumed, stood over her. She was a solid woman, fueled with quiet rage. She thanked us for coming and told us her daughter's name was Robin.

Grayson started his prayer for the sick. "Lord, you invite all who are burdened to come to you…" Jed's hands were clasped in front of him, looking thoughtful, and I dropped one hand onto the woman's arm as I mouthed the words.

Grayson's words disappeared into the background, as did the room and the grieving mother across from me as I focused on the spirit that lurked inside Robin, curled like a confused child as if it had gotten in there and didn't know how to get out now that the body was failing.

I murmured along with the prayer that I'd heard Grayson say out loud enough times to learn by heart, and let a tiny sliver of my energy pass through to her.

The spirit fought for a moment and then weakened as my fire reached it. It dissipated inside her, into nothing. She took a deep breath as if she felt relief. There was a moment of silence and I waited for the next breath but it didn't come. Then her heart monitors roared to life as the alarms registered her faltering heartbeat. Robin's mother raised her head in panic as a code blue sounded in the hallways and I heard the sound of feet racing towards us. The mother started screaming.

This wasn't my hospital and I had no legal authority to help this woman, but that didn't stop me from checking her airway for obstruction while I yelled at Jed and Grayson to get out of the way.

The cardiac arrest response team came through the door in a rush of bodies and equipment before I had the chance to start CPR. I plastered myself back against the wall, watching in horror. I had killed her.

A blond nurse who looked like she couldn't be more than twenty-three was straddling Robin's still form, hands planted on her chest while she did compressions with clinical brutality. They were charging the paddles and Grayson was forcefully ushering the distraught mother from the room. This was a scene he had witnessed before.

"Anna." Jed extracted me from the wall and pulled me out of the way, dodging equipment and people. I collapsed in silent agony in the hallway and he scooped me into his protective arms, carrying me from the noise so I wouldn't be there to witness Robin's death.

John found us in Katheryn's room. I was in one of the plastic-coated chairs, head buried in my hands. I hadn't spoken and I didn't know how long we'd been back. The list of people who had died because of me in the last month was long and it had a new name on it.

"Are you all right, Anna?" He touched my shoulder with hesitant fingers as if he thought I might jump. When I didn't react, his hand settled there. "What's wrong with her?"

"She was quite distraught when the young woman, Robin…" Grayson's voice drifted off. He wasn't sure what to call it either.

When I murdered her. The words were stamped on the inside of my mind so that I couldn't escape them.

"I guess she doesn't experience many code blue's anymore." Maybe John was trying to explain my reaction to the room.

More than you'd think, John. The snarky voice in my head wouldn't let up.

John's hand on my shoulder tightened and he gave me a gentle shake. "She's still alive, Anna."

I opened one eye and looked at him through the grid work of my fingers. He crouched on the floor in front of me and transferred his hands to the chair arms on either side of me to balance himself.

"We resuscitated her." He spoke intently as if he knew this was his one chance to reach me before I let my grasp on humanity slide away.

"That is welcome news," Jed spoke from behind me. I could feel his presence there like a beacon of light in my darkness.

"She's conscious again, and I spoke to her," John informed me in an odd tone of voice. "She says she's better now that you all healed her." *Healed her? I killed her.* "All of the patients the three of you prayed for yesterday are still improving." His words fell like lead in the air around us. Ned's boots shuffled against the linoleum across the room.

"I'm relieved to hear that so many of your patients are finally getting better," Grayson said. I shifted my fingers so that I could see him, perched against the foot of Katheryn's bed, one hand on her lower leg.

John took to his feet again. "I'm a man of faith, Father Harwell, but I've never seen anything like this."

"Not everything can be explained." Grayson's cryptic answer wasn't the best but we didn't have anything better. The religious tenor of the conversation made me nervous even though I'd done all I could to encourage it.

"Fighting this epidemic will take both our skills as physicians, and our faith." My voice was shaky and I sounded vulnerable instead of confident.

"I've got patients who have been ill for longer than the ones you prayed for. They aren't getting any better."

"There could be a variety of factors impacting that." Out of habit, I tried to turn his attention back to the medical facts. Individual immunity and overall health played a role in how people reacted to the same diseases in ways we didn't begin to understand yet, so it was a valid argument even if it didn't apply in this situation.

There was a long pause while John considered my response, but he wasn't a stupid man. He suspected I wasn't being up front with him, and he didn't like it. He turned away from me.

"The people from your diocese are asking to speak with the three of you," he informed Grayson as he reached the door. "They're in the chapel."

We found the chapel down the hallway past the lobby. It was larger than I expected it to be, the space decorated in muted reds and golds. Situated right next to the cafeteria, it was filled with the incongruous aroma of baked chicken. Three men in black clustered next to the alter in hushed conversation as if they were planning the best way to perform a sacrifice. When the door closed behind us they turned as one and I wondered which of us was the lamb. A tall heavyset man stepped away from the other two and extended a hand to Grayson.

"Grayson." His tone was warm as if they were the best of friends but Grayson looked stiff, as though he was uncomfortable with informality from this man.

"Bishop Doyle," Grayson replied. "It wasn't necessary for you to make the long trip."

"This is a serious request you've made, Grayson." The bishop looked over the rims of his spectacles like a father lecturing an errant child. "I believe you know Father Matthew Costas from our own diocese and this is Father Roberto Lombardi from the Holy See in Rome."

Why is a guy from Rome here? I sent Jed a curious glance and he shrugged.

"You're a long way from home, Father Lombardi." Grayson shook both their hands but directed his implied question to Lombardi. He didn't get an answer to it.

"It's my pleasure to be here." Father Lombardi had a delicious Italian accent that matched his black curls and rugged features. He didn't look like any priest I'd ever seen before. He looked like dessert.

Grayson gestured to Jed and me. "These are my friends, Dr. Anna Roberts and Mr. Jedediah Peters."

The moment I shook Lombardi's hand, I felt the ghost lurking inside him and jerked my hand away in surprise, chastising myself for not checking before I touched him. The Roman priest being possessed couldn't be a coincidence. Lombardi's dark eyes met mine and his lips curved up in a slight smile, acknowledgement of my discovery. He knew who I was. My photo must be up in some ghost bathroom. *For a good time, call Anna.*

"Dr. Roberts, I am pleased to meet you." He held eye contact longer than was necessary. *Should I release him now, in front of everyone?* Lombardi's body wasn't in danger. He looked healthy, unlike the patients we'd been working with. The spirit inside him must be strong because he'd apparently been able to just take the body over, like Adonijah had Chaz. Jed had said we needed information, and this might be an opportunity to get it. I clasped my hands in front of me in order to restrain myself. The urge to free his soul was strong but I wanted to get Jed's take on it. In the meantime, I didn't want to be too close to Lombardi. I backed away, trying to figure out a way to alert Jed to the situation.

"What brings you to Unionville?" I asked Lombardi but Bishop Doyle answered.

"It's a pleasure to meet you, Dr. Roberts. We came to discuss some church matters with Father Harwell."

Father Lombardi was still staring at me, his dark eyes disconcerting in their attentiveness. The other two priests were clean but who the hell was in control of Lombardi?

"What brings you here from Rome?" I tried again.

"It was quite provident," Lombardi answered this time, "that Father Costas and I were attending a retreat at Conception Abbey when he got the call from Father Harwell. I asked if I might join him."

"How convenient." I glared at him.

"Father Grayson." The bishop called our attention back to him. "If your friends will excuse us, we need to discuss this situation with you."

"No," Lombardi intervened without taking his eyes from me. "We need all of them here. Dr. Roberts and Mr. Peters are involved, are they not?"

"They are," Grayson admitted, startled by Lombardi's perceptive judgment of the situation.

Jed's demeanor turned wary and he shifted his position so that he was in between me and the contingent of priests. He must have picked up on the ghost. I placed a hand on Jed's arm in an effort to communicate that I'd noticed it too.

"Why have you come?" Jed was bristling with awareness and the bishop took a step back as if he sensed that Jed was dangerous.

Lombardi was unfazed. "There is no cause for alarm, Mr. Peters." He enunciated each word in careful tones so I could understand him even with his thick accent. "We are on the same side, you and I."

"What side is that?" Jed challenged.

"The side fighting against evil." Lombardi's words settled around us and the bishop shifted as if surprised by the direction the conversation was going.

"I think Father Lombardi is referring to the evil of sickness," he clarified but Lombardi didn't allow his correction.

"No, Bishop Doyle. I beg your pardon, but what afflicts these people is more than an illness." He turned to Grayson as if they had known each other for years. "Is it not, my friend?

"I know it's unusual, but this…illness seems to be a sickness of the spirit as well as the body." Grayson was skirting dangerously close to the reality of the situation, but it was pretty clear that Lombardi was well aware of what was going on.

"You called for an exorcist," Father Costas spoke with curiosity and doubt. "I've been asked to perform the Rites of Exorcism many times, but I must tell you, it's rare that they are truly needed."

"I think in this case we will find that they are indeed," Lombardi informed him.

"This is Missouri, Father Lombardi." The bishop looked grave. "We do not suffer often from cases of demonic possession. Perhaps it is different in Rome."

"Evil is opportunistic," Lombardi purred, "and not always visible."

Who the hell is this guy? Jed glanced back at me as if he could hear my thoughts and answered them with a little shake of his head. He didn't know either. I wasn't going to let this spirit keep a body that wasn't his, but I hoped to find out who he was and what he was doing here first. Maybe get a clearer view of what we were up against.

"Excuse me." The voice came from behind us and I turned to see John. How long had he been listening? "I need you three for a few minutes, Anna."

"Is Katheryn all right?" I was already moving.

"I've got another patient whose condition is deteriorating. I started him on steroids this morning but it isn't helping." His voice was filled with urgency. "You've helped the others. Will you come?"

I froze. I'd nearly killed Robin, my power separating her soul from her body, along with the parasitic ghost. Only the modern miracle of medical science had brought her back and kept her alive.

"You know what happened last time," I objected.

Jed took me by both shoulders and looked down at me, his voice an urgent whisper. "This person may die if you don't try."

"Try what?" Bishop Doyle was confused.

"You are doing something," John said with a tone of determination, "and you know it will help them. I don't know what it is but I need you to do it, now."

I gazed up at Jed, the conviction in his eyes dissipating my doubt. "All right. Let's go pray."

"We'll come," Grayson assured him.

"And then you'll tell me what's going on." John sounded adamant and I nodded my agreement, though I didn't know what I would say. The list of people who knew my secret was getting too long but I couldn't avoid this conversation with John any longer. The truth, though, was liable to get me evicted from the hospital. Would he believe me? He already accepted that something outside of the scientific realm was going on, which was an important step to accepting that his patients were possessed by ghosts bent on taking over the living world.

"Good. I've got to get back there." He told Grayson where the patient's room was and hurried out.

"We'll join you," Lombardi informed us and the bishop had the perplexed look of a man who has lost control of a situation and can't figure out how it happened.

Jed turned his attention to Lombardi. "Your presence is not required. You will stay here," he ordered. Lombardi gave him a casual smile and held both hands palm side up.

"I mean her no harm, Jedediah."

Father Costas disregarded the conversation between Jed and the Roman priest. "Grayson, if this is one of your curious cases, then I'd like to join you, too."

"Of course," Grayson agreed. I gave him an exasperated look. "Anna, this is why I called Costas. We need his help."

I didn't want them to come along but I didn't have time to argue with Grayson about it. I gave Lombardi a level stare so he'd know that I wasn't afraid of him and then followed Grayson.

He led us down a long corridor, filling me in on the man's vital signs while we walked. We were a strange procession, Jedediah and me in blue jeans and four priests.

When we got to the patient's room, I followed Grayson through the doorway and stood for a moment letting my eyesight adapt. With the blinds pulled closed it was dark enough that it took a moment to adjust. The only light came from the small television mounted in a corner near the ceiling, the announcer's voice a low murmur of white noise. The room smelled of hospital disinfectant with an underlying stench of fear. Jed walked over and pulled open the blinds and I blinked at the sudden shock of daylight. A reed-like young woman with a red-tinged mass of curls shifted in the plastic chair in the corner and stared at him. She might have been nineteen. John stood next to the monitors at the head of the lone hospital bed and I joined him.

"Armella, these are the people I told you about, who are going to pray for your brother," John told her. She laughed a shrill sound that echoed against the hospital walls.

"He's not much of one for prayin'," she informed us.

"He doesn't have to be," Grayson assured her. "He is still one of God's children."

"Our own parents don't want Brendan, and I don't think God wants him either," she sounded like she'd had more hardship in her short life than most.

Brendan was in his twenties, with cropped hair as dark as Jed's and a straggled beard. Tattoos lined both arms in full sleeves and swirls of ink curled up his neck from the lining of his hospital gown. Like most of the other patients we'd seen, he was tied to the bed in four-point restraints. The monitors displayed a heart rate of 112 beats per minute and his blood pressure was 190 over 120. I eyed the IV bag, analyzing the beta blocker cocktail with metoprolol, designed to bring his pressure down. It wasn't working. He was close to being in a hypertensive crisis.

"He's about to stroke." I kept my voice low enough that I wouldn't alert Armella. "When did you start him on steroids?" I asked John.

"He got his first dose this morning, but it's not helping yet."

"We should have the crash cart and a resuscitation team standing by," I whispered, and John looked surprised. "We almost lost the last one, John. I can't guarantee that that won't happen again."

John looked like he was full of questions I wasn't ready to answer but picked up the phone and called the nursing station. "The team is on the way", he assured me after he hung up.

"Thank you."

"What the hell is going on with these people and what are you doing to them?" He kept his voice low so we couldn't be overheard and I shook my head.

"We don't have time right now."

"You'll tell me, though," he insisted.

"I promised I would," I agreed.

"What's this man's illness?" The bishop asked from behind me, his voice low.

"His blood pressure is dangerously high," I explained, answering the only way I could.

I leaned over Brendan, evaluating the ghost clinging to his soul like a leech. His eyes flashed open as if I'd touched him and he started yelling and fighting the restraints with enough violence that the monitors beeped in warning.

"Fucking bitch." His voice was a hoarse scream.

I was getting quite the reputation among the living and the dead in Unionville.

His blood pressure ticked upwards while I watched the monitors, conscious of all the people watching me. I hoped I could find a way to release his ghost without it being obvious that I was affecting him.

"Whore, get away from me!" He'd be needing the crash cart without my intervention if he kept this up.

"Grayson, we need to get started." I reached for Jed's hand across the bed and he took it while the priests clustered at the foot of the bed.

"I know you," Brendan informed me, his eyes wild. "He's coming for you. He'll kill you if I can't do it first." *How very pleasant.*

"I'll sedate him." John turned for the door as the bishop started to pray. I didn't want this many witnesses, but I couldn't wait. I dropped Jed's hand and grasped Brendan's thigh.

"Eternity is mine," Brendan shouted.

Grayson and Jed started in on the Lord's Prayer while I concentrated on my power.

"Get your fucking hands off of me!" He bucked his hips with enough force to dislodge my hand and I moved to his ankle, right next to the restraint.

I had a hard time focusing on my energy with Brendan's brutal thrashing, but I found the core of it and allowed a controlled line of that burning fire to sear through my skin and into his, hoping it was enough for the ghost, but not enough to affect the soul that belonged there. His voice turned from violent curses to screams as my fire crawled through him. I knew what it felt like, that burning in the bloodstream, routing out a festering spirit.

The ghost burst out of his body as my power released it, crashing into the heart monitor with enough energy to push the equipment back into the wall. Brendan was still shrieking, his body jerking back and forth as if he was having a violent seizure.

John jogged back in with a prepped needle as Grayson's prayers rose alongside the noise Brendan was making to form a strange ritual that sounded like the joining of heaven and hell.

"Don't give it to him." I tried to stop John, but he was already depressing the plunger into the IV port. Brendan quieted as his thrashing morphed into a rocking motion. His eyes rolled up in his head and his screams turned to moaning pain. John righted the equipment which appeared to still be functional despite the beating it had taken.

"What just happened? Is he alright?" The bishop whispered from over my shoulder as Brendan quieted. His sister was still in her plastic chair but she was sitting upright and her eyes were wide with surprise.

"That was an exorcism," Father Lombardi supplied and I gave him a startled glance.

"That's preposterous." The bishop sounded confused.

"Is it?" Lombardi asked.

"Father Harwell wasn't even reading the rites."

"It wasn't Father Harwell," Costas interjected. "It was her."

"I didn't do anything," I protested automatically, keeping my eyes trained on the heart monitor. I could feel them staring at me.

Brendan's blood pressure was dropping fast but his heart rate was stable. John was dialing down the metoprolol drip. I didn't think we were going to need the crash cart but he wasn't out of the woods yet.

"He'll develop low blood pressure now," I warned John, thinking of how Chaz had reacted when I'd forced Adonijah out of his body. "And you'll need to continue the steroids." I glanced over at John to find he was staring at me.

"What did you do?" His voice was filled with suspicion.

"She got rid of the thing inside him." Brendan's sister surprised me, her eerie voice singing out from the corner chair. "I saw it."

She had everyone's attention but I was shocked. She saw the ghost. This young woman, curled up in a worn plastic covered chair in a hospital near the town I'd grown up in.

"What did you see, child?" Lombardi asked in his lilting accent. The words alone could have been condescending, but he said it with kindness.

"One of the demons in him, it left when she touched him." She gave a strange smile. "Didn't you see it?"

"Not everyone here has the gift to recognize the devil," Lombardi intoned.

"You have one, too," she told him and Lombardi smiled back at her, unfazed.

"What's going on?" John's tone was flat but demanded an answer.

"Children sometimes recognize the weakness in adults."

"I'm not a child," Armella informed the bishop with a surprising amount of strength for her waifish form.

"No, you're not." Costas intervened with the soothing words of the church. "Except in the eyes of God. We are all His children." I thought it wasn't the first time he'd had to cover for this bishop's brash words. Costas crossed the small room to her and knelt beside her. "Will you tell me what you saw?"

Jed edged me around the corner of Brendan's bed so I was on the same side as John. It was a defensive move that allowed him to see the whole room and put an additional barrier between me and the priests.

"The demon was in him. Has been for weeks," she explained, "I told the doctors, even him," an accusatory finger pointed towards John, "but they didn't believe me."

John glanced at me and I shrugged. Not many medical professionals would have done much with that accusation. The world was full of all kinds of crazy.

"You see them too, don't you?" She asked me and I hesitated, wondering how much I wanted to share.

"I do." She deserved to know she wasn't alone.

"How did you get rid of it?"

"I don't know," I told her. Which wasn't a lie. I didn't understand the power I wielded.

The machines blipped a warning and I glanced over at them. Brendan's heart rate was still tachycardic but his blood pressure had dropped below normal. His breathing was rapid, indicating that his respiratory system was under stress.

"Give him a dose of steroids now," I advised.

John stared at me for a long moment, looking confused, which was a reasonable reaction to what he'd just witnessed. He looked like he was considering objecting but decided to go along with my suggestion.

"I'll order it." He stepped through the sea of black robes and disappeared into the hallway.

"The power of prayer is immense, Armella." Father Costas was still squatting next to her so that he was on her level. "But I'm afraid there's no way of knowing how much we were able to help your brother."

"It wasn't the praying. She did it." She turned her fevered gaze back to me and I saw the nervous rustle of black as the cluster of priests in the doorway shifted.

"Why won't you tell them what you did?" she asked, her face reflecting genuine innocence.

I avoided looking at Lombardi but I was sure he was watching me.

"Armella," the form on the bed croaked as if he'd strained his vocal chords when he was screaming.

"I'm here, Brendan." She unfolded herself from the chair in a motion that showed her exhaustion and went to stand beside him.

"Why am I tied up?" He pulled on the restraints.

"You weren't being very nice." She unfastened the strap around his left wrist and he looked at the indentation of red where he'd pulled against the cuff. "You're better now, though, aren't you?"

"What was it?" He whispered sleepily and I didn't think he was aware the room was full of people.

"One of your demons," she answered. The door clicked open again and John slipped in with another syringe.

"I could feel it, inside me. It made me do things I didn't want to do." Brendan's eyes closed again. "Did I hurt you, Armella?"

"Not much." She rubbed his arm in forgiveness and I wondered what he had done to her.

Jed put his arm around me and I winced from the pain his touch caused. I'd gotten strong enough that I could still stand after releasing a couple of ghosts, now that I'd figured out how to avoid draining my reservoir of energy. I had enough left that I could take out Lombardi when the time came. I just hoped I could do it without damaging the body's native soul.

Brendan looked up at me, his eyes squinting as he tried to focus. After the dose of sedatives, I was surprised he was conscious at all.

"Thank you."

What could I say? "You're welcome." I gave his arm a reassuring pat, like his sister had.

John was evaluating Brendan, how dilated his pupils were and how rapid his pulse was while he digested the rapidly shifting numbers on the electronics that monitored Brendan's physiologic indicators.

"I've never seen anything like this," he murmured. I knew he was grasping for a scientific explanation, and I also knew that there wasn't one. Our training as physicians didn't prepare us for the metaphysical.

"The hospital is on TV again." Armella's lyrical voice cut through my reverie.

Glancing up at the screen, I saw the shot panning across the front of the hospital and read the banner out loud. "Mystery disease in Unionville kills five, dozens more infected. Health officials investigating."

"There's Anna's favorite person from the health department," John remarked as Leonard Chambers walked out of the front door of the hospital and toward the waiting reporters. An alarmed looking man in a suit hurried after him "Hospital CEO," John offered.

The priests clustered closer to the bed so they could see the television and Jed edged me backward. "Stay over there," he reminded Lombardi with a growl and the man shrugged.

"I have done nothing." He bowed his head in a manner that reminded me of Jed. "I came here only to help."

That earned him a sharp look from Costas. "What's going on?"

"A private conversation," Lombardi assured him.

"He's got a demon," Armella informed Costas. "I told you already, just like Brendan."

The bishop gave her a concerned smile. "We all have our demons to fight. Even priests."

"You don't have one," she protested. "At least not one like his." She cocked her head towards Lombardi. Lombardi eyed Armella like she was a painting that he wanted to buy and I hoped he wasn't thinking about trading the Italian priest's body for hers.

The reporter, an attractive middle-aged man, was introducing Chambers and the CEO but I couldn't hear. "Can you turn up the volume, John?" He was closest to Brendan's bedside controls and had the volume raised before I could finish the sentence. I'd have done it myself but Jed wasn't about to let me any closer to Lombardi. I was fine with that. I needed to know more about him before I freed his soul. I *would* release him after I talked to him, though. Whoever was trapped in there deserved their life back.

"A mysterious epidemic has struck the small town of Unionville," the reporter intoned, "where dozens are sick with an illness that appears to cause insanity. At least five people have lost their lives." Chambers was purple faced and mouthing his objections as he tried to interrupt him, but the volume on his microphone wasn't turned on. All we could see was him looking apoplectic while he spoke.

"Mr. Chambers, how concerned are you by this outbreak?" the reporter asked and his mic went live.

"…not an epidemic," Chambers gurgled mid-sentence as if his words had bottled up in his throat. "There is no evidence to suggest that these illnesses are connected, nor is there any known disease that this is associated with."

The reporter was undeterred. "Mr. Chambers, how contagious would you say this illness is?"

"There's no evidence that there is a contagious disease at all," Chambers insisted at a decibel range that suggested he hoped he could convince everyone simply by drowning the reporter out.

"How do you explain the number of cases in this area?" He pegged Chambers' weak spot with the ferociousness of a shark sensing blood in the water.

"There are a number of factors that could explain this coincidence without using inflammatory language like 'epidemic,'" he insisted.

"Do you think it's environmental, then? Something in the water supply?"

I groaned and Chambers turned a deeper shade of purple. After recent city water contamination issues in not one but two major metropolitan areas, I didn't appreciate the reporter needlessly frightening the residents of Unionville in order to gain ratings. The banner running at the bottom of the screen scrolled: *water contamination may be to blame in Unionville epidemic.*

"I can't believe he said that." John was shaking his head, looking as angry as I felt.

The hospital CEO stepped in with a confident and forceful tone. "We definitely do not believe that the water supply in Unionville is compromised in any way. I drink the tap water here every day and I'm not sick." He paused to make sure that everyone listening absorbed that. "What we do know is that this appears to be a virus that we are unfamiliar with. Standard antiviral treatments have been unsuccessful but we are identifying a new steroid treatment regimen that is showing early signs of success."

"And what about the power of prayer?" he asked him and my blood froze.

"Excuse me?" The CEO looked perplexed and the reporter pounced.

"We're getting recent reports of a prayer group in the hospital healing these patients, making their insanity go away. What do you think about these miracles?"

Chambers had gone from looking furious to baffled and the CEO was trying to deflect the conversation. I stopped listening. The banner changed to scroll the pronouncement: *Miracle at Unionville Regional.*

Costas let out a hiss while Grayson's face was unreadable. The bishop looked strained but counseled reason. "Easy gentlemen. Those who do not understand sometimes use the word 'miracle' lightly."

I wanted no part of a conversation involving miracles, but the power of prayer was my cover. I didn't know what to say.

"The fact remains, we have witnessed a few extraordinary recoveries here after we prayed for the patients," Grayson remarked, his tone neutral.

"Grayson," Bishop Doyle advised, "It's easy to mistake the everyday progress of mankind as a miracle of God."

"What I have seen occur in the last two days defies scientific explanation, and that which cannot be explained by the scientific world belongs to the realm of God."

"Or the devil," Costas remarked, eyeing me. He looked like he was thinking about trying me for witchcraft. If this was the 1700s, I'd already be on my way to the bottom of a lake, pockets filled with rocks.

"I was there," Grayson reminded him. "There was no evil in our prayers."

"This prayer group that the reporter referred to," the bishop clarified, "who has participated in it?"

"The three of us." Grayson indicated Jed and me with a quick hand gesture. "Bishop Doyle, the Church will have to have a response to this reporter's question. They will find out that I was there, and they will ask." The bishop nodded, and I hoped they had a good public relations team to help deflect any scrutiny.

"Why did you call for an exorcist, Father Harwell?" Lombardi asked, his tone innocent as if he didn't know full well what was going on.

Grayson didn't skip a beat, confidence ringing through his words. "Because I believe these people aren't sick, but possessed."

Bishop Doyle took a moment to gather his thoughts before speaking. "You would have us believe that there is a mass possession event occurring?" I couldn't blame him. It was easier to dismiss the things that were difficult to accept.

"I know there is," Grayson answered, and John shot me a look of disbelief. If he was expecting to share an incredulous moment with a colleague, my pragmatic stare may have confused him.

"There's no evidence of that," Bishop Doyle argued.

Grayson responded with calm conviction. "You watched her free this man from the spirit that possessed him."

"I saw nothing of the sort."

"I felt something," Costas inserted, shooting me another strange look. "I can't explain it, other than to say it was similar to the feeling I get when I'm doing an exorcism." That was very interesting. I hoped I could get Costas to talk to me later, maybe tell me more about what he experienced during exorcisms.

"The bigger question, Father Lombardi,"—I leaned around Jed so I could better see him—"is why you insisted on coming here."

"I came for you, Anna."

"Why do you seek her?" Jed kept his large frame poised to protect me from any threat Lombardi might pose.

"That is a conversation for later." Lombardi glanced at Costas and the bishop. Whatever he planned to tell us, he didn't want them to hear.

"You brought them in on this," I pointed out, "when you came with them."

"Perhaps you all should retire to the family waiting room," John suggested. He was right. The things that were happening didn't need to take place over Brendan's sick bed while his curious gifted sister absorbed every word.

"It's down the hall to the left," I supplied helpfully for the priest clan. "Grayson, can you show them?"

He might have been outranked but I didn't think that Grayson was ever outclassed. He escorted the fussing bishop out along with Costas and Lombardi. The latter shot a look our way on his way out.

"You are coming?" Lombardi asked.

"We will be there," I assured him. I wanted to talk to Armella first. She was the first living person I knew that could see spirits. I had a hundred questions for her. From the casual way she lingered at her brother's bedside, I didn't think she was as shocked as I was.

"I want to speak to the priest," Jed informed me.

I wasn't surprised. "Let me know what you find out."

"Stay here until I return," Jed instructed before following the priests. I shrugged my agreement. He wasn't going to let me go anywhere until he knew the hallway was secure. With Lombardi running around, I didn't feel inclined to argue about it.

John let out a breath as the room cleared. "What the hell is going on?"

No time like the present to be blunt. "Ghosts," I told him, "taking over the bodies of living people. Possessing them."

He looked as skeptical as I expected him to, and Brendan's head swiveled back and forth against his pillow as he looked up at us, trying to figure out what was going on.

"Is that what you think they are?" Armella leaned into the conversation.

"It is what they are." I looked over her wispy form, dressed in a gauzy blouse and blue jeans that had seen better days. *How do you fit into this, or is this a coincidence?* "Have you always seen them?"

"Yes." She spoke as if she were in a dream.

"Can you get rid of them too?"

"What are you talking about? You aren't making any sense." Disbelief ruled John's voice but I understood his objection to anything that didn't fit into his rational world.

"I might be crazy," Armella informed us without a hint of shame, which made me admire her more than a bit given the stigma associated with mental illness. "But I can see them. I thought they were demons." The sincerity of her words sounded strange spoken in the high pitch of her voice. "I can't make them go away like you did," she advised me. "At least I don't think I can."

"I think you'd know by now if you could." Or would she? Maybe Jed would know how to tell if she could and didn't know it. I trembled at the thought that this woman might be able to banish ghosts. Such a fearsome power, but to have someone to share the burden with would be a relief.

"How do you know they're ghosts and not demons?"

"I've seen them since I was young. A lot of the ghosts I've seen don't mean anyone harm, and I think if they were demons they would always be evil. I'm a doctor, too. I've seen a spirit rise from a dying body."

"Oh." She accepted this news with a smile and a nod, as if I'd taken a weight off her mind.

I switched my attention back to John and braced myself for rejection. "It's what causes the personality change. A ghost taking possession of the body."

"That's ridiculous." John's face was set determination.

"What else could it be, John? What viral process causes a personality change?" His jaw clenched and he didn't answer, because he didn't know of one. Neither did I.

"Maybe you were giving them some experimental drug, something fresh from a random study." He was grasping.

"You were willing to accept the miracle of prayer; are ghosts that much harder to believe in?" He turned away from me so he was staring out the window.

"Do you know how this sounds to me, Anna?"

"I do." I gave him a sympathetic smile.

"What's your explanation for the physical symptoms?"

"I think the extra spirit has some sort of electrical charge that messes up the body's adrenergic responses. When it leaves, it causes the tachycardia, low blood pressure, the electrolyte imbalance."

"And the steroids?" he prompted.

"Help stabilize the receptors while we get the body's sodium and magnesium back in line."

"That's an unusual treatment regimen." His tone had gotten colder, his expression blank.

"Think lightning strike victim therapy," I suggested.

He pondered my words before replying and when he spoke his tone was detached. "I don't know that I believe you, but I can't disprove your theory. I do believe you are somehow helping them. Katheryn and the other patients you visited yesterday are showing clear signs of improvement, the first improvement I've seen in any of these cases since the first one showed up."

"They all had ghosts and I released the spirit that was inside them. That's why they're getting better."

"I hear what you're saying, but I need some time." He sounded adamant. "I have patients to see. I'll talk to you later." John brushed around me on his way to the door.

"Wait!" I touched his arm, backing away when he recoiled. He thought I was a freak too. I was hurt but I didn't want to show it. "I need to see the rest of the victims. I'm afraid they'll worsen if I can't release the extra spirit that's in them."

The look he gave me could best be described as incredulous. "I'll see what I can do," was all he said.

I couldn't stop him.

CHAPTER NINE

"**Y**OU DIDN'T HAVE TO tell him," Armella observed in the awkward silence after John's departure. "Not everyone can understand the things we do."

"The existence of ghosts can be a hard thing to accept." I agreed with her as I sat on the cracked plastic chair at the window. Someone must have thought that pairing a dusky green chair with mauve curtains was a good idea, and maybe it had seemed like it was, in the seventies. I wasn't sitting because it looked like a nice spot though; the interaction with John had frustrated me and I needed to rest while the burning of my power eased through my bones.

"It wasn't hard for me to accept them," Armella spoke with a calm inner strength that I wouldn't have guessed at from her wispy voice.

I sat in the chair across from hers, aware of how tired I was. "No, not me either, although I was pretty surprised when I realized they could possess people."

"I just figured that was what demons did."

"I guess. I've never met a demon."

"Are you sure?" She asked, her blue eyes assessing the truth. I felt like she could see more than I wanted to show her, which was unsettling.

I thought about Adonijah and wondered what the difference was between a demon and a ghost with the power to start a supernatural war to take over the living world. Maybe there wasn't a difference at all. Or maybe Adonijah was a demon in his own right. "No," I admitted, "I'm not sure."

"Thank you, for helping Brendan." He was fast asleep, mouth partway open. I remembered the exhaustion I'd felt for weeks after getting rid of Adoni.

"I'm happy I could help him."

"I wish I could have done what you did."

"Perhaps you can learn how."

"Maybe." She was looking at me but I thought she was seeing something else, envisioning how to banish a ghost. "There are others here, with demons like he had," she informed me, her voice grave.

"I know," I assured her. "I'm going to try to help all of them. Will you be okay here with Brendan?"

"Oh, he's better now."

"You said he has other demons."

"The rest of his demons aren't quite like this one, but the last few months he's been trying to fight them. Until this happened."

"All right." I didn't know her at all, but I worried a little for her safety after the interactions she'd had. "Look, I have to go check on some things but I want to talk to you more. I've never met anyone else who could see ghosts." Except Jed, who was a ghost, so he didn't count.

She settled back into her chair and pulled a jacket over her lap. "We have a lot to talk about," she agreed.

"We do. There's a lot going on right now."

"I've noticed." Her tone was wry.

"I'll come back later. I think Brendan will be here for a day or two while he recovers." I backed out, closing the door gently behind me so I wouldn't disturb his rest.

"Anna." Father Lombardi was lurking in the hallway like some sort of creepy stalker and I took a reflexive step back, running into the door I'd just closed.

"Where's Jedediah?"

"It's time for us to talk."

"What about?" I glanced up the hallway, sure that Jed must be coming, but he wasn't there. He didn't like to leave me alone when there were ghosts running around and I fought a pang of fear. I could handle Lombardi myself, but for some reason, I was worried about Jed.

"The end of the world."

"I thought a plague of locusts came first." Sarcasm was a great defense mechanism but he ignored it.

"The end has begun."

"You dead guys love to be cryptic, don't you?"

"This is a plague of ghosts…do you not understand?" He sounded exasperated. "It's the dead taking their world back. Life as you know it is ending."

"Starting with you, right? I see you have your body." I inched to the left so that I was out of reach. "I expected the end of the world to be more dramatic." I could defend myself but I didn't feel comfortable with him that close.

"The dead returning to life is one sign of the world's end."

"That's comforting. Thanks for sharing." I stifled my annoyance that there didn't seem to be any normal, good ghosts involved in this possession event. Of course, all of the ghosts I'd run into were crazy, evil, or both. Except for Jed.

"Do you not believe me?"

"I don't know. For now, I guess I'll have to trust you on that one. You're the priest." I took another step back but he closed the distance between us, his expression intense.

"Lombardi is Catholic, as was I when I lived. Now I serve God in my own way."

I tapped my foot in exasperation. "Which means what?"

"For one, I will assist you with the Council." He gave me a charming smile as if his presence alone was worth my gratitude. "They grow impatient. You must join them. Too much time has passed."

I was so tired of the Council that I couldn't stop my eyes from rolling. "Who are you?"

"I am Blaise."

"Is that a first name or a last name?"

His lips twitched into a lopsided smile. "The living, so hung up on the formality of names."

"The dead, always taking over living people so they can annoy me in person."

"Anna." Jed rounded the corner and I shot him a glare. Where the hell had he been? He took his place next to me and I stepped into him, ignoring the remaining traces of my power that made my skin hurt where he touched me. He settled a proprietary hand on my upper arm. Even though I could defend myself against one ghost like Blaise, Jed made me feel safer. "Lombardi." His hand rested on his lapel, near the hilt of his sword. "Why are you here?"

"He was just telling me about the end of the world," I answered.

"I took the opportunity to properly introduce myself to Anna," Blaise explained.

"What do you want with her?" Jed demanded. "Who are you?"

"Be at peace, Jedediah. You and I, we have no quarrel."

"Prove it." Jed sounded ominous.

"I could release him," I offered with a malicious grin but Jed tightened the fingers on my bicep in a cautionary squeeze. Blaise drew himself upright in an effort to match Jed's height which he couldn't do without growing six more inches.

"Stand down, Jedediah," he commanded and I was impressed that Jed didn't laugh at him. "We serve the same masters, you and I."

"You presume much," Jed replied. An older couple shuffled past in the hallway, darting curious looks our direction. I opened my second sight and checked them for ghosts but they were clean.

"Have you given up on the Council, then?" Blaise asked.

"I have."

"That's a shame. You were one of our most dedicated soldiers."

"I no longer serve the Council."

"Stop with the games," I insisted and Blaise looked surprised as if he hadn't expected me to be so confident. "He says his name is Blaise," I informed Jed.

Jedediah straightened with respect and I thought he was surprised. "Bishop Blaise?"

Blaise seemed pleased at the reaction. "Of Sebaste, yes. You do remember me."

Lucky me, a plague of bishops.

"He's Council," Jed muttered and I wondered if he was telling me or warning me.

"He said that earlier. I'm not overly fond of the Council." I kept my tone congenial as if I wasn't twitching with the urge to release him.

"I have heard that you and Christiana did not see eye to eye." Blaise gave me a conciliatory nod. "It's unfortunate that she failed as our envoy."

My eyebrows knotted together in disbelief. "Did she misrepresent the Council?"

"If she has made you wary of us, then she did." Blaise was

being cautious as if he could sense the heated core inside me and the strength of my desire to use it again.

"Do you trust him?" I asked the mountain behind me and felt Jed's resignation in his reply.

"I hesitate to trust anyone, but I have no reason to believe that this man would work against us. His reputation is"—Jed seemed to search for the right word—"pure. He's the Saint of Sebaste, canonized by the church." Saintly and pure weren't good descriptors for a man who'd taken over another person.

"I don't care who you are. You need to free Lombardi."

Blaise smiled at me. "Do not fret for him. He is being well cared for."

I watched as a nurse pushed a patient by us in the hallway, the patient's head lolling in the wheelchair. She definitely had a ghost in her, and I wanted to follow. She didn't deserve to be held captive in her own body any more than Lombardi did.

"That's not good enough." I heard the hard edge of my tone as the panic of my memories caught at me. I fought them back.

"You and I have a war to fight, Anna." Lombardi's voice was persuasive, his demeanor priestly. "The time is upon us and I needed a body in order to help you. I did not have Jedediah's luxury of time to go looking for an empty house."

Something about him made my skin crawl. Maybe it was the fact that he was holding another human being hostage. I narrowed my eyes and crossed my arms.

"At least hear what I have to say before you send me to my final release," he requested, palms again outspread in a gesture of peace. He looked so innocent in his white collar and black shirt, dark curls framing the edges of his neck. His appearance made me doubt him all the more. Jed caressed my arm in encouragement and I backed down. If I couldn't trust Jed, then I was lost.

"Fine." My eyes narrowed into slits as I glared at him. "I'll let you be for now."

"That is kind of you." Blaise looked amused rather than relieved which annoyed me more.

"The Council gathers. It is past time that you joined us."

"Where are they?" I couldn't keep the defensive tone from my voice.

"They are close by." He said it like he thought I'd find that news reassuring. I didn't.

"Is that why so many of these people are possessed?"

"The end of the world is not the Council's work. We have tried to prevent it. Others, though, seek the last days. Adonijah is one of those. These people are his work."

Hearing Adoni's name from Blaise's lips made me shudder and I leaned closer to Jed. He'd proved that he'd do anything to protect me when he'd saved me from Adoni the first time.

"Where does the Council want to meet?" I made it sound like we'd all sit down for a cup of coffee but the thought of having a chat with a group of super ghosts gave me chills.

"We have acquired property nearby." I wondered who their real estate agent was. Did they have living staff or did they just take bodies over in order to do what they wanted?

"Is Christiana there?"

Blaise hesitated before admitting, "She is."

"Then I'm not going."

"Jedediah." Blaise turned to him with a sigh, as if he expected the big man to make me see reason.

His face was set in stone. "Christiana has not represented the Council's interests well. You should reconsider the faith you have placed in her."

"I will deal with Christiana, if that is necessary." Blaise crossed his arms, eyes narrowed. "I assure you of Anna's safety."

"I protect Anna. Your assurances are meaningless."

I looked up at both of them. "Blaise, if your ghost group wanted to help me with Christiana you would have done so a long time ago. I don't have any reason to trust you now."

If the world was really ending, though, I was going to need some help. "Is Scipio with you?"

"He is."

"I'll meet with you and Scipio alone. At a location that Jed and I choose."

"Jedediah, you must make her see reason. The Council is ready for her. There is no more time to waste," Blaise implored. Jed and I remained silent, and Blaise continued with a steely edge in his tone. "Your attendance is not optional."

"Anna," Grayson called down the hallway, his voice filled with urgency, "we need you in the chapel."

I turned to follow him and registered a distant buzzing of souls, like the beehive that moved into my uncle's truck engine when I was thirteen. Voices rose and fell as I rounded a corner to find the walkway filled with people in wheelchairs.

Is this high school? Who set off the fire alarm? Jed and I followed Grayson through the packed lobby while Blaise trailed us. Patients and their families crowded the halls, clutching at Grayson's sleeve as he neared them, asking for his blessing.

"What's going on?" I asked as Jed tried to shelter me from the crush. The patients with ghosts became more agitated when I neared them and I sensed the spirits roiling inside like caged wild birds. *How do they know who I am?* Maybe my picture was on a milk carton in hell.

"Bishop Doyle has decided to hold Mass." Grayson turned back to me when we were partway through the crowd. "He has no choice. After the news story this morning, these people are insisting upon it."

I saw Chambers, John, and the hospital CEO having an argument a little distance ahead of where we stood, but I couldn't quite make out what they were saying. Chambers stalked away, disappearing through the doorway that led to the administrative offices. The CEO followed him with a shrug.

"Insisting on what?"

"A service, Anna. They think we healed the others with prayer and they want our blessing." Grayson gave me a gentle smile as if he feared he would startle me. "They aren't entirely wrong about that."

That prayer healed them? A little bit wrong. "The bishop was never involved."

"No, but he'd like to be now. He thinks it's his responsibility, as the bishop of this diocese."

Ah. The bishop plans to take responsibility for this. Which could work in my favor. "We'll have them all together?" My mind was analyzing the physics of it, the number of patients left and the amount of energy required to banish each ghost. Could I do it?

What would we do if another patient decompensated after having their second spirit released? *We need to have a team standing by.* At *least this time we're in a hospital.* Which was a serious improvement from the crashed helicopter.

I shook my head and took a calming breath. Even if they were at risk of dying, I couldn't hold off. The longer the leech-ghost was in them, the sicker they got. This was the rare opportunity in medicine when I was guaranteed to help someone who was sick. Success as a physician came in spurts but this was a sure thing. As long as I didn't kill anyone else.

"Can I have a snack first?" I asked with hope, and Grayson patted my arm.

"I'll find you something," he promised.

"Thank you." I breathed in relief. "I've got to catch up with John." He looked at me warily as I approached him. "I know you aren't sure about this, but I think you should have a team standing by during the service. In case."

"I'm not bringing a crash cart into the chapel. There isn't room." That was true enough. The chapel was pandemonium as people crowded in.

"Agreed. You'll be here, though, in case someone gets into trouble?" He grunted and I took it as an agreement.

The chapel had space for around fifty people, but we had surpassed that number a dozen or so ago. Hospital staff brought in extra chairs and set them up in the back, taking care to leave the center aisle open. Relatives leaned against the walls while nursing staff locked the wheels on people's wheelchairs. I nibbled on the snack that Grayson had brought me, something that claimed to be a beef stick. I wasn't sure if it had any beef in it, because it tasted like a salt lick. Either way, it had calories and I was eating it.

"What the hell is going on now?" Ned appeared at my elbow, eyeing the crowd.

"A prayer service," Jed said simply.

"That's a lot of people." He was right. Was this what the beginning of the end of the world looked like? A bunch of sick people, praying for God to help them? Maybe it was.

"I'm hoping I can banish more of the ghosts during the service."

Ned quirked an eyebrow. "Sounds exciting."

"Are you going to stay for it?" I wished he would, I felt like I needed the extra support.

"I'll go tell Carrie and Katheryn what's happening. I'll be back in a bit." He gave me a sympathetic look before swiveling on the heel of his boot and walking away.

"This is your chance to save them all." Blaise nodded at the crowd.

I eyed the packed rows of chairs. "Yes, but I have to be able to touch each of them."

He gave me an odd look. "You don't have to touch a spirit to release it."

I glared at him. "I know that. When it's possessing someone, though, it's the only way I can see to banish the ghost and not the person who belongs there." My right eyebrow lifted in an effort to remind him that his time would come but he just smiled.

"Anna, there are too many for you to take care of in the span of an hour." Jed looked over the crowd with concern.

"You're always telling me that I can do more than I know," I reminded him.

"Yes, but this may be different. How many people are left?"

"There might be twenty, I'm not sure." I surveyed the room with my second sight and saw the blurring light of extra ghosts. "It depends on how many more cases have come in."

"You can relax for a while, Dr. Roberts." Bishop Doyle came up behind us with a benevolent smile, Costas on his heels like a trained dog. "It's time that we let God care for the afflicted."

"I'll let you handle the preaching. I'll take care of the healing."

"The bishop cleared his throat, and when he spoke it was with firm kindness. "If you were a member of the clergy you would be welcome to participate in a non-denominational service…but you aren't." He looked like he was trying to figure out how to turn down a date without causing offense.

He's dismissing me? My inner voice was laughing while I fought to school my expression. "I'll try to not be too much of a distraction, Bishop."

"We need her," Grayson interjected in a quiet tone.

"These people need God."

"You saw what happened with that young man. Praying together helped the other patients, and I believe it is because of Dr. Anna Roberts' presence. If you want to help them, she has to stay in here."

Bishop Doyle looked mildly frustrated. "Dr. Roberts, I didn't mean to imply you shouldn't join us. Everyone is welcome."

"The Holy Spirit inhabits us all," Costas quipped, earning a smile from me.

"As does idolatry and the devil," the bishop was quick to remind him, but Costas didn't seem intimidated.

"I trust Grayson's judgment," Costas insisted.

"As do I," the bishop agreed, thoughtfully discussing Grayson as if he weren't standing right in front of them. "I've known him for many years." He appraised the crush of humanity crowding into the chapel with concern. "We aren't equipped for a full Mass."

"It doesn't need to be a Mass." Grayson smoothed over the interaction. "We just need to pray for them."

"Many of them aren't Catholic." The bishop sounded like he'd suddenly realized that he would be dealing with the unclean ranks of Baptists and Episcopalians and he wasn't sure that he should be bothering with them.

"The Pope washed the feet of Sunni Muslims in Palestine last month," Costas noted.

"I am aware of that." The bishop sighed in a way that seemed to convey his concern with the Pope's dedication to taking care of the poor, but when he turned back to Costas it was with a different concern. "We should have reached out to the other local clergy and had a multi-denominational service."

"If we had more time, we could have."

"We can arrange for that in the future," Costas suggested.

"Which rite should we perform?" Costas bent his head towards the bishop to answer.

Blaise nodded his head towards the crowd and spoke quietly to me. "Go and do what you must while you have time." He turned towards Costas and the bishop to take part in the liturgical conversation, and I turned to survey the room.

"I know he comes across as pompous, but he's a good bishop." Grayson shrugged.

"He's not the first guy I've met that thinks highly of himself."

"He's a good man. He set up a small homeless shelter in St. Joseph, and he makes sure that the Feed the Children initiative always has enough funds."

It was a good program, one that was close to my heart as well. I gave Grayson a grudging smile.

"I'm sure he has many redeeming qualities." I noticed John standing just outside the chapel doorway with two nurses. The medical team was in place, then, which was all I'd been waiting for. I caught Jed's attention. "Will you walk with me?"

"Are you starting?" Grayson stepped around an empty wheelchair.

"This will be taxing for you," Jed noted.

Thanks, Captain Obvious. Sarcasm was the best way to keep myself from thinking about how much it would hurt to release this many spirits. This was what my life had come down to. Fighting the dead while trying to save the living by causing myself pain. There wasn't much there to look forward to.

"How can we help you?" Grayson asked and Jed answered for me.

"All we can do is stand by her."

Since I didn't have a better answer, I stepped into the last row in the chapel with Jed behind me. We had to step sideways to get between the extra chairs they'd brought in and take care not to trip over anyone's legs.

Grayson kept pace with me behind the last row. He started in on his prayer, raising his fingers in a blessing over the head of the man in front of him, pausing to touch another patient on the shoulder. The third person in was possessed. I murmured the words to Grayson's prayer out of habit and let my fingertips fall on her arm. She moaned and I gasped as power arced from my skin into hers. Her ghost fizzled and the one in the woman next to her made the wise choice to depart its host before I had the chance to annihilate it. I eyed it as it fled through the ceiling of the hospital, sending it a mental warning to not possess anyone ever again. I checked both patients' pulses and breathed a sigh of relief when I found them both stable.

Three priests made their way in a small procession to the front of the chapel. The formal service started with a blessing for the sick as I released the second ghost. The woman's body convulsed for a moment and then quieted while I tried to ignore the fire in my bones. We crossed the narrow aisle to get the back rows on the other side, continuing our prayers in whispers while I laid my hands on the possessed.

I released the third ghost without incident, but the fourth

person I reached out to tried to bite me when I got close to him. Jed planted a hand on the man's chest, holding him still while I avoided the gnashing teeth long enough to release the ghost. The fire in me burned so hot I thought I might be consumed by it like a phoenix, only I wouldn't be reborn. If my gift turned into a volcano and consumed me, these people would have to find someone else to save them. I squeezed between two chairs and reached out and banished another ghost.

Number six's wrist ID read Shonda Rheams. Shonda was polite enough to just heave a sigh of relief. The seventh person screamed, interrupting the bishop's prayer. He glared at me from the front of the room, but I ignored him. Blaise was keeping a close eye on me, I noticed. I repressed a shudder and crossed the narrow aisle again to the eighth patient, who scrambled from his wheelchair with a surprising degree of agility. He marched down the tight middle aisle in his flopping hospital gown as if he planned to outrun me. When I caught up to him and put my hand on his shoulder, his ghost incinerated and the man collapsed into Grayson's arms. He gently lowered the writhing man to the floor. Bishop Doyle paused mid-prayer as the floor show became too much to compete with.

A couple nurses helped Grayson boost the man back into a wheelchair and wheeled him out of the room. I paused to catch my breath, happy to see that even though my lungs were on fire, they weren't emitting smoke. I looked up when Jed cleared his throat and realized that everyone was staring at me. I was attracting too much attention. I nodded at the bishop, urging him to continue with his service. When he began speaking again, I moved on to a young woman. Grayson was in the aisle behind mine, and Jed was at my side.

The woman stretched thick fingers towards my face, her eyes gleaming with desperation. Her cracked lips were mouthing words and I allowed her to draw me closer so I could hear what she was saying. Her whispers were still too faint to understand and I braced my weight on the arm of her chair so I could place my ear next to her lips. Air brushed my earlobe as I tried to focus on her words.

"It's your…"

"My what?" I encouraged in a whisper, almost as soft as hers.

"It's your turn to die." She reached out her meaty fingers and wrapped them around my arm. *What the hell does she think she's going to do to me?* I let my power course into her and she shook with the effect of it before passing out as if she'd had a seizure. I knelt in front of her, supporting her lolling head while I pressed my fingers to her throat to check her heart rate. Someone shouted something from the back of the room, and then there was a scream, but my attention was fully on the woman whose heart rate was erratic and breathing shallow. I needed to get her out to John so we could start monitoring her heart rate and begin steroids and fluids.

"Anna." Jed made my name into a warning.

"Not now." I lifted my head from the woman and noticed that the room was in chaos. People were standing and pushing on each other in a panic. *Was there a fire?*

Jed's hand gripped my shoulder and he shoved me to the floor, his body kneeling over mine. Grayson went down in front of us as staccato sounds of alarm carried through the room like an ocean wave. There was a loud *bang* in the air followed by silence, as though someone had set off a large firecracker, followed by an acrid smell.

What's happening? An explosion? Is Grayson okay? Time seemed to slow, and everything felt brighter. There was no space to move in between the rows of chairs. I tried to stand, and suddenly my face was pressed against a pair of faded blue sneakers, Jed's hand gripping the back of my neck in a vise. The shoes smelled like hospital disinfectant, damp soil, the lingering odor of a stamped-out cigarette butt.

Adrenaline, the sweet drug of panic, swept my system. My mind started to process rational thought again, and the burning fire in my bones receded to the background. *Not a firecracker, gunfire.* I tried to shift underneath Jed so I could see, but his knee settled on the back of my calf. The pain from that pressure held me still. I forced my neck sideways so my nose was pressed against the tennis shoe owner's jeans. I could somewhat see past their leg, through a sea of limbs and chair legs. There were other people, like us, seeking sanctuary on the floor. A pair of black laced work boots were planted in the middle of the aisle, all the other feet in my vision backing away from the boots. I couldn't see above the top of the boots but I was certain this was the shooter. *Is there more than one?*

"I know she's here. Give her to me," a man's voice demanded. I searched my memory but I didn't think I'd ever heard it before.

My sixth sense identified two spirits, twined together in the direction of the voice and was pretty sure the gunman was possessed. The boots moved two steps towards us and fear mixed with disbelief swept through me as muffled cries sounded around us.

"I don't want to hurt anyone. Just do as I say." The voice rose above the commotion. If the words were meant to be reassuring, they weren't. There was no doubt in my mind that he was looking for me, though why I didn't know. There was a rustle of motion above me and I saw a glint off Jed's sword as it was released from his coat and tucked next to me. I tried to move away from it, panic rising in my throat at the thought of him getting close enough to the gunman to use it. He could get shot.

People were trying to flatten themselves away from the boots as they stalked down the aisle and I could hear the exodus at the back of the room as those that could escaped to safety. Jed shoved my face harder into the shoe and I felt the shoelaces imprinting themselves onto my cheek. I feared for the people in wheelchairs who weren't well enough to hide on the floor like the rest of us were trying to do.

Fear drifted among us in a palpable haze. I looked between the tennis shoe owner's legs and locked eyes with a middle-aged woman lying on the floor in the next aisle, fraught with panic. We shared the certainty of fear, of life, and of death between us. The link of humanity seemed to calm her and she nodded at me, as if in thanks.

"Give her to me," the voice insisted. I saw feet behind him, edging in on the gunman in soft steps and my breath left my body in a rush. *Oh, dear God.* Some brave soul was going to tackle him.

The boots swiveled and the gun discharged, momentarily deafening in the small expanse of the chapel. My other senses compensated for my lack of hearing. Someone kicked me in the cheek, temporarily blinding me in a flash of pain. There were a few muffled shrieks and when my vision cleared there was a body lying on the ground and the black lace up boots were facing away from me, standing over the body.

"May I tend to him?" I didn't fully register what was said until a few seconds after he stopped talking. Blaise's accented English was calm, as if he was used to seeing people shot. Then again, Blaise was already dead. What did he have to lose? I turned my head the other direction and saw black dress shoes making their way down the central aisle.

"No." The gunman's feet swiveled back towards Blaise and he stopped moving.

"He may die. Let me tend to him. Let us take him out."

"I'm a nurse. May I help him?" A woman behind me spoke into the veritable silence, and my heart quelled at her bravery.

"No!" The gunman roared and the boots loomed closer. He definitely had a ghost inside of him. Jed shifted his position so that he was clear of me, and then he crouched in front of me. I felt vulnerable without his body covering mine.

"A sword against a gun?" The voice had a nasal hint of a laugh to it. The man's face was out of my sight but the gun gleamed in a flash of gray that I glimpsed between bodies. A handgun. A Sig maybe. Ned would know but I wasn't sure.

I didn't hear any sound from the man who'd been shot. He might be dead, might be dying now as other people parlayed to save him, but I was a doctor. He'd taken a bullet because he'd been brave enough to try and stop this.

Now that Jed was off of me, I could act. My chances of disabling the shooter using my power were better than if we waited for the police to show up. I forced myself to my feet in a move slow enough that I hoped it didn't alarm him.

"Get down," Jedediah ordered, reaching back for my wrist. I twisted away from him before he could touch me.

The gunman almost looked familiar, in an everyman sort of way, with nondescript sandy hair and an average frame. I was pretty sure I'd never seen him before. He wore a brown canvas coat and had a semi-automatic rifle over his left shoulder. I swallowed as his blue eyes took me in. Now that I had an unobstructed view of him, I knew he was the one I'd sensed with the ghost.

"There you are," he confirmed with satisfaction. *Lucky me.* I looked past him to the body splayed on the floor, a stain of red on his belly. Half the crowd that had gathered for the service remained, anyone who wasn't in a wheelchair was on the floor. A couple of people were trying to crawl slowly towards the door. There were still so many people. If he switched to the semi-automatic rifle he could kill everyone in the room in moments. I felt nauseous and tried to figure out how to get him away from everyone so that I could release his ghost without hurting anyone else.

"Let them go and I'll stay," I offered. My legs didn't want to move, but I forced them to. I stepped over an empty chair and around my protector, narrowly avoiding stepping on a man's hand.

"Get back," Jed hissed as I put myself into the path of danger. I was sure that Jed would have done more if it weren't for the gun that was now sighted on me.

"No deal. I'm not giving up my hostages." He gave me a grin that didn't seem to fit his face.

"Please let them go."

"I could shoot you," he offered with a casual tilt of his head. He was in the process of committing a dozen felonies, but the threat of prison time wasn't much of a deterrent for the already dead. His host would be the one who suffered.

"You could," I agreed, glad that my voice was steady even though my body was shaking like a brittle leaf before a storm. "But whoever you work for would be pretty pissed off if you killed me." I took two more steps and I was in the aisle, clear of the mess of bodies seeking shelter on the floor as if the chapel's folding chairs offered any protection.

"Why do you think I'm working for someone?" He looked affronted.

"Because the one you work for doesn't do his own dirty work." I sounded braver than I felt. It was easy to be a big talker when you were probably going to die anyway. I didn't see many ways out of this one. I had to release the parasite without harming the host, or anyone else in this room. I had to be close enough to touch him. I wasn't confident enough in my control to blast him from a distance. He might be okay with collateral damage but I wasn't.

"Makes no difference to me if you live or die, you little bitch." He shifted the position of the gun in his hand and I tried not to flinch.

"If you shoot me, at least you'll know I can't hurt you."

"You don't look dangerous," he sneered.

"I'm not." I tried to look harmless. "But what will he do to you if you don't deliver me?" I took a step closer, my eyes flicking between the gunman and the motionless man on the floor.

I recognized the victim. He'd been in the hallway earlier and we'd smiled at each other. I couldn't see his chest moving but the shimmery light of his soul was still there. I was worried that the bullet might have nicked the abdominal aorta. If it had, it wasn't bleeding too much yet. If it ruptured, then we had a window of about thirty seconds to get him to the operating room before he bled out. There was only one way I could think of to help him.

Removing the gunman from the chapel was the fastest way to help the man on the floor, and the best way to keep him from shooting anyone else. And I might get an opportunity to lay my hand on him.

"Let's go then," I suggested, taking another step. The gunman responded by stepping back from me, keeping the distance between us around three feet.

"You first." The gun stayed trained between my breasts and I edged past him, careful to not make any sudden movements.

"Anna." Jed's voice was strained. I glanced back at him, trying for a reassuring expression.

"Don't move," the gunman commanded Jed, and I hoped against hope that he would listen.

"Don't go with him," Jed ordered and my eyes filled with tears in response. I was afraid to look at him again, afraid to say anything.

I kept my hands raised a little as if that would help keep me from getting shot and took another step forward.

"Towards the door," The gunman growled. I moved forward in a shuffling gait towards the man on the floor. We'd have to step over him to get out. I felt each blink of my eyes and registered the tiny details of air entering and leaving my lungs. Little sounds echoed like claps of thunder and the smell of fear overwhelmed me. The shooter took one step after me, but he didn't discharge his weapon again.

I reached the injured man and knelt beside him, feeling the hot warmth of his blood as it soaked into my jeans. A nurse, maybe the one who'd spoken before, watched me from a few feet away and I gave her a nod as I briefly pressed my fingers to the side of his throat. His pulse fluttered under my fingertips, thready, but still there.

"I didn't give you permission to help him." His voice was filled with the frustration that I seemed to cause everyone.

"I'm just checking his pulse." The nurse's eyes met mine and I drew fortitude from her look of determination. She was going to take care of this guy no matter what; I just needed to get the guy with the gun out of there. He was in good hands. I leaned back, wiping my bloodied hands on my jeans as I stood.

Something hard brushed the back of my head and I froze. I'd made the mistake of focusing all of my attention on my patient and lost track of the gunman. He was right behind me and I was pretty sure that the hard thing that I felt was the barrel of the gun.

"Keep your hands in front of you," he ordered and I clasped them together in front of my waist. I fixed my eyes on the reddish-brown streaks of drying blood on my hands. I could envision the barrel of the gun he held against my scalp. If he pulled the trigger, the entrance hole would be as small as the one on the man's belly, but the front half of my head would be gone in an instant. I didn't dare speak. A small part of me had whispered for the serenity of death, but it wasn't enough to overrule my body's instinct to avoid it.

"He will die anyway, you know," he informed me as if we were having a casual conversation. "But I let you help him, so you're going to help me now." Every word from his mouth was a threat.

I nodded a fraction, to let him know I was cooperating, and shivered at the feel of the metal skittering against my skull.

"We're going to walk, ever so slowly, to the door." Another push of adrenaline flooded my body, enabling me to move. As I took a step I felt the gun lose contact with me, and then regain it in a gentle bump. "Very good," he crooned, encouraging me like an errant child while I tried to figure out how to use my power against him without hurting any of the innocent bystanders around us. I could direct it through my hands, and I knew from experience it would conduct from my hands through metal, but could I direct it through that metal contact in the back of my head? I didn't know, and the circumstances weren't ideal for experiments. He might have enough time to pull the trigger as he felt my power enter him.

"Anna." Jed's voice was a harsh whisper. If he moved now I was dead, and he knew it. I hoped he stayed put. It was the only way I could protect him.

"Stay back, guardian." My escort gave the gun an emphatic knock against my head and I fell forward, more startled by the blow than harmed by it. He let me fall to the floor and laughed. "Get up. I'm not going to help you."

I grimaced and wished he was dumber. I needed skin to skin contact.

A hand appeared in front of me and I looked up into the eyes of a dark skinned, middle aged man in a wheelchair, hunkered low to offer me his hand. His brows were furrowed in anger. Helping me up was his way of rebelling against the gunman. If I didn't hurry, a mob would jump this guy, and one or more of them would get shot. They'd be able to overpower him, but not without more injuries. My chances of dealing with him without getting hurt were better.

I took his hand, the contrast of our skin less noticeable since mine were darkened by dried blood. I squeezed his fingers in reassurance, willing him to stay in his seat. The fury in his eyes gave me the strength to get up. I didn't break eye contact with him until I was standing again, with the gun pressed to my head.

"Let's go," the gunman said. I moved slowly forward, hoping that he wouldn't hit me with the gun again. The people closest to me cringed away, moving as far from the walkway as they could.

"Stop," he ordered before I reached the doorway. I looked out into the empty hallway, hoping that the police, or hospital security, were hidden just out of sight.

"Walk through, Anna, but be careful. They may be waiting for us." The fact that he knew my name made the situation feel scarier. It was validation that it was me he'd been hunting.

I held up my hand a little to warn my captor that I wasn't ready to move yet. The pressure of metal against my head eased. "Don't think about doing anything stupid," he warned me.

"I just want to make it into the hallway without dying." I was amazed that I managed coherent speech with a gun aimed at me. "We're coming out into the hallway," I announced, raising my hands. I didn't want to alarm the man with a twitchy trigger finger behind me. I swallowed against the dryness in my throat and hoped I could get a sip of water before I died.

I anticipated a SWAT team with guns trained on the door but when I stepped through it the hallway was silent, devoid of anything except a lone wheelchair, abandoned in the middle of the hall, its occupant vanished. I felt as if I'd entered the set of a movie because none of it looked real.

"Go right," he ordered with a little push against my head. I took a few steps in that direction and noticed that the fire doors to the lobby were closed. The hospital had started to lockdown in response to the active shooter incident.

He kicked the door to the chapel shut behind him. There wasn't any way for him to lock people in there, but it would be harder for someone to sneak up on him if they had to open the door. I could release him without hurting anyone else now, but if I did I'd kill the host along with the parasite.

I kept walking, wondering if the police were here yet. I didn't hear sirens, and the incident couldn't have taken much time, although it felt like an eternity to me.

We were thirty feet from the lobby when a white phone on the wall started ringing. We both froze. The gun against my head twitched away from my skin and I felt off balance as if that deadly contact was all that kept me upright.

"Answer it," he growled. I thought about arguing with him and decided it wasn't worth making him angry. I took two steps and grabbed the handset.

"Hello?"

"This is Officer Andrew Walker."

"Yes."

"I'm with the Unionville Police Department. I see you on camera."

My eyes rotated around the ceiling until I spotted the half-moon in the corner. "Right."

"Are you okay?"

Other than the fact that I'm a hostage with a gun pressed to my head? "Yes."

"What does he want?"

He hasn't said yet, but I'm very scared. "I don't know."

"Will he talk to me?"

I pulled the phone away from my head a little and held it out to the side. "It's the police. They'd prefer to speak with you," I offered.

"No. You tell them we need a car, one with a full tank, around the north side of the building." That was the same entrance that Jed and I had come in, but I wasn't going to offer him my car. I relayed his instructions into the phone and Andrew stalled.

"I'll see what I can do but I have to clear that with a few people. Are you injured?"

"No, I'm okay," I told him. "There's an injured man in the chapel, though. He needs help right away."

"Shut up," the voice behind me growled and a hand pushed me into the wall. His hand was gone again in almost the same moment, as was my opportunity to use my power against him. I rested my face against the aging wallpaper and closed my eyes while I clutched the phone to me. I'd never met him, but Andrew suddenly felt like my tenuous link to life.

"Move into the lobby. It's secure there. We'll find him a car."

"They say that if we go to the lobby and wait they'll find you a car." My words were muffled against the wall but he heard me.

"That's bullshit. I want the car now. Tell him I'll shoot you."

I was sure the policeman could hear him without me passing on every word. "He says he might shoot me, Andrew." I was just able to keep my voice from trembling.

"Let's keep that from happening, Anna. Move to the lobby or I can't do anything about the car."

"If we don't go to the lobby they won't get you a car."

He grabbed the phone from my hand and shouted into it, putting his knowledge of the English language to creative use while the gun jabbed into my head with emphatic motions. He slammed the phone down, the gun barrel dropped away and he grabbed my hair in a fist at the base of my skull, dragging me away from the wall.

I panicked with the shock of pain and helplessness as I tried to keep to my feet, controlled by the grip of his hand in my hair. My hands went to his arm to try to free myself, rage swelling in me as he yanked me along like an abused dog. My power burst out of me in a fiery torrent.

The burst of it threw me backward and flung my captor away from me. My head gave a vicious yank as my hair ripped from his hand.

I heard a gun fire as I hit the floor, and then again, and finally one last time. My eardrums vibrated with the noise. I lay still for long moments as flames seared through my veins, attempting to take inventory. I wasn't sure if I'd been shot or not, but I still had enough of a power core in me to keep me safe.

The gunman's body was sprawled on the floor next to the far wall. There was blood on his shirt. Had my power blown him open? Was that possible? Either way, I'd killed the innocent man trapped inside.

The floor vibrated beneath me and a familiar form, handgun at the ready stepped past me to the shooter, nudging him with a booted foot. Ned raised his weapon to the camera in the corner, and then laid it on the floor by the far wall and held both his hands out so that whoever who was watching could tell they were empty. He stepped away from the gun and knelt next to me.

What is Ned doing in here? I hadn't seen him in the chapel. His lips moved, but my ears were ringing too much to hear him.

"Ned?" I tried to talk but felt the word gurgle in my throat.

"Are you hit?" He was shouting but I could barely hear him.

"I don't know," I managed to articulate. I tried to focus my energy on the words, willing my ears to hear again and grateful when snippets of words filtered through to me.

"How can you not know?" He rolled me roughly to one side and then the other, hands searching my body for wounds.

"Is she injured?" I felt Jed's presence over me before Ned rolled me back so I could see him standing there, sword drawn.

"I don't think so."

Jed's look of relief spoke volumes. He gave the body a dismissive glance and slid his sword back into the sheath built into his coat.

I grabbed Ned's hand. "What are you doing here?"

"The police aren't here yet, and I thought I might be able to help. I came around the back way, past the cafeteria." He looked grim.

"I just talked to the police," I protested.

"Hospital security, maybe." Ned shrugged.

Voices yelled in the distance, urgent missives I couldn't quite make out. The floor vibrated again as feet pounded down the hallway.

"Police! Hands in the air!" an authoritative voice yelled. Ned dropped to his knees next to me, his hands outstretched.

"I'm sorry." Ned was speaking softly enough now that I had to supplement the bits I heard with lip reading. "This may be ugly. But I couldn't let him do that to you."

"Couldn't let him?" I was confused.

Jed lowered himself to his knees as well, copying Ned's stance with arms raised.

"The Colt next to the far wall is mine,"—Ned's words were clipped and concise—"which I used against Anna's attacker. My conceal and carry license is in my wallet in my back pocket."

Jed's shoulders hunched slightly. "I have a sword in my coat." *Wonder if he has a conceal and carry license for that?*

"Don't move, Jed," Ned instructed. "Let them get it."

"On the floor! Hands behind your backs."

Ned dropped to his face and assumed the safest position possible. Jed stayed on his knees.

"Jed." Ned's voice was urgent while his words were curt. "Do as they say or they will shoot you."

"Anna—" Jed started.

"Lie down," I ordered. He lowered himself onto the linoleum floor next to me and I reached for his hand as four officers rushed upon us. One of them relieved him of his sword.

"Be cautious." Jed's voice was a firm warning. "The blade is sharper than it looks." Two of the officers looked the length of metal over with care and then they removed it from reach.

"These two are my friends. They aren't involved," I tried to tell them, but my voice was as weak as my body. They hadn't had time to get their full tactical gear on, but if they'd been watching the camera, they knew the shooter was down. I didn't flinch at the sight of their guns aimed towards us. After having one pressed to the back of my head, this didn't seem as bad.

I looked again at the gunman. He was gone. There was no doubt about it, no need for me to rouse myself to CPR. His eyes were open in the shock of death and his soul had long since fled. The only question was whether I had killed him, or Ned had, but I was pretty sure it was me. He had been a human being, a living soul that wasn't ready to go to the next world but had, because he'd run into me. I wished him peace in death.

He did hold a gun to your head and threaten to shoot you. He shot that man in the chapel, probably killed him. My inner voice had a different moral compass than my conscience did, and didn't care that the soul controlling the body wasn't the only one that was gone.

An officer removed the semi-automatic weapon from his body and picked up the handgun as if they worried that he'd come back to life, while another officer secured Ned's Colt. This wasn't a horror film, but I'd seen enough of them to be happy that the weapons were well out of the corpse's reach.

A policeman was on one knee next to Ned, snapping a circle of metal around his right wrist. Another officer was standing over us.

"Ma'am, I need you to release the suspect." The words were remarkably gentle given that they were spoken by a man handling a large gun.

"He's not a suspect. He's my…boyfriend." I stumbled over the word because it wasn't the right one, but it was the simplest way I could answer.

I thought the gun wavered for a moment in sympathy but his words were firm. "Sir, I need you to put both hands behind your back right now."

Jed complied, his fingers slipping from mine. I felt the loss of our connection and kept my head turned so I could watch him. I was too weak to stand, so I lay on the floor, our eyes locked as they cuffed him.

Jed and Ned were shackled like criminals, their respective weapons bagged and labeled. The police spent some more time murmuring with each other over Jed's sword. I watched with chagrin as my car keys went into the personal property bag from Jed's front jeans pocket, along with his wallet. He stared at me while they searched him as if it were more humiliation than he could take, and I begged him with my eyes to cooperate.

We were all seated on the hallway floor, a few arm lengths from each other while the police strung yellow tape across the hall. A medical team with a stretcher entered the chapel and emerged a few minutes later at a brisk pace. I hoped they could save the man who'd been shot. Wheelchairs started emerging in a slow trickle. Jed and Ned looked uncomfortable, cross-legged and hunched forward at a slight angle to accommodate their hands cuffed behind their backs. I was helpless to do anything for them, other than telling the officer who took me aside to interview me what had happened. I left out the part where I blasted my attacker's soul into the next universe.

After what felt like an eternity, I was allowed to go to the bathroom to clean up, though an officer accompanied me. She stared through me as I scrubbed the dried blood from my hands and patted my face with damp paper towels. When she led me through the lobby I stopped to watch as Ned and Jed were settled into the back of police cruisers. My status as victim had been well documented on the hospital's security cameras, and I hadn't been carrying a weapon, so I didn't earn the proverbial ride downtown.

My escort led me to a small conference room where she pointed to a chair and left me there once I sat. I found my cell phone still in my pocket and flicked it open, surprised to see that it had yet again survived unscathed. As much as I was putting it through, I should buy one of those shock-proof phones that contractors and the police used. I didn't know if I was allowed to make a phone call, but I texted Chaz one quick line. *Jed and Ned arrested in Unionville. Both innocent. Please help ASAP.*

"Anna?" I glanced up to see John in the open doorway. His face was drawn and his eyes had dark circles underneath them. I probably looked just as bad, if not worse.

"Are you injured?" He asked in a detached clinical tone that struck a nerve.

"I don't deal with being doctored well. If you can't talk to me like you know me, then go away."

His features shifted and he forced his lips into a thin smile. "I hate guns. My best friend was killed in a gun accident when we were kids."

"I'm sorry." I allowed the genuine emotion to show on my face, so that I didn't hide behind the same professional facade he'd tried on me.

"It's okay. Just easier to distance myself. That's one of the reasons why I work out here. Less violent crime." He glanced around and laughed at the irony. "Until today, anyway."

"I understand."

"Are you okay? I assume that if you were hit I'd know by now but that was a lot of gunfire in a little hallway."

"I'm fine." The reality was that I felt like I'd run a marathon after using all my energy. I needed to eat and to sleep for about a week, but there were more pressing matters. "What happened to the man in the chapel, the one that got shot?"

"He's in surgery, but I don't know if he'll make it." John let me absorb that for a moment. "I'm sorry I couldn't check on you while you were in the hallway. I tried to but they wouldn't let me."

"It's all right." I took a deep breath and voiced the fear I could only share with another clinician. "I was afraid he was done for, that the bullet had nicked his aorta."

"He had a lot of blood loss, and we're worried about organ damage," John admitted. "I'll let you know how he does. Do you need anything right now?"

"No, I'm okay."

"Our patients, I'm treating them all with steroids. We're seeing improvement in most of them."

"Thanks, John."

He squeezed my shoulder and then left the room.

"Dr. Roberts?" A woman in crisp black pants and a pressed blue button-down shirt walked through the conference room door carrying a laptop and a big white box that smelled like sugar. She placed the items on the table and offered me her hand with a smile. "Detective Alicia Gutierrez. Formerly Miller. We were in high school together; I was a year behind you."

"Right, of course." I had a momentary flash of a scrawny girl with glasses who'd played on the basketball team, which in no way represented the solid blond woman in front of me now. "How are you doing?" The platitude seemed out of place given our surroundings, but I needed to convince myself that I was still a human being.

"I'm doing really well. Husband, three boys. Made detective a few years back."

"Congratulations." I meant it. Juggling a career and family had to be a challenge.

"Thanks." She slid a pastry box towards me. "We grabbed some stuff from the cafeteria. I thought you might be hungry."

"Oh, I am. Thank you." I opened the box, inspected the contents, and chose a blueberry muffin for starters. The back door opened and a man walked in with a tray of coffee cups. He was a little older than Alicia and me.

"This is my partner, Detective Walker."

They each had one soul shining with bright energy. I'd used my second sight so much I wasn't sure I could turn it off again. Given the events of the last few days, I wasn't sure I ever wanted to.

"Nice to meet you, Detective."

"Call me Andy, Dr. Roberts."

"It was you, on the phone with me?"

He nodded. "You know, it's a small town. I'm the negotiator, when we need one."

"I hope that's not too often."

"More than you might think."

"I'm sorry to hear that."

"It's the job. It was pure luck that I happened to be here at the hospital when the incident began."

"I guess so. I'm Anna Roberts. Thank you, for what you did today." I felt a strange kinship with the man that had been on the other end of the phone. When I reached out to shake his hand, I got a cup of coffee in return. He even pulled a bunch of sugar and creamer packets out of his pocket. I took two of each because I needed the calories. Andy apparently did too, since he pulled a sizable cinnamon roll out of the box and went to work on it.

"Are you married, Anna? Any kids?" It sounded like Alicia was making casual conversation, but she slid a recording device onto the table and turned it on. This was official.

"No, I'm not married. No kids."

Alicia nodded and then for the purpose of the recording listed off the people in the room. "We've got to ask you some questions about what happened today. We're recording our conversation so we don't have to write everything down. It helps us remember everything later. Is that okay?"

I nodded and then spoke up when she gave the recorder a glance. "Yes, that's fine."

"Anna, the alleged gunman's name was Marcus Wilson, though he went by Mark." She shuffled through a pile of papers in front of her. "He lived in Des Moines. Did you know him?"

"No, I didn't." Part of me didn't want to know his name because naming him gave him humanity. I'd killed him and I didn't want to face the reality of that. It was easier to leave him a nameless face instead of an innocent man who'd been possessed and then murdered.

"You've never met him before today?"

Being held at gunpoint didn't qualify as a formal introduction but I didn't argue the point with her. "No, I haven't."

"A lot of people in that room seem to think that he was there looking for you."

"I got that impression, too."

"How did he know who you were?"

"I don't know." It was an honest answer and she nodded.

"Why do you think he was looking for you?"

"I'm not sure." Not quite true.

"We've had some pretty strange stuff going on here lately, but it seems like you have too, Anna."

"Do you mean the virus, or is there something else that's been going on here?"

"We can get to that in a minute." Her words were a rebuke, reminding me that she was the one who got to ask the questions. "I was thinking of the helicopter that crashed in your yard. We heard about it, of course." My farm was in the Grundy County Sheriff's jurisdiction. Even though it hadn't been the responsibility of the Unionville PD, our towns were close to each other.

"That was a terrible accident." I was surprised by the sudden rush of tears and had to brush them away.

"It was," she agreed in a tone of voice that said she thought it was an odd coincidence that I'd been involved in these two violent events. "What were you doing at Unionville Regional today?"

"I was visiting a patient." Taking a sip of sweet coffee gave me time to phrase the rest of my answer. "My boyfriend,"—I had to pause and remind myself to use Jed's legal name—"Tobias Peters, and I also joined Father Harwell while he visited some patients."

"You were praying for them?" She gave me an encouraging nod.

"Yes, we were."

"Do you belong to Father Harwell's congregation?" Andy inserted into the conversation.

"I don't belong to a church," I replied. "I believe it's possible to be spiritual and still not adhere to any organized religions." That was as much of an answer as he was going to get out of me. I couldn't confess to being an atheist since I'd been running around the hospital with Grayson's prayer group. I wasn't sure I *could* even qualify as an atheist anymore; I just hadn't had a moment to sit down and figure out what I believed at this point. Jed's firm belief in the existence of God and my brief experience with death was changing me.

"Who were you here to visit?" Alicia asked.

"Ned Joules's wife has an aunt that's in here. Katheryn

McPherson." Alicia gave me a nod to confirm she knew who I was talking about. "I came over to see how she was doing."

"What can you tell us about your prayer group?"

I felt confused. "Why is that important?"

Alicia gave me a disarming shrug that said she was grasping at straws. "We're trying to figure out why Mr. Wilson came here today. Maybe he's connected to someone else here at the hospital. We're looking at every possible angle."

"I understand. I met the hospital clergyman, Father Grayson Harwell, yesterday and he invited Tobias and me to join him yesterday." That was true enough, but if they started pinning people down on the details they'd have a lot more questions.

"Anna, there are a few people here who think you are responsible for saving their lives." To her credit, she said it with a straight face.

"Me?" I tried to look surprised.

"They say that when you touched them, or their loved ones, that you healed them." Again, I was impressed she was able to say the words as if she found them believable.

"I'm a physician, not a miracle worker."

"Fair enough." She took a breath. "Why don't you tell us about the service?"

"I was in the chapel with the priests: Grayson, Bishop Doyle, Father Lombardi and Father Costas, and Jed. I'm sorry, I mean Tobias Peters."

"What's his name again?"

"That's the big guy we have in custody, the one that had the old sword," Andy reminded her and I could tell from the flash of impatience in her eyes that she knew exactly who we were talking about; she just wanted me to clarify it for the recording.

"His name is Tobias Peters, but he goes by Jedediah."

"Why?"

"I'm not sure." I doubted that was pertinent to their investigation. "Anyway, the priests were putting together a service for everyone who was sick."

"What was your involvement with that?"

"Nothing official, but Father Harwell invited me to join him."

"I don't know if this is related,"—Alicia hesitated like she didn't want to bring it up again—"but the hospital staff, patients, everyone we talked to seem to think that you're healing people. Can you tell me why they think that?"

"I'm just a doctor," I protested. "But I had this virus a few weeks ago. I know what a toll it can take. I was trying to be supportive. If that made them feel better, that makes me happy. As a physician, we can't always fix what's wrong with people. It's one of the many frustrations of being a doctor."

"Do you believe in miracles?"

I can banish ghosts and I know for a fact that the spirit of a saint is walking around the hospital in a priest's body...does that count? "I don't know."

"I've got a dead gunman in my town, and we could have been dealing with a mass shooting today." Alicia looked troubled. "From what I can tell, he came here looking for you. I'm not trying to be difficult; I just want to understand why."

"I don't know how he knew who I was, much less what he wanted with me."

She stared at me as though she was trying to read my mind. "Do you know anyone who'd be upset with you? Jilted lovers? Fights with your family?"

"No and no," I answered with a glare.

"Random attacks do happen," Alicia explained, "but it's unusual."

"I didn't ask for this." I sounded defensive, which wasn't how I wanted to come across. Defensive was too close to guilty.

"I'm not suggesting this attack was your fault." Alicia was quick to reassure me. "We just need to know why this happened. That's why I'm asking so many questions."

"I understand." She seemed sincere so I took a deep breath and told myself to stop assuming she was attacking me.

"The FBI is at his house now. They're afraid it might be booby trapped, so they're going in slow." Andy leaned back in his chair and stretched as if to show how low key he thought the interview was. "Maybe we'll have more answers after they get in there."

What would they find in Marcus Wilson's house? Ghosts? Would there be clues to Adonijah's whereabouts, or the name of the ghost he was working for? If so, would the police know how to interpret it and would they tell me? What if the ghost possessing Marcus had been working for someone other than Adonijah and his master? How many bad guys was I up against?

"Will you tell me, if you find anything?" I asked.

Andy seemed to find my question interesting and I had the feeling that I'd done something wrong. It was the same feeling I got when I passed a policeman on the highway while I was driving the speed limit.

"If we find anything pertaining to you, we will tell you about it," Andy reassured me while Alicia scrolled through something on her laptop.

"Why did you ask Marcus Wilson who he was working for?" Alicia pulled this one out like it was her trump card, a bit of knowledge she'd been holding onto so she could trap me with it if I didn't confess it first, which I hadn't.

"Did I?"

"Several witnesses say you did."

"It was a pretty scary situation. I was just trying to think of a way to get him out of there, so he didn't hurt anyone. Trying to keep his attention on me, so no one else got hurt."

"I'm sure it was scary, but these statements make it sound like you knew him, or knew why he was there."

"I'd never met him before today."

"What did he want with you?" I'd lost track of how many times I'd answered that question.

"I don't know. But I'd like to know if you guys figure it out. This is awful." I rubbed my eyes to get rid of the tears that were blurring my vision.

Andy gave me a sympathetic smile before turning his attention back to his cinnamon roll.

"I know this is hard. I'm sorry, but I need you to take a look at this, Anna." Alicia turned her laptop so I could see the screen. She clicked on a grainy video and hit play.

A woman entered an empty corridor, a man behind her, his arm outstretched to the back of her head. The pictures were distorted but it was good enough to tell that this was the video from the hallway security camera. The woman took disjointed steps as if she was a marionette controlled by a machine's jerky movements instead of the fluidity of human motion.

The man closed the door behind them, and they took a few more steps. I picked up the telephone receiver in the video and stood still for a moment.

"This is where it gets interesting," Alicia explained, clicking a button that slowed the tape down so that each second of real time lasted several seconds. I saw the gunman shove me into the wall, and then a moment later grab me by my hair. The violence of it made me feel queasy and I reached back and rubbed the sore patch on the back of my head. A figure stepped into view at the end of the hallway with his arm outstretched.

"We believe that that is Ned Joules, based on the statement he provided us," she supplied helpfully.

Marcus Wilson's body jerked backward with enough force that it lifted him off his feet while I fell back in the other direction. There was a flash from the gun in Ned's hands, then another flash, and another. The body jerked with the impact of the bullets as it hit the ground.

"We don't have the autopsy results back yet, but I'm hoping you can tell me what went on in that hallway."

"Ned shot him?" I tried not to phrase it like a question, but failed.

"We all agree that Ned Joules discharged his weapon three times, but that happened after you both fell in different directions. Did something happen there before Ned's gun fired?"

"It's curious," Andy added, backing the recording to the moment when Marcus' feet lifted off the ground and freezing it. "It's like a grenade went off under you two." Without the detonation that would have blown us to bits. I'd never been so glad that my power wasn't something most people could see. There were no visible flames arcing from my hands to him.

"Do you remember anything else?" Alicia asked.

I wasn't going to lie to the police, but this wasn't something I could tell them about. "I can't explain it. It looks like something knocked us over."

"Do you know what caused that?" His tone was patient.

"I just remember him dragging me by my hair and then the gunshots went off. And then he let go of me."

Alicia gave her head a little shake. "I was hoping you would know."

"I'm sorry."

"Maybe the video is wrong," Andy suggested. "Maybe Ned Joules squeezed off a shot we didn't see on camera."

"That's possible," Alicia admitted but her tone told us how remote a possibility it was.

"What's going to happen to Ned?" I asked.

"Wilson shot a man in front of fifty people, and looks like he was prepared to do much worse. Ned Joules deserves a gold star, as far as I'm concerned."

Ned wasn't in trouble. I exhaled with relief. "What about Tobias?"

"Did you know your boyfriend was carrying a sword?" Andy gave me a perplexed look.

"It's an antique." I hoped that made it less awful.

"It's illegal to carry a concealed blade in Missouri."

Uh-oh. "I didn't realize that."

"We understand he's foreign, but that's not an excuse."

"Of course not," I agreed, wondering what the penalty would be. How long would they keep him and would Chaz be able to help him? "Are you guys done with me?"

Alicia glanced at her watch and sighed as if she were just realizing how much of the day had passed by. "I'm sorry, but we still need to do a walk-through with you and Ned, once the team is done processing the scene."

They probably had every right to hold onto me. Not that they were giving me a choice. I peered into the now empty pastry box. "Can you guys have someone fetch me some real food? I'm really hungry."

CHAPTER TEN

"**FOR GOD'S SAKE,** Anna." Chaz waited until the door was closed to start talking, but didn't wait for me to finish my mouthful of food. "I leave you guys for a couple of hours and you get into more trouble than I could have imagined."

"It wasn't my fault," I protested.

He sank into the chair next to me ran his hand through his cropped hair. He didn't look very much like a lawyer in his stylish jeans and black zip-front sweater, but that didn't wouldn't affect his ability to help us. "What happened?"

"Where are Jed and Ned?"

"Ned will be released soon, but Jed's been charged for having the sword in his coat."

I buried my face in my hands, rubbing it vigorously. "Are they keeping him?"

"Not for too much longer, maybe another hour. I took care of the bail for him." I coughed, attempting to hide the swell of emotion I felt at having Chaz come in to take care of everything. "Thank you for coming back."

"My pleasure." His voice was filled with sarcasm, but he softened his tone. "He'll be okay. Don't worry about him right now. Tell me what happened. It's safe to talk. They aren't recording us, and I haven't been able to have a private conversation with Ned yet."

"We were having a service; I was trying to banish all the ghosts, one at a time, when this guy, Marcus Wilson, walked in and started shooting."

"That had to be scary for you."

"It was."

"Was Adoni there?"

"No, it wasn't him."

Chaz breathed a short sigh of relief. "What happened next?"

"Jed pushed me onto the floor and I hid behind him for a while but it was pretty clear that the shooter was looking for me. Wilson shot a guy who challenged him so I came out, to keep him from shooting anyone else."

"That corresponds with what Jed said."

"I didn't realize that you were testing me." I was a little hurt, but Chaz gave me a tired shrug.

"It's a habit, Anna. Please don't take offense." I cut him some slack—this had been a rough day for everyone.

"The guy led me out into the hallway. He got rough with me and I blasted him." I let that sink in. "I killed him, Chaz. It wasn't Marcus that was causing trouble. I killed the ghost possessing him, and I killed Marcus."

"You know he probably would have killed you, right?"

"I know." Even as I agreed with him I felt my eyes fill with tears again. I wasn't the kind of person who killed people.

"This is a war you are fighting." Chaz attempted to temper his anger at the situation. "There will be casualties. It's your job to make sure you aren't one of them."

"The ones I'm supposed to be killing are already dead. This guy wasn't a ghost," I emphasized.

"I get it; it sucks. This is the way it is, though. You didn't choose to hurt him. The ghosts chose him. They're the ones who killed him." He gently touched my chin, ensuring I was looking him in the eyes. "You did the right thing." He gave me a moment to let me wipe the tears off my face. "Tell me about your interview with the police."

I walked Chaz through everything I could remember, including the viewing of the tape and their questions about what happened in the hallway.

"Did you tell them what you did?"

"No. I don't know how to explain it and they wouldn't believe me anyway."

"You can't tell them," Chaz agreed.

"So, what do I do?"

"We leave it. As long as your and Ned's story is the same, there shouldn't be any major problems, other than the possible weapons charges. They saw the video; the guy had you by your hair. What can they think happened? After all, you aren't superwoman, are you?"

"I'm not. It would be useful, though."

"They'll release you as soon as all the interviews are over."

"Will they charge Ned with Wilson's death?"

"For protecting innocent people by taking down a shooter with his own legally licensed concealed weapon? I don't think so." Chaz shrugged. "The hospital has a 'no weapons' sign posted, so he may face charges for carrying it in the building, same as Jed."

"I won't let Ned take the fall for something I did."

"I wouldn't ask you to. But they aren't going to incarcerate someone for shooting a guy who was in the middle of a gun rampage."

"I was pretty surprised they arrested the guys."

"They had to, if only because of the weapons issues. They did need to make sure that you all weren't part of the crime Wilson was committing. Mass shooters sometimes work in teams." Chaz reminded me.

"Good point."

"Right. So, we'll let them do their job. Tell them as much of the truth as you can without getting a three-day psychiatric evaluation."

"Got it." I laughed. "Now that you mention it, the hallway floor was slick. We must have both slipped."

"That's a pretty lame answer, but better that than something they can't understand," Chaz murmured with sympathy. "Don't use it unless you have to."

"Do you understand?" For some reason, it was important to me that he knew the truth, that I hadn't turned my whole life into a lie.

"You know I do, chica." He gave my arm a gentle pat and walked to the door. "I'll go see what I can do to get you out of here a little faster."

"I'm ready to go now," I told him.

The door closed behind Chaz, and I turned my attention back to the Styrofoam container Alicia had brought me. The baked chicken breast reminded me of how the chapel had smelled earlier in the day, but it was all I had, and I needed food.

Around an hour later Chaz escorted me out of the conference room with one arm around me and the other holding my bag. The police let us out through a side door so we didn't walk through their crime scene, and I blinked in surprise at the waning light of day. More time had passed than I realized, sitting in that windowless room. Jed was waiting on the other side of the police line. I gripped Chaz's arm tighter to keep myself from running to him.

"What are you waiting for?" Chaz asked.

"I need to know."

"Know what?" He sounded cautious.

That was a good question. "I guess I need to know if it's love, or infatuation, or my gift."

"Anyone can see that he's crazy about you."

"I should have told him about Christiana sooner. It's because of his Council. I don't want them to play any part in why we stay together." I softened my tone and slowed my steps. If we got much closer Jed would be able to hear us.

"Don't screw things up just because you're scared." Chaz smiled while he said it, and I answered it with one of my own as if we shared a private joke. Our masquerade so that Jed didn't know we were talking about him.

"I'm not scared."

"Then don't act like it."

A few steps more, and Jed was within speaking distance.

"Anna." My smile faded at Jed's tone, and I looked up into the intensity of his eyes. He reached out and took my upper arm in a firm grasp.

"Thank you, Chaz, for obtaining our release." Jed pulled me towards him, an inexorable force that I had no more power to resist than the moon did against the earth's gravitational pull. I leaned against his chest, overwhelmed with emotion while he held me tight. "We must go," Jed whispered into my ear.

"Where are we going?" I glanced back at Chaz in confusion but the only answer he gave was to nod his agreement.

"Away from this publicity," Jed informed me. At his words, I looked up and realized that every reporter in the parking lot was heading our way, and there were quite a few of them.

"Shit," Chaz muttered and stepped up to my other side.

"She has been all over the news," Jed informed him. "They call her the Miracle Doctor."

"Do they know who she is?"

"They do," Jed confirmed.

"How'd they get her name so fast?"

Jed shrugged as if it didn't matter. "They quote anonymous sources."

"Do you have a plan to get her out of here or do I need to make one?" Chaz asked.

"Dr. Roberts!" The reporter's cries caught me and I turned towards the noise. Chaz guided me forward with a gentle hand to my back.

"Ignore them," he ordered. "We have to get you out of here."

Jed's cell phone rang and he answered, listened, and then searched the parking lot until his eyes rested on a black SUV pulling up two rows over. The lights on it flashed once and Jed headed that way. "We're coming," was all he said to whoever was on the phone. "Black SUV," he told Chaz in terse tones, guiding me along in front of him and pushing reporters out of the way.

"Whose is it?" Chaz asked even as he waved off the first microphone in his face with an efficient gesture. "No comment." I knew whose car it was. I could see the white collar on the man in the passenger seat.

"I don't want to go with him." I pushed against the mountain of flesh next to me and found myself moving forward anyway. I might as well have been pushing against a brick wall for all the good it did me.

"Get in the car," Jed ordered. "I don't like this either but I must get you away from here. This is the best method I have right now."

"No," I protested. "I'm not going with him. Get my car."

"The reporters have surrounded your vehicle and the Saint of Sebaste has promised our safety," Jed spoke into my ear so the reporters couldn't hear him. "Please trust me."

"He's right. We have to get you out of here." Chaz was quick to agree with Jed. "Those reporters are like piranhas. They'll eat you alive, and there might be more crazies where Wilson came from hunting you." Before Chaz switched to corporate law, the cases he'd worked on had gotten plenty of publicity but I hadn't ever been exposed to that. I didn't have the same fear of reporters that he did. They did have us surrounded, though, and they kept yelling my name, so everyone in the area knew where I was. But that didn't mean I wanted to go with the Council.

I didn't get the chance to protest further because the SUV door opened and Jed lifted me into the backseat and then closed the door with a decisive thump.

"Hello, Anna." Blaise smiled at me from the passenger seat, half turned towards me. The driver was in a black priest's cassock, but he was possessed by a ghost just like Blaise. He hit the door lock button and alarm blossomed over Jed's features. He tugged on the locked door he'd just closed. The SUV slid forwards and he jogged next to it, banging on the window with forceful thumps and yelling my name as the truck started to pull away.

"What about Jed?" I shouted, tugging on the door handle. The smooth metal responded to my touch but failed to activate the door mechanism.

"Jedediah is no longer necessary." Blaise's calm demeanor frightened me. This was planned.

"Let him in, or let me out!" I ordered, pulling on the handle again and again.

Blaise clicked in disapproval. "I believe they are called child-proof locks." The vehicle turned out of the parking lot and picked up speed. "I can't have you getting away from me."

"This is abduction." I glared at him, gathering my power inside me so I could release him. Blaise made another disapproving sound.

"Don't be hasty, Anna. I have a gun pointed at you and I can fire it before you can reach me with your power." He shifted a little in the seat so that the folds of his cassock uncovered it. It looked a lot like the one Wilson had used. *Does everybody have a gun today?* I sat back with a shiver. He was far enough away that he'd have time to pull the trigger before I finished releasing him. Blaise watched my reaction with satisfaction.

"We'd both die if you shot me," I pointed out.

"As we both would if you attempted to banish me. This is the truce I offer you. A chance to live, if you give me one as well."

Jed was running after the truck as if he thought he could catch a moving vehicle. Chaz was chasing him, followed by the crowd of reporters.

"What do you want with me?" The distance grew between Jed and the SUV, and I calculated my options. Jed would never give up, but he couldn't catch us.

"The Council has business with you, Anna. Business you have failed to attend to."

"The Council isn't my problem." Jed slowed in the middle of the street. He bent over his knees as if to catch his breath and then straightened. Chaz reached him and they conferred for a moment, and then Jed collapsed. Chaz caught him, half falling as he lowered him to the ground.

"Jed!" I wanted to scream, but it came out as a whisper. I was reaching over the seat back as if I could save him. Chaz was kneeling next to Jed. *What happened? Did he have a heart attack? Is he still breathing? Is he alive?* I needed to get to him, to help him. I might already be too late.

"Jedediah has outlived his purpose," Blaise informed me.

"What is that supposed to mean?" I demanded, my voice verging on hysteria.

Blaise gave me a small smile. "He was meant to bring you to us. In that, he failed."

"He protects me, like your Council sent him to," I argued.

"You do well enough taking care of yourself, as you proved a little while ago."

"Jed is mine. You can't take him from me."

"You have no idea what we are capable of, child." The priest's voice was dismissive.

"And you shouldn't forget what I'm capable of." The heat of my anger illustrated every word. "Take me back. Now."

"I have gone to great lengths to procure you today given your lack of willingness to cooperate." Blaise sounded bored. "I will not take you back until you have spoken with the rest of the Council."

The driver turned a sharp corner, tossing me onto the other half of the seat bank. Jed, Chaz, and the crowd in the street around them disappeared from view as the vehicle accelerated.

"What do you mean you went to great lengths? Did you have something to do with the man in the hospital, the one with the gun?"

"That was not my doing. You saw me try to intervene."

Blaise had been one of the brave ones that spoke to the shooter in the chapel, but that didn't mean that everything he was saying was true. I dug my fingernails into the palm of my hand and thought about trying to climb over the last seat to open the back door and jump out. Even with the locks engaged, I should be able to unlock the back hatch thanks to the new security features to keep people from locking themselves in their trunks.

We were going at least thirty miles an hour, though. How much damage would I do to my body if I jumped? If he stopped the car, I might have a chance, but with it moving I could kill myself in the process. If I released the ghosts, we'd wreck, which would kill me and Lombardi, and the driver's host. Blaise was watching me as if he could see my thought process playing out.

"You don't want to banish me, Anna." Blaise's persuasive tone wasn't convincing me.

"I'm quite sure that I do," I informed him. "You haven't earned this life." I could do condescending too, and talking distracted me from the situation I was in. *Jed. What happened to you?*

"I'm a saint," Blaise reminded me with a puzzled smile as if his canonization in the Catholic Church meant anything to me.

"Maybe you did something once to deserve that title, but what have you done to help humanity lately? I think you have to continue performing good works to qualify."

"I have spent centuries serving on the Council, and I give comfort to the citizens of Sebaste that pray to me."

His tone offended me. Even if he had done good things in wherever the hell this Sebaste was, he'd just snatched me from the safety of Jed's arms, so I wasn't impressed. I didn't even know if Sebaste was a real place at all. For all I knew, he'd made it up. *Jed knew about it. It must be real,* I reminded myself.

"Please, let me out." I appealed to the driver, but he ignored me. I was sick of dealing with the dead.

I held on as the driver took the turn onto the county highway too fast and the vehicle swerved. Suddenly it felt very important to buckle my seatbelt. I cinched it tight as he accelerated in a burst of speed. A lot of people had just witnessed my abduction, whether they realized what was happening or not. Hopefully, Chaz would call the police because I didn't have my cell phone with me. It was in my bag, and the last time I'd seen that, Chaz had been clutching it as he escorted Jed and me to the car.

"By the way," I continued my discussion with Blaise because it made me feel like I was doing something to resist, "existing doesn't mean you're doing anything to save the world, and I'm pretty sure that your God knows the difference."

"You want me to give you a miracle." He sounded bored, like it might be something he could do, if he wanted to.

The miracle I wanted had collapsed onto the street in Unionville. "I don't believe in miracles, and I haven't seen you perform any." Baiting him gave me a small sense of pleasure.

"The living." Blaise shook his head with a sigh. "Always looking for proof."

"The dead," I shot back, "always trying to take over our lives. You had your chance. This is our time."

"You have such anger. I know my method may seem extreme but you must meet with the Council. Had you been reasonable, this would have been unnecessary."

"Your method involves getting gunmen to come to the hospital to abduct me?"

"As I have told you, that was not my doing. Strange, isn't it? How many people seem to desire you harm?"

I gave him a glare and then diverted my gaze out the window. Did I believe that Marcus hadn't been sent by the Council? If it wasn't them, then it was Adonijah, but was he working with the Council?

"Why are you so hung up on me meeting the Council?"

Blaise sighed as if I were simple and he doubted I could grasp the situation. "The situation you have here, so many of the dead possessing the living, would have been avoidable if you'd been working with the Council instead of against us."

The SUV accelerated over a steep hill with a surge. The driver looked angry.

"What's your problem, asshole?" I was too angry to be polite. This guy hadn't done anything, except help kidnap me. He wasn't getting any respect from me.

The man gave his head a bitter shake and I laughed at him. He used the rear-view mirror to glare at me, the blue of his eyes filled with hate.

"His name is Scott," Blaise informed me.

"His name, or the ghost's name?" I got a shrug in return as if it was an irrelevant question.

"You say it's your time," Blaise slid back into our earlier

conversation, "but look what you are doing to your world today. Your age is destroying it. Morality is dead; you have turned away from God."

"You don't have the right to pass judgment on us." I didn't care if they did have a gun, I was mad and felt like arguing. As long as Blaise wanted something from me, I felt safe. "You think that bringing back murderers and psychopaths is going to make the world a better place? It's a good thing I got rid of Wilson's soul or you'd probably let him have another body too."

"You deserve whatever they do to you, bitch." Scott spit out over his shoulder. I wasn't sure if I was more surprised by his anger, or the fact that he'd finally spoken.

"And here I thought you'd taken a vow of silence."

"I'm not a priest," he informed me.

"Yeah, they don't usually kidnap people."

"It's a disguise." He smirked at me. "No one suspects a priest."

"You know, I don't think this conversation has anything to do with you," I noted.

"I'm in it now." The man gave me a raw grin that chilled me and the vehicle swerved over the yellow line. We were lucky that there wasn't oncoming traffic.

"Easy, my friend. You will have your reward." Blaise's voice had a relaxed cadence.

"I could kill you both," I reminded them, gripping the side handle in alarm.

"Shut up," Scott snarled, his hands tightening on the steering as though he wished it was my neck.

"Keep your dog on a leash, Blaise, or I'll take care of him for you."

"Don't allow him to antagonize you, Anna. Aside from the fact that you would die, what would happen to our poor hosts? You would kill them too?" Blaise mused, calling my bluff. If I released the driver while we were going this fast, he'd take all of us with him. I didn't care if Blaise died again, in fact, I planned to release him myself as soon as I got the opportunity, but I didn't want to hurt the rightful owner of their bodies, the ones trapped in there. Not to mention myself.

A few weeks ago I wasn't sure if I wanted to live or not, but now that I know I want to live...

"These cars have pretty good safety ratings, so Lombardi's chances are good," I threatened while I tried to figure my own odds. It was very high-speed for a crash but it was a newer vehicle. How would we fare if we struck a tree or rolled down a ditch? Between Blaise's gun and the speedometer ticking upwards of seventy miles per hour, my chances weren't looking very good. Scott didn't seem concerned with following the speed limit. I'd seen some pretty bad car crash victims that had made it to the ER before they died. I didn't want to die that way.

The desire to survive burned a hot fire inside me, reaching through to my nuclear core. Maybe it was just the adrenaline but my recently-remembered love of life surged, mingling with my feelings for Jed. Jed, who had collapsed in the street, and might now be gone.

Blaise had hurt him somehow by taking me away from him. Anger coursed through me. I should have blasted both of them in the parking lot before the car was moving fast enough to hurt me. I could have risked the gunshot wound while I was right next to the hospital. *If only I had responded earlier.* Chaz and Jed should have reacted faster too, should have listened to me. I was mad at everyone, myself included.

Ned had shot Wilson at his first opportunity. Why had Jed trusted Blaise with me? He should have known I'd be in danger. *It's not completely their fault. You took too long to think about what to do.* If I'd thought of the back hatch earlier, I could have escaped before the car was going too fast. I wasn't a warrior like Jed; I was trained to save lives, not take them.

"I don't want to fight with you, Anna." Blaise twisted around to watch me again. "I'd like to make peace with you. A truce." We must be getting close to our destination if Blaise was trying to make a deal.

"Why would I agree to that?"

"I will protect you if anything goes wrong, but the Council needs to work with you, not against you."

"I have a strict rule against believing people that abduct me, and if the Council wants to work with me, why do I need your protection?" His silence frightened me. "Why do I need protection from the Council? Is Christiana planning something?"

"I do not know," Blaise admitted.

"Why do you really want me here?"

"You are the one with the power," he reminded me.

"You want me to release the members of the Council that you don't agree with. It's a power grab."

He gave a soft laugh. "Ruling the Council is not my goal." His head lowered as though he were tired.

"It's about restoring balance then? You said when I met you that we had a war to fight. I thought you meant against the ghosts, but you were talking about the Council."

"The Council's role is to maintain the harmony between the dead and those that live. One of your roles is to monitor the Council, to ensure they do not abuse their power."

"Christiana kept me away. What about the others like me?"

Blaise shook his head. "They are lost to us."

Something made me think he was telling the truth even when I didn't want to believe him. Had Christiana driven all of us away or had she killed the rest of them? "Give me the gun. Then maybe I'll trust you."

"I don't think that's a reasonable option." He wasn't stupid.

"I won't release you if you give me your gun. You have my word."

Blaise sighed. "I would like to believe you, but I think this is how I best guarantee my safety now that I've taken you against your will."

"It's a stalemate then, either we both live, or we both die. You said you need me."

"Indeed," Blaise mused.

Scott slowed and turned down a simple gravel road. I listened for the sound of sirens but didn't hear any. I wished the cavalry was coming after me but I knew they weren't. Without my cell phone signal, there wasn't any way for them to locate me.

I sensed a hover of souls clustered over the next ridge. The Council was waiting.

As we came down the final hill I made note of the solitary dilapidated cottage, the dead-end drive, the thick trees, and pastureland. There wouldn't be anyone who could help me. *If I release them all, then I can have the car,* I mused as we pulled into the driveway, but the cluster of souls was like a school of fish swirling in the ocean. I'd imagined the Council had a dozen spirits in it, but there were many more than that here. According to Jed, they were strong ghosts, fallen angels, in fact. They might be harder to banish, put up more of a fight.

The house was a dark unkempt cottage that might have been built in the 1930's. It didn't appear to have been painted since then, and the roof had a concave shape that made me worry it was ready to collapse. A junk pile of twisted metal and trash lay in the front yard while a haphazard stack of logs adorned the flower bed next to the steps. There were no other cars in sight. Maybe Blaise was the only spirit here that had needed to steal a body.

Blaise opened my door for me and stepped back out of reach, the gun trained on me. I was angry enough to eliminate him on the spot and he knew it. He wouldn't let me get close enough to touch him, and I couldn't safely release just his spirit without touching him. If I blasted him from afar, I'd kill his host too, and I wasn't willing to kill another innocent man.

Blaise knew he had the upper hand. "Let's go inside," he suggested, gesturing the way to the stairs with the sleek metal weapon in his hand.

I eyed the roof and the cluster of souls inside the small space and decided I preferred my chances outside. "I don't think so."

"They're waiting for you." He smiled reassuringly.

"No." If I ran, what would they do? Shoot me?

"This doesn't end," Blaise spoke as though he had all the time in the world, "unless you finish it with us."

His words had the ring of truth to them. I wouldn't be free of the Council unless I worked with him.

A woman with honey-colored hair in a black dress stepped through the front door onto the decaying porch with the regality of a queen entering her ballroom.

"Christiana." I paused and decided that being nice to her wouldn't help. She'd interpret it as weakness. "I almost didn't recognize you with clothes on. You look a lot better."

Blaise choked back a snort of laughter.

She ignored me, her attention on the priest next to me. "So nice of you to grace us with your presence, Saint Blaise."

"Your beauty is never great enough for me to overlook your venomous heart. It's no wonder that God rejected you from the gates of Heaven."

"Just as He embraced you." She snorted and Blaise's eyes narrowed into angry slits. According to Jed most of them were souls that had been tossed from heaven by a God I didn't even believe in. If the story was true, then they were supposedly watching after the human race, trying to protect us in an effort to earn their way back into God's favor. I guessed some of them were tired of the effort after centuries of it. I shivered as the winter wind filtered through my sweater.

"We should go in. The outside air is too cold for these bodies," Blaise informed us.

"I'm not going in there," I protested. I was cold, not stupid.

"Shoot her," the driver prompted, and I reconsidered my policy of not hurting the hosts of the possessed. If it came down to them shooting me, would I kill again to protect myself? I would, and hoped I didn't have to.

"That wasn't polite, Scott. Anna is my guest. Please remember that." Blaise's words were nice, but he still had a gun. He turned to me and lowered his voice as if that would prevent the ghosts from hearing him. "Let's start with the porch. Christiana is not the one you need to be concerned with," he added with more volume, "and she wouldn't dare harm you when you are under my protection."

I took a few careful steps that brought me onto the porch, Blaise following me just out of arms reach. There were a lot of spirits here. Strong ones, if Jed was to be believed, and some that might be more dangerous than Christiana. I needed to be cautious.

Blaise and his driver were the only ones who had bothered hijacking a body, and Christiana had clearly materialized her own out of thin air again. At least this time she had clothing on. She looked me over.

"Now that you are here, we are ready to begin." She turned on her heel and walked into the house.

"Now we follow her." Blaise encouraged with a nod and I gave in. I wasn't any safer outside, and it would be warmer. We navigated the small hallway past the kitchen to the living room beyond it.

The inside of the house was a swirl of spirits. The blurring lights of their energy made my head ache, and it felt colder inside than it did outside. If Blaise and Christiana weren't careful, I'd freeze to death before anyone had a chance to kill me.

"Please, sit." Blaise waved towards a couch that had once been a light brown but was now riddled with stains. I eyed it with distaste and stepped to the far side so I could put my back against the wall next to it. That put me farther away from the front door, but there should be a back door. The driver took up a spot next to a fireplace blackened with years of soot. A dirty chandelier with three functioning bulbs and strung with pink plastic beads swayed overhead as the spirits raced around it. Blaise held the entryway, eyes fixed on the ghosts darting around the ceiling.

Christiana stood in the middle of the room, head cocked. If she was listening to the voices of the dead, it was a conversation that I couldn't hear.

One spirit descended from the ceiling and settled before Christiana, the brightness of its soul becoming opaquer with each passing second. This ghost's body didn't appear as solid as Christiana's was. Did that mean it was less powerful than she was? I wished Jed were here so I could ask.

This new ghost had a woman's body as well. I watched in horror as a second set of arms sprouted out of her armpits, right below the first set. Her skin tone turned midnight blue and her head formed into a sort of fierce Chinese dragon with green flowing hair. She looked like she was grinning, but that might have been due to the tusks that curved from the edges of her lips. Scales covered her face, shimmering with iridescence in the dim light. Two species merged at her neck with incongruous ease. She didn't bother with clothing but her blue skin looked so strange to me it didn't seem like she was naked.

I'd never seen a human spirit take a non-human form, but if you were a centuries old ghost I supposed you could choose whatever shape you wanted. She looked fearsome and amazing all at once. I pressed back against the wall to stay as far away from her as I could while I stared at her and tried to figure out what she was. This dragon woman had never shown up in my dreams.

Something darted around me, tugging at my hair with invisible fingers and I flinched away.

"Don't touch me," I warned it, and then reiterated my demand to the whole room. "None of you will touch me."

"You are safe here." The dragon's voice resonated with nasal overtones. The tusks in the side of her mouth must interfere with her ability to speak. That, and having the head of a dragon.

"I was abducted and I'm being held at gunpoint against my will. You'll have to forgive me for not believing you." I tried to keep an eye on the ghost that pulled my hair but it disappeared into the swarm of souls above us.

"Saint Blaise," the dragon chastised, "is this true?"

Blaise shifted but the gun didn't waver. Was he afraid of the dragon?

"Jedediah was in the way. This seemed like the most expedient manner given that she wasn't willing to come meet with us."

"Indeed. Her watcher is most dedicated." Christiana's voice dripped with sarcasm that the dragon ignored.

The dragon inclined her head to me, folding both sets of hands in front of her in a gesture of reconciliation. "My apologies for the lack of respect that my fellow Council members have shown you."

"Oh, please." Christiana rolled her eyes but the ghosts crawling along the ceiling seemed to settle with the dragon's words as if hearing her speak calmed them.

"I am Simhamukha Dakini." She waved both sets of arms in an encompassing gesture to the ceiling and I realized she looked like a statue from the Asian collection at the art museum. "We are the Council."

The ghosts buzzed like a swarm of agitated bees.

"We aren't yours, Dakini." Christiana made the name into a three-syllable reprimand, and from the churning above her, I wondered if Christiana was giving voice to their thought.

"I am the oldest," Dakini chided, "the wisest. The only one of us that is a deity. Therefore, I lead." I got the impression that it was a conversation they'd had before.

"If you were worthy of leading then we might follow you." The scraping of the ghosts along the ceiling intensified and a piece of dislodged plaster fell to the floor with a dusty thump. If they got any rowdier, they might tear the roof down.

"Do I need to be here for this argument?" I inserted between chattering teeth. I didn't want to freeze to death before these two figured out who got to be their spokesperson. I hoped none of the others wanted to stake a claim to leadership. They might have all of eternity, but I did not.

"Patience, child." Dakini's retort was sharp, and she turned away from me back to the blond beside her. "I am a god," she spoke as if this were a detail she was tired of reminding everyone of.

"Or a demon." Christiana snorted. "And Scipio a general, Blaise the patron saint of throats." she gave an incredulous laugh. "And me nothing but a lady and a whore."

"Precisely." Dakini the dragon woman didn't hesitate. I thought she looked smug but it was hard to tell what her expression meant since I'd never seen the face of a dragon.

"But now we are all dead," Christiana reminded her. "And who we were while living means nothing, despite your insistence on clinging to it."

"Nothing to you, perhaps, my lady," Dakini emphasized the last two words with a sneer and Christiana's skin rippled with anger while a new blast of cold filled the room.

I stuffed my hands into my pockets to warm my fingers and noted that Scott's lips were turning a bluish hue.

"Is this going to take long?" I enquired as politely as I could muster.

They swiveled towards me like great cats remembering their prey. "Do we bore you?" Christiana managed to sound both condescending and menacing.

"A bit." I wasn't going to give her the benefit of the upper hand if I could help it. "Do you think you could move it along? At this rate, I could die of old age before you two finish."

"Oh, darling," Christiana drawled through the syllables as if they tasted like fine wine, "that would be just fine."

"Don't you need me alive?" I managed to counter.

Dakini looked as apologetic as a dragon could. "Anna, you have spirit. There is much you could do to help us." She shook her great head and her green hair swirled back and forth around her like a living tail. "Your power while alive, though, does cause us some concern as we don't know where your loyalty lies." She cleared her throat, a sound that was part human, part growl, and managed to make it a regretful noise. "Some on the Council would prefer to eliminate you."

"Not all of us," Blaise assured me.

"I see," I replied, though I didn't.

A ghost detached itself from the ceiling like a bat and swept down, zigzagging a menacing path between Christiana and Dakini.

It failed to adopt a full body, the top half materializing in black and white as if color were more effort than it could bother with. Still, I recognized him from his curly black ponytail and flat nose.

"Scipio." Dakini did not sound pleased. "We agreed you would wait."

"You embarrass yourself, Dakini, trading insults with this," he paused, "member of the Council. It's unbecoming of a goddess."

"Western manners were not the greatest invention of your era," Dakini informed him and Scipio looked confused.

"In this, we agree, Dakini." Christiana's laugh made the hair on my neck stand up.

Scipio rallied. "I will not be sidelined while you derail the Council's first attempt at a relationship with our magos."

"What did you call me?" *Did he say maggot?*

"You are a magos," he informed me and I gave him a blank stare.

"A sort of witch," Christiana supplied with a helpful smirk. "Like we used to hang back when I was alive."

"I'm not a witch," I informed them.

"You have a power that no one else has, Anna," Scipio said kindly. "Whatever you choose to call yourself, you are indeed one of the magoi."

That was hard to argue with. I absorbed the word, trying to decide if it changed what I knew about myself, and decided it didn't.

"The witch doesn't want to work with us, she has made that clear," Christiana drawled.

"Whose fault is that, Christiana?" I asked but they ignored me.

"She has not been given a fair chance," Scipio protested.

"We have tried to contact her for decades now, Scipio." The dragon lisped around her tusks. "Have you forgotten how she rebuffed us?" Both sets of hands gesticulated like a cartoon character and I found it difficult to suppress a nervous laugh.

"Your messenger did little to secure her trust," Scipio informed them.

"How so?" Dakini demanded, her head swiveling to Christiana. "We sent one of our strongest members to meet with her and Christiana was threatened, her pet Silas banished. Have you forgotten Christiana's report to us?"

"I too met with our magos. She told me a different tale. One where Christiana threatened her. Where Christiana spoke of an alliance with a spirit we have vowed to destroy."

"The witch lies," Christiana bellowed.

"Scipio is not the only one of us who doubts you, Christiana." Blaise's voice was calm but the dragon lifted her head in a roar that shook the house. I didn't know which part upset her but the mass of ghosts dipped and flew above us with furious energy, several of them showing their form. More plaster fell from the ceiling and the lights flickered in sequence with the buzzing.

An upset spirit threw a book and it hit Blaise in the arm. His gun fired twice and I dropped to the floor and hunkered next to the couch hoping none of the bullets would hit me. I didn't know if he meant to shoot, or if it was an accident.

The noise died as quickly as it started. I opened one eye and saw the black shoes and pants that the priests wore planted a few feet in front of me. I looked up to see Blaise, gun in hand as he surveyed the room. The spirits swirled around, resembling the aftermath of a disturbed nest of hornets. My ears felt hollow. If I was going to continue being around gunfire in enclosed spaces, my hearing would have permanent damage.

Christiana was staring at her upper arm, where a chunk of flesh had been shot out. Blood flowed in rivulets down her arm, dripping off her fingers onto the floor. I started to get up so I could help her, an instinctual response to help anyone who is injured, but stopped myself. She was a ghost and she didn't need my help. Her eyebrows crushed together in concentration and I realized she was healing herself, stitching her flesh back together in much the same manner as she had created herself in my bedroom a few nights before.

"What happened?" I demanded, shouting to hear myself.

"Blaise shot me," Christiana exclaimed and Dakini launched into an angry tirade in a language I didn't understand but reminded me of the Bollywood films that my college roommate watched.

"I want you to kill him," Christiana responded and I wondered what Dakini had said.

"He is one of our own," Dakini reminded her in English. "To destroy him would bring war to the Council."

"Revenge is futile," Blaise pontificated.

"Revenge is all that we have left." Christiana gave him a sweet smile. The flesh of her arm was knitting itself back together, which didn't seem to bother her. Maybe her reconstruction didn't go as far as creating nerve endings.

"It's our duty to protect those that live, not avenge ourselves on them," Scipio debated. He appeared to be almost enjoying himself, and I wasn't sure if he was more interested in my well-being, or the philosophical discussion. The three of them stood in front of the dragon, who listened to their argument, though I didn't know if she was an indulgent parent, or the judge. I feared a ruling that came from someone who seemed to be more beast than human, who thought herself a deity.

Christiana wiped a hand across her upper arm, now whole again. "The living destroy each other. They cannot be saved."

"Have you abandoned our purpose, Christiana? Fallen from the path of the righteous?"

"Your preaching bores me, Blaise."

"We all swore the oath." Scipio came to Blaise's defense.

"God rejected each of us. Cast us from heaven. Or have you forgotten that?"

"He will forgive us. He will take us back if we show we are worthy." Scipio's blind faith was admirable, if stupid.

"Do you still believe that?" She seemed to radiate light when she was angry, or else her soul was so dark she was reflecting the feeble light in the room.

"You must have faith," Blaise insisted.

"Centuries have passed since you were cast out of heaven. You have waited patiently for God to forgive your sins and take you back into His grace, and yet here we stand. I am done waiting," she announced, and the rafters buzzed with her words.

"That was a pretty good stump speech," I commented.

"What?" Her icy glare turned on me and I ignored my fear hoping she wouldn't sense the weakness in me.

"Have you been practicing for a while?" I kept my tone light.

"What is it talking about?" She asked Dakini, but I didn't give the dragon a chance to respond.

"It's pretty clear that you think you should be in charge of your little Council. What better way to get support than convince your fellow ghosts that God has forgotten them, that you're the only one with their best interests at heart. It's a ploy used by politicians everywhere."

"Shut up, you nosy bitch. We don't need you."

"Tell them the truth about who you really work for. Tell them about your alliance with Adonijah," I insisted.

"These accusations are ridiculous." Christiana laughed. "You know nothing, human."

"She and I argued one night," I shouted up to the swirling bright mass of souls overhead, gambling that not all of them were on her side. "She told me about Adonijah, and about her allegiance to the Master." *Were they one and the same?* "That's who she's working for."

The buzzing in the rafters turned to a roar and the floor boards rumbled. A tarnished brass lamp fell off the table beside the sofa and onto the floor. The lightbulb shattered, scattering a thousand shards of glass across the floor, and I trembled with fear.

"Shit," I muttered. This wasn't a conversation with the Council; I'd stepped into the beginning of a civil war.

"Join me," Christiana raised her voice over mine, "and we will live again. God has forsaken us but we can make our own heaven here."

Dakini roared, levitating off the ground for a moment and the lights flickered in response to her anger.

Blaise screamed over the furor. "We swore an oath together to do good on this earth so that we could all return to what lies beyond." He'd abducted me, but he seemed like my best hope for survival.

"I tire of being reminded of your saintly works, Blaise. You are no better than the rest of us." Christiana sneered.

"You belittle me, but I protected a city for centuries, kept war from its gates."

"Do you like it when they light candles and pray to you, Blaise? They almost gave you as much strength as our dragon god has."

"Christiana." Dakini's voice resonated with authority and she seemed surprised when the woman ignored her.

"You were all thrown from heaven, evicted by the one who rules there. Why do you try to go back? This is our paradise, our world to rule."

Voices rose from the cloud of ghosts above us though if they were cries of support or disagreement I couldn't tell.

"Join me," Christiana cried up to the ceiling. "Take up life again however you choose it. Be a king, have wealth, live as you will. And when that life is over, take another, and another. This is our heaven."

"No," Scipio roared. "That is not our way."

She laughed at him. "Scipio, you hypocrite. Everyone knows how many lives you have lived. Did you think we didn't notice when you were defeating Hannibal and finding glory? Your most memorable life, but you have lived many, and we turned a blind eye."

"Everything I did was in the service of this Council."

"Yes, the Council," she murmured and the room quieted to listen to her. "I too serve this group. I have for centuries and I will continue to do so, in my own way."

Blaise stepped forward. "In the name of God, I banish you, Christiana, from this Council." His words stirred the ghosts back to action. They looked like a colony of bats, hanging from the plaster and dipping down to whip past us.

"You don't have the power, Saint Blaise. The Council is already mine."

"It will never be yours!" Scipio leaped at her, but instead of tackling her body and them both falling to the ground, his light simply sank into her skin. The two souls merged together, burning hotter in some sort of battle inside her form. Her body collapsed, writhing on the floor as they fought each other. The light of the souls burst and her body stilled, one soul inside of it, the other gone. Ghosts shrieked and moaned. In the kitchen, I heard dishes hitting the floor and shattering as one of them gave physical action to his rage.

"What happened?" I demanded.

"Scipio fought her, and lost." Blaise took a step back.

"Ghosts can do that?"

"The strongest among us can absorb another soul," he explained. "We should go."

"Why?"

"She is stronger than I realized. She shouldn't have been able to destroy Scipio. He was one of the original fallen, and she was not. Even Dakini may not be able to hold her."

The dragon was bent over Christiana now. The blond woman appeared unconscious, and I hoped that the fight had hurt her.

"Will Dakini try?"

"I am not sure," Blaise admitted. "Who can predict the minds of gods? Though they do not care for each other, they have spent many years working together. I had thought Dakini would come down on our side but they may yet forge an alliance."

"And you? Are you strong enough?"

"Me?" Blaise gave me a regretful look. "If Scipio couldn't...I don't think so."

"I'll do it." I took one step forward and the dragon's head lifted, hooded eyes staring at me. She opened her mouth, flicking a forked tongue over her snout, and then flames licked up out of her mouth as she exhaled.

She can breathe fucking flames! I took two hasty steps back, bumping into Blaise. Even with the gun, he seemed much safer.

"Reconsider your actions, magos," Dakini advised, smoke curling from her nostrils like she'd been indulging in a cigar.

"She's working against the Council." I tried to keep my tone clinical so she wouldn't hear fear in my voice. "She doesn't respect you; she just wants to control you."

"It is not for you to decide her fate," Dakini growled. "This is a Council matter."

My legs trembled. "I could release all of you," I threatened, but I didn't present a very ominous figure, hiding next to the patron saint of sore throats. I could release the regular ghosts, but there was a blue-skinned fire breathing dragon god in the middle of the room. Would my power affect her at all? If I failed, how angry would the dragon be?

"There are some here that do great things for your world, Anna. To destroy them all would be a mistake," Blaise spoke into my ear. "I had hoped we could convince Dakini to help us, but now..." Christiana was stirring and I was willing to bet she'd be mad as hell when she woke up.

"Aren't the ones who are with Christiana doing far more harm?" If there were good members of the Council, what right did I have to release them? Was it my duty, since they were dead anyway, or would I be overstepping my moral bounds?

"Do you have the strength to slay a dragon?" Blaise peered down at me.

"I don't know," I stammered. "You have a gun; can't you shoot it?"

"That might make her angry."

Oh.

"I didn't realize things had come so far. If Dakini takes you, she will have your power and hers." He put an arm around me, and now that we were finally touching, I didn't feel the need to release him. "I shouldn't have brought you here." He guided me away from them.

"I tried to warn you about them," I reminded him as he ushered me into the hallway.

"Yes, my dear," he murmured as we passed the doorway to the kitchen. I stopped for a moment in amazement. It seemed as though every dish in the house was broken on the kitchen floor. The faucet was running into a stopped-up sink, based on the sound of the water, and the stove was at an odd angle, dislodged from the wall.

"Blaise." The dragon's voice roared behind us.

"Do you smell gas?" I asked as I caught a whiff of the toxic smell.

"I do." His voice filled with concern.

"The gas line to the stove," I said as the scent increased.

"One of our friends has disrupted it." I thought it was a fair guess given the angle of the stove, but wasn't ready to go as far as calling whichever ghost who'd done it a friend.

"Where are you taking her?" Christiana's voice was sweet sounding and made the hair on the back of my neck stand up.

"Run." Blaise turned back to Christiana and shoved me behind him towards the door.

"Take her," Christiana roared.

I didn't look back. I darted down the dark hallway and ran directly into the driver with a thump as he came back in through the front door. His arms immediately wrapped around me, and I took advantage of the skin contact to deliver a small dose of my energy, releasing the ghost. He hadn't been entirely on Blaise's side, which was apparently also now my side, so I felt no guilt in sending him on.

The man collapsed and I grabbed his arm, dragging him through the door with me, aware of how much stronger the smell of gas was. Ghosts poured out of the house, flying over me and around me, tearing at my hair and clothes as they passed me by. I released a small burst of my power to remind them to stay away from me. Two spirits caught my flame and burst on contact. I heard windows shatter in the house behind me as the ghosts who remained in the house chose other exits.

I pulled the man down the steps of the porch, ignoring the beating his body was taking as he slid onto the snow. A quick search of his pockets didn't produce the car keys. I heard heavy steps fall inside the house and I abandoned the driver to run towards the SUV. I flung the driver side door open, cursing when I didn't find the keys in the ignition, either.

Ghosts hurtled through the air high above me, stirring the wind and blotting out the dim light of the half moon. They all looked the same to me, bright spirits of the dead. I couldn't differentiate between those aligned with Christiana and any that sided with Blaise. How far could my power reach? Not as high as they swirled, almost as if they knew what my limits were.

One darted down to attack me and sizzled into a thousand sparks of light as I released it. Something metallic hit the SUV and I ducked as it bounced off the door. *Did they throw something at me?* My leg was struck from behind and I fell to my knees, landing on top of a log that hadn't been there before. The ghost who'd thrown it darted back up into the sky.

This was their tactic. Stay out of range of my power but pelt me with large objects until I was too injured to resist. From the feeble light of the open front door, I saw another chunk of wood levitating from the woodpile, and crawled into the SUV, pulling the door shut just as a second piece of wood slammed into the car where I'd knelt moments before.

Blaise and Dakini were on the front porch with Christiana. She appeared to have recovered from her battle with the general. Dakini gesticulated with all four arms and Christiana looked like she was bristling with anger. Blaise, who'd been unflappable even when facing down the gunman in the chapel, stood rigid before them.

A piece of plastic bounced off of the passenger side window and I felt around for the keys, hoping that the driver had left them here somewhere. They weren't in the seat or the cup holder. I checked the visor since in the movies that was where bad guys stored their keys, but was left empty-handed. Had the driver lost them or set them down in the house?

Hot-wiring an automobile wasn't a skill I'd learned in medical school, though in hindsight it would have been a more practical skill than the section I'd had on chiropractic manipulations. If I lived through this, I'd try to get it added to the curriculum.

A hunk of wood hit the windshield with a decisive *thunk* and I crawled into the backseat as the glass cracked into a thousand pieces. It sagged inwards but didn't outright shatter thanks to the safety glass.

Blaise was being attacked. I saw him on his knees in front of the dragon as if he was praying to her. He'd betrayed her when he decided to rescue me and there was nothing I could do to help him. I hoped he was stronger than he realized.

The vehicle swiveled in a half circle as the ghosts gave it a push and I remembered the flying tractor. I wasn't safe in the SUV, either. I needed to get them close enough to me for me to use my power against them. The vehicle lurched into motion again and I climbed over the seat rows into the cargo space and held on while it slowed. I hit the electronic button to open the back door and waited until the back end neared an old tree with twin trunks that split in a V shape just off the ground.

I leaped, rolling into a snow bank and knocking the breath from my lungs. I scrambled to my feet as the truck started towards me. When the SUV was almost on top of me, I jumped through the center of the trunks into the safe space on the other side. It smashed into the tree, its grill implanting on them. The tree shuddered, but held.

The ghosts were on me. One attacked me from above and when I blasted it, two more flew down. They chose the perfect moment to enter me, in the aftershock after my power had left my body, the energy having dissipated.

I panicked at the familiar pain, my heart declaring how afraid I was in a rapid staccato. It was like having two serpents inside me, roiling inside a space too small for them, biting at me with venomous teeth. In my rush of fear that they would be able to control me, I used a larger blast of my power to destroy them than I needed to.

Christiana's laughter was victorious. It was a good plan. Weaken me as Adonijah had, and then control me.

Take a breath. They can't take you over as long as you still have power left. Don't use it all.

The reality was, there were enough of them that it might work. If the remaining swirling ghosts were all willing to sacrifice themselves for Christiana, I would be too weak to resist.

"Whoever takes the magos controls her power. I will bow to you," she yelled across the clearing and another soul raced towards me. I released it as a chunk of debris hit the tree trunk next to me. I cursed the owner of the house for leaving so many convenient missiles laying around.

I gauged the spirits darting above me. There were twenty or so of them. Did I have enough power to release them all, one at a time? I didn't think so. And Christiana and Dakini still needed to be dealt with. I wasn't inclined towards mercy for any of them.

A new soul rushed in, darker than the night sky, attacking the melee of ghosts above me, the souls merging as they fought. Two exploded, and the darker one remained.

Something struck my head and I fell to my knees. My hand came away from my face wet and I knew I was bleeding. I didn't have time to apply pressure because another spirit took my moment of distraction to dive inside me. I tensed and let my energy pulse, dissolving it while another crawled in right afterward. They were good at judging the gap when my energy was dissipating and when I would be able to use it again. *I'm not the first one with my power they've battled. And if they fought someone like me and are still here, they killed them.*

It wasn't a pleasant thought. I breathed through the pain of the ghost inside me until I could release another thread of my energy. It died. Some of the ghosts in the sky above me were fighting each other, and I hoped they saved me the effort of destroying all of them.

There was a commotion at the front of the house as the dark soul that joined our party late attacked the dragon. Dakini, the dragon deity, writhed with the battle inside her. Blaise stood, and then his soul jumped from Lombardi's body into Dakini. Lombardi collapsed off the porch like a lifeless puppet. The dragon roared a sound that merged fury and pain as her form launched from the porch into the sky above us. The cacophony of souls quieted as they watched their dragon goddess fight for her life. Dakini's form with three souls inside it flew high until I couldn't see them at all. Even gods weren't invincible. There was an explosion, a supernova of light. Two souls came back to earth, but Dakini wasn't one of them.

Christiana jumped from the porch into the snow, shouting commands to the wind. A handful of ghosts ambushed her, having decided that they weren't on her side.

The dark soul, the one that helped beat the dragon, went after Christiana.

"Are you ready to die, Jedediah?" She screamed as he tore into her.

Jed. He'd left his body and followed us. Followed me and killed a dragon god.

I pulled myself to my feet and found a rock, launching it towards Christiana. Growing up on a farm, I'd learned to throw and I had a good arm. I hit her in the side and she shrieked with rage. I grabbed another rock and pitched that one at her head. She threw Jed from her and the other souls came to her defense in a rush and swept him up to the cloudless sky, too far for me to be able to help him.

I blasted a couple spirits who'd ventured too close and a third entered me but tore out the other side faster than I could release it. The pain was so immense that I gagged from it. My hands went to my abdomen and back, certain they had holes from the force of its exit.

It swirled back down on me so fast that my blast of energy was too late. The wasted glitter of my power bathed the tree trunk in front of me as the soul tore through me a second time. I writhed on the ground and waited for it to come back. I was ready for it this time, and when it did, and I released it in a rush. My reservoir of power wasn't endless, they were picking away at it as they were me.

"Bring her to me," Christiana commanded and a handful of souls broke away from Jed and swooped down towards me. He was still up there, I hoped he was giving them hell. I banished the first one with a thread of my ebbing power. I couldn't let it run out like I had before Adonijah possessed me.

A ghost picked me up, and I floated through the air with nothing supporting me. I didn't release it because I needed to be smart and I didn't want it to drop me. I landed in the dirt at Christiana's feet with a solid thump, dizzy and unsettled.

She grabbed me by my hair and yanked me off the ground while I grasped at nothing. "She is weak." Christiana proved it to them by dragging me into the yard. "Who will take her?" If I were her I'd be damned careful about who got ahold of a power like mine, but maybe she knew all of them were on her side. Still, absolute power tended to corrupt. Even the best ghost might be susceptible. "Who wants this power?"

"I've been saving something for you," I gasped, grabbing Christiana's ankle and releasing her with a decisive burst of power. I gave her everything I dared, enjoying my brief moment of victory. The sky filled with howls as the dead roiled above me.

A pack of ghosts descended but a rush of heat and air tossed me backward as the kitchen exploded. *The gas line.* Fire raged so close I could feel the heat of it scorching my skin. I crawled to the driver and tried to pull his body farther from danger but I was too weak to move him very far. If the gas line caused another explosion, we were too close. I tugged again, grunting as I shifted him a few more feet. Finally, we reached a safe distance. Fire consumed the old house. The last time I'd seen Lombardi, his body had fallen off the porch but I didn't see him there now.

Using my second sight, I located the bright glow of a soul lying still a few feet away. I moved towards it and found Lombardi, unconscious on the far side of the junk heap. The explosion must have knocked him there but he didn't appear too damaged. Blaise wasn't in him. Had he been destroyed? I dragged Lombardi to join the driver, collapsing next to them. They had pulses, but they were unconscious. They needed more help than I could give them.

A ball of souls swirled from the flames like a tornado, so entwined with each other I couldn't tell if one of them was Jed or not.

There was a second explosion of light as one of the souls triumphed and the others vanished. A ripple of green ricocheted along the night sky like the northern lights. Two more ghosts swirled to attack me but were intercepted by other spirits. I watched them battle each other, nurturing the final embers of my power with fear.

A few spirits floated down over me, like a sentinel guard. They weren't attacking so I decided they must be on my side. I stared up at the flickering lights above me, the souls of people who had lived and died, and who had come to my aid.

"Thank you," I called. It didn't seem like enough but I didn't know what else to say. I didn't know if they heard me or not, but they dissipated, returning the night sky to the stars.

There was one soul left, the dark one that had fought Christiana briefly. He came to me slowly, as if his energy was failing. I held out my hands and he settled in front of me, the outline of two hands coming to join mine. I saw a fragmented flash of a man's face, one I'd never seen before. The rugged face of a king who had lived three thousand years before. The light of his spirit dimmed. He was faltering.

He'd left the safety of his body to come fight for me. "Stay strong, Jed," I whispered. "I need you."

His light brightened for a moment and his hand tightened around mine, entreating. I understood what he needed. He'd held my soul in the cup of his hands, it was time for me to repay the favor.

"Don't you leave me, Jedediah," I ordered, drawing him closer. "Stay with me."

When his soul slid inside my body it was a cooling balm. There were no serpents and no pain because he made no effort to control me. I felt him resting deep inside me. *Draw your energy from my body, Jedediah. Let me nurture your soul.* I hoped he could hear me, but he didn't reply.

I pushed myself up off of the melting snow and walked away from the burning house. As I set off down the gravel drive, soaked clothes sticking to my skin, my nuclear core started to rebuild. It kept me warm as I walked towards the sound of distant sirens.

THE END

ACKNOWLEDGEMENTS

THE JOURNEY from the first words of *When They Come True* to publishing has been long, and one that I am fortunate to have not travelled entirely alone. That said, I realize that living with someone who writes her novels between the hours of 4 & 6 am isn't easy. Greg, thank you for the endless cups of coffee and wine refills while I was immersed in the story. M, I'm sorry about the games that I missed so I could write—and grateful that you both understand and have to witness the work it takes to achieve your dreams.

Dr. Turner, thank you for again adding your expertise to my writing process and helping to make Anna a credible clinician. To Mom, you are a ground-breaking inspiration as a deacon, lawyer, and a wonderful mother and grandmother. I hope to someday be half as good as you in scrabble, but until then you'll continue to beat me. For Hilary, my sister, dearest friend, confidant, and proofreader extraordinaire—who happens to be the only person who can make me laugh until I cry. To Krista K., whose life changing advice I took to heart in early 2016. Thank you, with all my heart, for your friendship. To P. Costas, my chief adviser on guns and weaponry. And to author Clare Meyers, for her friendship, camaraderie, and an impromptu round of editing.

For every person who enjoyed *When They Come Calling*—I keep writing for you. And a special thank you to everyone who supported our Kickstarter campaign! Without you, and Atthis Arts, editor Abigail Hodges and the folks at Quill Pen, this novel would be sitting in my hope chest.

And finally, to Barney, my heart and soul these last 3 years. I miss you.

ABOUT THE AUTHOR

SARAH FLEMING MOUNTFORD lives in the Midwest with her family, two rescue dogs, and three inherited cats. When she isn't traveling, Sarah is a runner, the family chef, and a reluctant soccer mom.

CPSIA information can be obtained
at www.ICGtesting.com
Printed in the USA
LVHW092113291120
672982LV00033B/256